PERSISTENCE IN FOLLY

Also by Les A. Murray

THE ILEX TREE (WITH GEOFFREY LEHMANN)
THE WEATHERBOARD CATHEDRAL
POEMS AGAINST ECONOMICS
LUNCH AND COUNTER LUNCH
ETHNIC RADIO
THE PEASANT MANDARIN (SELECTED PROSE)
THE BOYS WHO STOLE THE FUNERAL
THE VERNACULAR REPUBLIC: POEMS 1961-1981
THE PEOPLE'S OTHERWORLD

PERSISTENCE IN FOLLY

Les A. Murray

A SIRIUS BOOK

Published with the assistance of the Literature Board
of the Australia Council.

SIRIUS BOOKS
an imprint of Angus & Robertson Publishers
London . Sydney . Melbourne

This book is copyright. Apart from any fair dealing for the
purposes of private study, research, criticism or review, as
permitted under the Copyright Act, no part may be reproduced
by any process without written permission. Inquiries should
be addressed to the publishers.

First published in Australia by Angus & Robertson Publishers in 1984
First published in the United Kingdom by Angus & Robertson (UK) Ltd in 1984

Copyright © Les A. Murray 1984

National Library of Australia
Cataloguing-in-publication data.

Murray, Les A. (Leslie Allan), 1938-.
  Persistence in folly.
  ISBN 0 207 14948 8.
  I. Title.
A821'.3

Typeset in 10pt English Times by Setrite Typesetters
Printed in Hong Kong

Contents

Preface	1
The Human-Hair Thread	4
Cole of the Funny Picture Book	31
Of Phenicopters and Beccaficoes	34
The Aboriginal Poet — An Ecological Niche	37
The Year of Living Dangerously	40
Bruce Dawe	43
The Greater Metroland Anthology	46
The Big Loose Poems that Rule Us	49
Isaac Rosenberg	52
The Bonnie Disproportion	61
A Prose Diaspora	86
Poetry and School	90
Centering the Language	94
Starting from Central Railway — A Bush View of Sydney	100
Notes on the Writing of a Novel Sequence	105
Some Religious Stuff I Know About Australia	109
Locum at Lyons Road — My Years at *Poetry Australia*	130
Eric Rolls and the Golden Disobedience	149
On Being Subject Matter	168

Preface

This, my second collection of prose articles, comprises those written between 1977 and 1982 which I have wished to preserve. With a very few exceptions, the articles are presented in the order in which I wrote them. Emendations have included the restoration of my original titles for some of the pieces, and also the restoration, sometimes from rough memory, of bits cut out by editors. I am ruefully amused by the variations in paragraphing in the book, likewise reflecting the efforts of different editors when the articles were first published. Left to myself, I do perhaps incline towards trying to write everything in one huge paragraph, out of a sense of the simultaneous interconnectedness of all things. I have updated a few of the pieces in ways which seemed appropriate; sadly, some of these updatings have been made necessary by the deaths of persons alive when the relevant articles were first published. Details of publication are given at the end of each article, recording its appearance or appearances in print. It should be added here that the final three essays comprised the Colin Roderick Lectures for 1982, commissioned by the English Association of James Cook University of North Queensland, in Townsville, and first delivered at that university. I would like to thank the Association, and especially Elizabeth Perkins, for their kindness and hospitality to me on that occasion.

This book differs from my earlier prose collection, *The Peasant Mandarin*, (University of Queensland Press, 1978) in a number of ways. It contains fewer short book reviews on widely differing topics, a greater proportion of general essays, and fewer adverse criticisms of individuals' writing. Little or no rewriting was undertaken in that book, while in this one many things have been expanded and worried towards a more definitive shape. If thought is to be organic, there has to be room for expansions and afterthoughts. One article in particular, "The Bonnie Disproportion", has grown larger and more detailed with each re-publication, and I suspect it wants to grow into a full-length book. I have restrained it, however, and hope that it may be useful as source material for the person who does someday write the large history of the Scots

Australians which the subject seems to call for.

Another piece, "The Human-Hair Thread", was written in 1977, just too late to be included in *The Peasant Mandarin*; since then, I have drawn on Aboriginal tradition and art in one large and a few smaller instances, and my thinking on the use of borrowings from this source has slightly altered. I did think of writing an appendix to that article for this book, but I have found that some critics rather resent authors who seem to intrude into their province, and I am aware of the danger of imprisoning poems in authorial comment. Also, there is a lot of continuity between the concerns and themes of "The Human-Hair Thread" and those of *The Boys who Stole the Funeral*, the verse novel published in 1980 which constitutes the major instance referred to above. This is especially true of the main body of the story. New elements mainly occur in the delirium sequence near the end, which is as much as anything a fantasia on many different Aboriginal and other elements, bushrangers, escaped-convict cedargetters, swagmen, mad hatters, *Karadji* "clever men" and fragments of the ancient Bora religion of south-eastern Australia, as well as Central Australian echoes. Incidentally, I don't think Clancy Forbutt, the verse novel's main (living) character, really undergoes subincision, circumcision or any other literal operations during his visionary trip. He doesn't mention such traumata afterwards, and he would tend to notice if he had been cut about the generative parts in any literal way. As many have demonstrated, the dreamworld is a frequent and natural place for white and Aboriginal Australians to meet. Really, though, the emphasis in the whole poem is on what the races have in common, rather than on what divides them. Much of its action takes place in that rural world where being Aboriginal or white can sometimes be a matter almost of choice. Not always, sadly, of one's own choice. Mrs Ella Simon, mentioned in "The Human-Hair Thread", relates in her autobiography how she was sometimes told, when she was living at Purfleet Settlement, and before she had her Dog Licence (citizenship papers in her own country) to "Go and live in Taree with the other whites". Not that she would have been allowed to do so by the white authorities of the time. I should add, now that I seem to be writing that appendix after all, that my other main use of Aboriginal material since 1977 is in the poem "The Mouthless Image of God in the Hunter-Colo Mountains", which is based on a painting of the Supreme Spirit I was once shown in the mountains to the south of the Hunter Valley wine district. The figure has no mouth, and I was told that this referred to the time when birds and animals could speak, while humans were dumb. The creatures, however, told too many of their sacred secrets, and the Supreme Being took away their speech and gave it to the humans. The cautionary nature of that tale is clear, I think, though it saddens me. When I was very young, I used to think secrecy, or even ordinary reserve, was a little undignified and cowardly.

The very old review of Cole Turnley's biography of G. W. Cole, dating from 1974, is one which I unaccountably missed when compiling *The Peasant Mandarin*, and is included here out of liking for its subject. I would like to have met Cole, and used his great Book Arcade. We need such bookshops nowadays, and such booksellers. I think that a great bookseller, of whom there seem to be only a few in every age, is one of the key cultural figures in a nation. It is good to report that Cole's policy of unrestricted reading of the stock continues as a tradition in a few Australian bookshops. Sadly, most of them are small, and some are getting smaller. In the years since I wrote about Cole, I have often been moved by thoughts of Amos Cole, his farm-labourer father. Dying young and poor, in the anguish of leaving a family unprovided for in an age before social services, he is a face briefly glimpsed out of the millions of peasant Europe who were our ancestors. A moment of human tragedy reaches out from among the dry, branching names of genealogy to touch us. As will be obvious, this book continues many of the concerns of *The Peasant Mandarin*, the republicanism, the mistrust of elites. Concerning one of the later articles in it, an academic friend sneered affably the other day, "Ah, another chapter in your disguised autobiography, I see." I doubt the book is that, or that any autobiography I wrote would wear much disguise, but he may have a point. My own suspicion is that I am taking part in an experiment, one which I am not aware that I designed, to discover whether it is possible any longer to be an individual in Australia.

Les A. Murray
Chatswood, New South Wales

The Human-Hair Thread

It may seem strange, and immodest, for a poet to embark on a lengthy account of one of the elements in his own work. My justification for tackling it is threefold: first, I was asked by the editor of *Meanjin* to do so, second, it will tend to use my writing as a springboard for talking about matters of wider interest, and third, its centre of gravity is not so much what I have been able to do with one of the great Australian cultural heritages, but rather what that heritage has given me, and how it has contributed and may yet increasingly contribute to a richer and more humane civilisation in this country.

Since the demise of the Jindyworobak movement, this resource has been largely neglected by writers; the main effect of Aboriginal culture on the general Australian consciousness in the last twenty-odd years has tended to flow through the conservationist movement and, to a lesser extent, through painting and perhaps music. Growing politicisation of the Aboriginal question has also, perhaps, made many non-Aboriginal writers wary of charges of exploitation, paternalism and the like. It will be a tragedy if the normal processes of artistic borrowing and influence, by which any culture makes part of its contribution to the conversation of mankind, are frozen in the Aboriginal case by what are really the manoeuverings of a battle for political power within the white society of our country, or by tactical use of Third World rhetoric by jealous artists trying to damage each other professionally. Artistic borrowing is quite unlike the processes of finance from which the metaphor is drawn: it leaves the lender no poorer, and draws attention to his riches, which can only be depleted by neglect and his loss of confidence in them; these cause them to be lost. Borrowing is an act of respect which may restore his respect for his goods, and so help to preserve them. And he is at all times free to draw on them himself with the benefit of his own superior understanding of his treasures.

There has been an Aboriginal presence in my work almost from the start. This is natural enough, in one coming from the country. Until quite recently, the original Australians were almost exclusively a country people, and the white culture they had to resist or assimilate with was the Australian rural one. Growing up outside the cities, one couldn't fail to be conscious of them, living on the fringe of things, mostly in poverty, hanging around the pubs in Taree or walking the two hot, dusty miles back out to Purfleet Settlement. In my part of the north coast of New South Wales, they were not really poorer or more broken down than the poorest farm families or seasonal workers. All the same, one was dimly conscious of a difference that went beyond the often slight differences of skin colour. One knew there were special laws about the Aborigines — to some extent, the modern Aboriginal people is a *creation* of discriminatory laws working against the declared policy of assimilation — and one heard they could be treacherous, apt to repay slights exorbitantly after long and patient delay, though I don't remember any examples being given. They had a way of looking stately in tattered clothes, walking along the road to Taree, but one had no idea then of the warmth with which they supported and cared for their own. Nor any idea of their tradition of sharing. Ugly, contemptuous words were used to refer to them: coon, darkie, koori, black-gin. My mother, a city woman, prohibited these words in our house, and it was only years later, in the city, that I learned that *Koori* was what the black people called themselves. About the term gin, I remember hearing the story of Constable Crotty, of Taree, who was caught in flagrante with a Purfleet woman down at the Manning River car ferry, in the days before the Martin Bridge spanned the river; a six o'clock curfew was imposed on Aborigines in Taree in those days, and Mr Crotty was supposed to be seeing that all the black people were across the river by that hour. For a long time afterwards, in all the pubs of the town, a gin-in-milk was known as a "Crotty's"; the word drove Constable Crotty to leave town.

The Aborigines were partly a people, partly a caste, partly a class, though really that last term is inaccurate: they were actually part of a larger class of the rural poor, and it is still often more useful to see them in that light than in currently fashionable radical-racialist terms. We, my family, were in the same class ourselves. The Murrays were among the earliest white families in the Manning district, but my father was a tenant-at-will of *his* father, who, before letting him rent a hived-off segment of his large property and farm it, had exploited his labour as a bullock driver and timber cutter for eight years with no pay beyond gruff promises of future rewards, Grandfather John Allan Murray, called Allan to distinguish him from his wildly generous and hospitable, if feckless, father Johnnie Murray, the first white settler at Bunyah, was always a man to do well out of family loyalty, but he was not at all unusual in that, in his time and place. Until it was pulled down some years ago, our house on the farm never had a ceiling, or lining on the walls; summer and winter, the wind through the cracks in the plank walls provided us with air-conditioning. As my father says, "We were poor people — hardly had a roof to our mouth." I suppose we were heirs to the unadmitted guilts of the white conquest of Australia, though I don't remember our being conscious of them at all. Perhaps we were too poorly educated. A certain slight shyness on my part when meeting Aboriginal people may stem from subterranean feelings of guilt, however; indeed, I almost hope they come from there. They may be no more than an outgrowth of learned liberalism, or a residue of childhood fears. Really, I am not at all sure about white conquest-guilt; it may be no more than a construct of the political Left, that great inventor of prescriptive sentiments and categories. It certainly isn't a reliable sentiment for outsiders to invoke among country people.

We may also have been heirs, tangentially, to guilts about miscegenation, a topic on which many older country people of all colours are deeply and ambiguously touchy, in part because of real tension between racial scorn and ordinary decency, in part also because it has been a stick used by urban elites, past and present, to beat us with. Then, as now, the sunny, self-righteous, generalising confidence of urban commentators was inimical to rural Australians. When I was growing up, the injustice of urban attitudes was shifting from the black people (feckless, primitive, a doomed, inferior race) to the white rural population (bigoted, conservative, ignorant, despoilers of the environment, a doomed, obsolete group), though it had not reached its present levels of intensity.

I grew up in what had been the country of the Kattang people, a region lying between the Manning and the Karuah Rivers and extending westward towards Gloucester and Dungog. This is the country which formed me, and I have celebrated it many times in verse. When I was a child, though I did not know it then, there were still initiated men living at Purfleet, men who had risen through the ceremonial stages of the Bora, that ancient religion whose name means resurrection and rebirth. I read about these men much later in the memoirs of Mrs Ella Simon of Taree, who was one of the last fluent speakers of Kattang, as well as a recognised keeper of family trees and traditional lore. Mrs Simon was one of the informants in Nils M. Holmer's study, published in two parts by the Australian Institute of Aboriginal Studies in 1966–67, of the Kattang and Thangatti languages. Her autobiography, titled *Through My Eyes*, will correct and greatly amplify anything I could say here about the life of the Aboriginal people Up Home, and people wanting an account, from the inside, of relations between the races in the Manning region are advised, most warmly, to look out for this book, which was published by Rigby in 1978. Mrs Simon was a great lady of my country, the first Aboriginal Justice of the Peace in New South Wales, and a person of immense wisdom and justice; she knew where all the corpses were buried. She would certainly have known who the old black man was who stood by the roadside in Purfleet with his hat in his hands and his eyes lowered the day my mother's funeral passed by on its way out to Krambach cemetery. I was twelve then, but that man has stayed with me, from what may well have been the natal day of my vocation as a poet, a good spirit gently restraining me from indulgence in stereotypes and prejudices. Or trying to. I don't know who he was. He could have been one of the Bungey family, a relation of young Cecil Bungey who jumped into the Manning from Queen Elizabeth Park in Taree one night when the police were after him and drowned. This tragedy, in the mid-fifties, was an important event in the district, because the indignation it caused among black and white people alike led to some curbing of police oppression of the Purfleet community and a beginning of social change in the settlement. He could have been a Saunders, or a Lobban, a member of that Scottish settler family of a century ago which seems to have no white members left now. Or he may have been one of the Syrons, visiting from Minimbah.

In tracing the black thread as it runs through my work, I am conscious of many mistakes, shortcomings and impositions of myth on the facts. Leaving aside a couple of short stories I wrote while at university, heavily programmatic tales which were really about the tension between individuality and community values, and not about real Aborigines at all, the first poem of those I have kept which deals with an explicitly Aboriginal subject is one titled "Beside the Highway", written in about 1962 or 1963. It is an outsider's view of an Aboriginal settlement of the old type, and is, of course, based almost entirely on Purfleet and the life I saw or imagined going on there, the heat, the ennui, the sense of dereliction and aimlessness — in other words, very much the conventional white liberal picture, enlivened by an eye for detail. The thing in this early poem which gives it some fleeting originality is the image of cars on the highway, which "approach like missiles/and scatter glare as they pass". Purfleet used to be bisected by the Pacific Highway, exposed to the constant intrusive passage of cars and trucks that violated its inwardness. It must have been a fearfully dangerous place for little children — though they grew up into public-spirited youngsters capable of putting out placards on the approaches to warn motorists of police speed traps — and one can

Persistence in Folly

imagine the disruption and chronic restlessness which the endless glittering stream of vehicles must have provoked in the people there. Mrs Simon says in her memoirs that Purfleet should be bulldozed now; it had value in its day, and was a step up from the squalid riverbank blacks' camp it replaced, but the need for a refuge, a separate community, in effect a ghetto, has now passed. The poem is stitched shakily together by the imagined figure of Mad Jess, who owes more to Wordsworth and Yeats than to actual observation; this figure is made to bear the burden of Significance in the poem:

> "And I was dreaming,"
> says old Mad Jess to herself, "flash cars was coming at me like hailstones, cutting me to pieces."

What this highly literary figure allowed me to do, I see now, was to use the rural dialect I had grown up speaking, but which I was as yet too conventional to employ in my verse. Perhaps the most perceptive touch in the picture of Mad Jess, though, is the image of her contemplating her shoes. This image, with its concomitants of remembered barefoot freedom and of lore and magical practices connected with tracks, recurs in a much later poem, "The Ballad of Jimmy Governor". Images of the ground and of tracks abound in the poem, and in one place the half-caste outlaw ironically refers to his full-blood accomplice Jacky Underwood as having "already give back his shoes". The implication is that the only footwear Underwood ever owned was that given to him by the prison officials in Dubbo for his appearances at court. Now he has been hanged and the shoes have been taken back. The Governor Ballad is written entirely in the dialect, or more properly sociolect, of the rural poor. I have heard it read in an Aboriginal accent by the actor Bob Maza, and the effect chilled even me!

In a poem written while I was living in Wales in 1967, entitled "The Wilderness", there is a reference to the day my friend Peter Barden and I, watched by curious peak-hour crowds, trotted down Wynyard Concourse in Sydney towards the railway ticket barriers, excitedly pointing out imaginary animal tracks in the dust and pausing to make more with our knuckles in the manner of Aboriginal hunters discussing the finer points of their trade, while all the time exchanging remarks in an Aboriginal-sounding gibberish. We even avoided sibilants in our mock-Aranda, knowing dimly that these don't occur in Australian languages. The yen for travel to the Outback and for what Barden called the "clean country" of the Centre was strong on us that day. And it was a good stir. In the poem, which is about a hitchhiking trip through the Centre which I'd done in 1961 to while away the hungry months of the Credit

Squeeze that year, I refer to our gibberish as mock-*Arunta*, and thereby fall into the same sort of error as the old Jindyworobak poets, Rex Ingamells, Ian Mudie, Flexmore Hudson, Max Dunn, Roland Robinson and the rest, who lacked the really first-rate scholarly sources available to us now. The spelling "Arunta" comes from the writings of Sir Baldwin Spencer and F. J. Gillen, who carried out valuable but faulty anthropological studies in Central Australia in the late nineteenth and early twentieth centuries. The people these men were principally concerned with were the *Aranda*, who pronounce their tribal name with the stress on the initial A. The common white Australian mistake of pronouncing the "Arunta" form with the stress on the medial *u* probably stems from popularising material derived from Spencer and Gillen.

The Jindyworobak poets were very prone to romanticise the Aborigines, but their really worthwhile project of fusing Aboriginal and diverse European elements into a new and genuinely Australian poetry was made more difficult by the shaky incomplete source material they had to work with. Roland Robinson, the greatest of the Jindies, is of course an exception, largely because he did his own original research. Many of the best modern studies only appeared at the end of the Jindyworobak period or even later, in the late forties and early fifties; T. G. H. Strehlow's monumental and superb *Songs of Central Australia* only came out finally in 1970. Before the Second World War, for those who read German there were accurate poem-texts in Carl Strehlow's *Die Aranda- und Loritja-Stämme in Zentral-Australien*, published between 1907 and 1920, and other accurate texts could be found in odd articles by E. H. Davies and the young T. G. H. Strehlow in *Oceania*. Other texts, whose reliability I cannot judge, existed in George Taplin's "The Narrinyeri", a chapter of *The Native Tribes of South Australia* (1897), in A. W. Howitt's *Native Tribes of South-East Australia*, and in a few other old books. Older texts were often clumsily literal, or else rendered Bill Harney-fashion into totally inappropriate English traditional rhyme and metre, which smothered their tone and flavour and usually made them look merely banal. Mary Gilmore's renderings are a partial exception, as Judith Rodriguez points out in a recent review article in *Contempa*. To digress for a moment, it would be wonderful if we could recover the transcriptions of native, probably mainly Wiradjuri, songs Mary Gilmore's father is said to have made; these were allegedly most painstaking, and were glossed by Mr Cameron in his native Gaelic so as to avoid missing nuances, before he made his English versions. It was not until 1945 that R. and C. Berndt published the results of their early field work in the Ooldea region, and not until 1951 that Ronald Berndt published his study, with sensitively translated texts, of the Arnhem Land Djanggawul cycle. Similarly, the younger Strehlow's authoritative *Aranda Traditions* only appeared in 1947. The Jindyworobak poets also suffered from too great an emphasis on only one Aboriginal tribe, the Aranda, important and fascinating as the traditions of the Aranda are. Pretty well their whole understanding of Aboriginal metaphysics and philosophy comes, it is clear, from Spencer and Gillen's often shaky understanding of Aranda belief.

If this last point is true of the Jindyworobak poets, it is even more true of the hazy ideas of Aboriginal philosophy and religion held by most white Australians. A particularly good example of this is the term "Dreamtime". This term, taken from Spencer and Gillen's studies of Central Australian tribes and applied indiscriminately to all Aboriginal groups in Australia, is analysed incisively by T. G. H. Strehlow in his *Songs of Central Australia* (pp. 614-15):

Spencer and Gillen's *alcheringa* (altered in *The Arunta* to *alchera*), which has been mistranslated as "dream time" and popularised by them and others in this sense, owes its origin to a confusion of *altjíra ráma* and *altjíranga* (*ngámbakála*). The English "dream time" is therefore a vague and inaccurate phrase; and though it has gained wide currency among white Australians through its sentimentality and its suggestion of mysticism, it has never had any real meaning for the natives, who rarely, if ever, use it when speaking in English. "Dreaming", or rather "dreamin", which is commonly used by pidgin English and Northern Territory English native speakers means *totem* only, and is a translation not of *altjíranga* but of *kngánakála* (= someone who has originated). Thus "emu dreamin" would be a translation of *ilia kngánakála* (= someone who has originated as an emu).

Strehlow discusses the word *altjíra* in some detail; it is apparently a rare word used only in a few fixed phrases, and its root meaning seems to be "uncreated, sprung out of itself". The suffixed form *altjíranga* means "from all eternity", and is given as an answer to questions about the origin of the world. In the Aranda view, the earth and the sky have existed *altjíranga*, that is, from all eternity. So have the supernatural beings who created the features of the earth and its human and animal inhabitants, and who continually reincarnate themselves in them. Some of the immense dignity of traditional Aborigines, when seen outside of degrading circumstances, obviously comes from their sense of being the present forms of eternally existing beings. A man who "owns" a certain ceremony or set of verses belonging to a sacred site does so because he *is* the supernatural being who indwells in that site. The only slight connection between *altjíra* and dreaming, in our Western sense of the word, is through the idiom *altjira ráma* "to see altjira", that is, "to dream".

I place great reliance on Strehlow's accounts of Aranda matters because unlike other scholars to date he spoke Aranda as a native; it was one of his mother tongues. In a private discussion, Emeritus Professor A. P. Elkin of Sydney University told me that Strehlow was really the only white man who had ever learned an Aboriginal language. Spencer and Gillen, on the other hand, had to rely on native informants speaking a limited pidgin English, because they themselves spoke no Aranda at all. This led them into many mistakes, notably their belief that the sacred chants attached to the different sites (for ritual scarcely exists apart from the places in which it must be performed) were in fact nonsense verses which the Aborigines themselves did not understand, a sort of ritual glossolalia! As an example of the long survival of misinformation, I remember in 1961 being told dogmatically by a well-read, rather pedantic and in fact somewhat scary truck driver that sacred Aboriginal verse was all meaningless noise-making. As we were crossing the Nullarbor at the time, I did not persist in arguing with him when he showed signs of irritation.

The first poem in which I attempted to capture some of the rhythm and feeling of Aboriginal poetry was "The Rock Shelters, Botany Bay", written in early 1968 (we were living in Scotland then) and published, like "The Wilderness", in my second book *The Weatherboard Cathedral*. It is a rather pallid poem, "poetic" in a bad sense, and reads like a counterfeit of another culture's poetry rather than a genuine re-creation of it. It fails to catch the tone and style of Aboriginal poetry of any sort, in the way in which, say, Tom Keneally caught them in the short extempore songs he put into the mouth of the young Jimmie Blacksmith in his fine novel based on the Governor outbreak. I was perhaps too far, in every sense, from my sources. The only real point of interest in the poem is the mention of people averting their eyes from the track of a "kingparrot man", the ill-omened spoor of a soldier dressed in a red coat. It was a guess of mine that, in the first days of contact, people accustomed to ritual body painting would take figures in red coats to be spirit-figures associated with a familiar creature. Apart from possum-skin cloaks for wearing in cold weather, most Aborigines in traditional times scarcely had a concept of what we may call secular clothing. Decoration with blood, paint and the down of birds was a festive or religious act. The poem alludes to the common eastern Australian idea, reminiscent of Melanesian belief, that the white invaders were actually ghosts, a truly horrifying thing for a people with as deep-rooted a fear of the dead as Aboriginal Australians possessed. Ghosts garbed as crimson rosella

Persistence in Folly

(kingparrot) men would thus be an attempt to make sense of white figures garbed in red upper-body decorations.

My next attempt to describe, amongst other things, the effect of absolute culture shock was in "The Conquest", written in 1969 and published in *Poems Against Economics*. This is a more successful poem, I think, and deals with black-white relations during the first years of settlement at Sydney Cove, the period of Phillip's governorship. This period is very important, in that events and reverses which happened then went far towards setting the pattern of black-white relations for more than a century afterwards; the poem outlines some of these and then, in its last two sections, moves into a more general depiction of white myth-making about the Aborigines, both in the past and today:

> A few still hunt way out beyond philosophy
> where nothing is sacred till it is your flesh
> and the leaves, the creeks shine through their poverty
>
> or so we hope. We make our conquests too.
> The ruins at our feet are hard to see.

Early in the poem, the failure of understanding on both sides is presented in terms of perception; neither side can *see* the other at all accurately, because neither side can understand what it is seeing. The failure is presented from both sides, with the Aboriginal side predominating in the early sections and then fading away as white incomprehension, brutality and myth-making take over. The tribesmen see, with difficulty, what look to them like "blue parrot-figures wrecking the light with change" (Royal Navy officers and bluejackets are meant) and they see "man-shapes digging where no yam-roots were", a solecism against the proper order of things in many ways, not least because most digging was women's work. Later, the Governor addresses the tribesmen in English and they reply, naturally enough, in Dhuruwal, the language of the people south of Sydney Harbour. Marines stand stolidly there, with their firelocks at the ready, obeying the customs of their culture and their service, and the warriors obey *their* customs by ritually biting their beards as a sign of defiance and challenge. Beard-biting with this significance was, it seems, pretty well universal throughout Australia, so it is not inappropriate to cite an Aranda example. It comes from the sacred song associated with Ankóta, a northern Aranda dingo-totem centre on the Burt Plain in the Northern Territory; "he" refers to the dingo ancestor Ankótarínja:

> Angrily sucking his beard into his mouth
> He follows up the scent, moving his head from side to side.

Nothing comes of the confrontation ("glass beads are scattered in that gulf of style"), and soon convicts are crying out for protection against the imaginary violence of naked "Indians", the common eighteenth-century term for all New World indigenes, who "circle them like birds". Exasperated with the unresponsiveness and menacing mien of the Aborigines, the Governor forgets his earlier unrealistic projects of racial harmony and orders that they be driven off, and so they disappear carrying the germs of unknown European diseases which will sweep through them like fire through blady grass. In the forest, dogs feed on the corpses; "it makes dogs furtive, what they find to eat". Later, finding that the colony cannot support itself, Phillip changes tack again and orders that some natives be captured, partly in order to get information about native food resources, and partly to train as emissaries capable of interpreting the benevolent white Governor's wishes and intentions to their fellow indigenes. The poem thus records Phillip's swings from benevolence to exasperation and back, and his final outburst of savagery when his personal huntsman, named McEntire, is speared. The punitive expedition he orders on that occasion is a complete failure, but it sets a deadly pattern for the future:

> The punitive squads march off
> without result, but this quandong of wrath
> ferments in slaughters for a hundred years.

As the Aborigines themselves fade from view as an independent "side" in the confrontation, their place is taken by various stereotyped European views of them. Paralleling the Governor's shifts from benevolence to anger, the image of the Noble Savage in very early drawings and accounts is replaced by scornful pictures of degraded black beggars in Sydney Town, capering drunkenly for pennies or rum in a now totally desacralised world. They have gone, in a few short years, from being unencumbered with possessions to being destitute, "poor for the first time", and their culture goes underground, becoming a matter of fading traditional lore spoken softly in languages which most white men do not trouble to listen to or learn. Colonial reality is something which can be, and is, expressed entirely in the conqueror's language. Perhaps because of a personal interest in linguistic things, I have made more, I think, of the linguistic dimension in black-white relations than most other Australian writers.

Matters of language are very much to the fore in the very next poem I wrote, a few weeks after "The Conquest". This was "The Ballad of Jimmy Governor", and the tension in this poem is between the rough nineties ballad-metre in which it is cast and the horrific anti-white and anti-pioneer sentiments of the Aboriginal outlaw who speaks it. I tried to write the poem, though, in the only poetic mode Jimmy Governor might have been expected to know, the rough folk-poetry of the settlers and battlers, and there is possibly some pathos in the way his language is precisely theirs, right down to the dialectal forms such as "give" for "gave" and "soon be" for "it will soon be", the slang is turn-of-the-century too, as in the use of "plant" for "hide". This, and the other forms, are still current among older people in my region today. There are cruel punning references to Black Velvet (Aboriginal women, as sexually exploited by white men) and White Lady, a dire mixture of methylated spirits and powdered milk still drunk in shanty settlements to this day. The only references to traditional belief are fairly oblique, and refer to traditional lore about the balefulness of tracks and other traces left by evil men and, more specifically, by traditional revenge parties. I've noticed that white readers don't tend to notice or "hear" these parts of the poem, though a couple of Aboriginal people who have heard or read it have reacted to them. I may just have got something right, and succeeded in creating a real Aboriginal character. Interestingly, Tom Keneally also refers to footprint-sorcery, and to the concomitants of shoe-wearing, in his *Chant of Jimmie Blacksmith*. Tom was writing his novel at the same time as I was writing this poem; this was a subject for mutual surprise and head-shaking later on.

The first poem in which I deliberately incorporated large amounts of actual material of a traditional sort was one called "Stockman Songs", which forms part of a long sequence entitled "Walking to the Cattle-Place". This sequence forms more than a third of *Poems Against Economics*, and goes into enormously ramified detail about cattle and their place in human history and consciousness. The element of surprise in the poem is that the stockmen aren't white Australians singing Country-and-Western songs, but black men chanting the sort of non-sacred nonce-verses which Aborigines compose on the spur of the moment to celebrate the casual events of the world around them. The only Aboriginal terms I know for this style of song-making are *djabi-dja*, which comes from one of the languages of the Kimberleys, or *tabi*, a term from Ngumal, one of the languages of the Pilbara. The place names in the poem are Aranda ones: Pmolangkinja is known as Palm Valley in English, Tnórula is Gosse's Range and Rúbuntja (or Urúbuntja) is Mount Hay. There is a reference, of a joking sort, to the grass-seed totem, and a couplet in near-traditional style referring to the semisacred Rúbuntja fire totem ceremony. Strehlow tells the story of this ceremony in an article published in the *Inland Review* (vol. 3, no. 12, September–November 1969):

The Human-Hair Thread

A large group of fire ancestors was living at the beginning of time around Urúbuntja or Rúbuntja, now known as Mount Hay. Some of the fire ancestors accidentally started a bushfire which rapidly engulfed the whole countryside. Finally the fire ancestors themselves were set ablaze. The older men among them thereupon turned into sacred objects. The younger men — who were still wearing their hair tied into long cones in the manner of Aranda novices — rose towards the sky. With their hair aflame and their bodies charred and blackened, they were carried by the fire-heated gales many miles away. Some landed near Tnorula, and changed into grass-trees; others came down in Pmolangkinja, where they turned into palms and cycads... The mountain of Urúbuntja never regained its trees, and the surrounding burnt-out country turned into Mitchell grass plains.

As well as being metaphorically vivid, this story makes good sense as history, and depicts what probably happened many times in the past as Central Australia dried out and became deforested. The Aborigines almost certainly assisted in the work of desiccation and deforestation by careless use of their firesticks — like the Bedouin, they may be as much fathers of the desert as sons of it — and even the picture of the grass trees and palms "flying" into sheltered places is an accurate image, when you consider that the flora of sheltered, well-watered spots in the Centre consists of remnants of sclerophyll forest and even rainforest. The description only lacks a time scale, but then mythologised history usually does. Written only a couple of years after "The Rock Shelters", and slightly revised in 1981, this poem works very much better, I think, as an attempt to capture some sense of the inwardness of another culture and its ways of looking at things.

There follow a number of poems, written over the next few years, in which there are passing references to Aboriginal themes and culture, or in which Aboriginal figures appear. In "Lament for the Country Soldiers" war memorials are called "The stones of increase"; they are, as it were, sacred sites from which a spirit, if not the spirits of the dead soldiers themselves, can be reborn, and the names incised on them are a sort of tjuringa of a past world. In one of the poems of the cattle cycle, "Novilladas Democráticas", "shirts of landless red" refers to the often gorgeous garb of black stockmen in the Outback, and in the last poem of that cycle, a black woman remarks, after the somewhat puritanical country women have explained the reasons for their narrowness and coercive use of the power of community feeling, that Jesus said all hidden things would be revealed, a profoundly true insight of His in which I have great and even sardonic faith. In "The Mitchells", I have a suspicion that one of the two Mitchells is an Aborigine, because of the "pain and subtle amusement" with which he announces his name. But this is perhaps a country point, and too much stress should not be placed on it, as some critics have tended to do. The point of the poem is its depiction, from the outside, of an Australian vernacular culture and its shared private understandings. The two Mitchells — if they *are* both Mitchells — know what they are conveying to each other. We, the readers, are never going to be told, since we don't need to know. In the poem "Escaping Out There" there are references to imaginary place names constructed on an Aboriginal model — the Flying-Fox Cooking-Place and Praising White Moth Larvae — along with other local names constructed on a not dissimilar rural white model: Where The Old School Got Burnt and Where The Big Red Bull Went Over. The latter is an actual place on the island of Tristan da Cunha in the South Atlantic, but it is so like nonce-names for familiar places Up Home that it fitted in perfectly. It may be evidence for a good deal of commonality in rural place-naming in widely separated parts of the world. The name All The Bloodwoods also occurs in the poem, but I would not like to speculate whether that one is white or Aboriginal. The same poem contains a reference to unadmitted, and therefore probably black, grandmothers, and their benign effect on mountain farm families who might otherwise have been too stiffly respectable and hard-working for their own good. In "The Action", finally, a meditation on history and minorities spoken by a man floating at his ease in Coolongolook River in my country, there is a reference to a sacred flying fox increase-site said to have existed nearby. Both Coolongolook River and the red-headed fruit bat are important sponsors of my writing. It was while sitting in the now-vanished timber mill at Coolongolook and contemplating the river, one evening in the mid-fifties, that I first realised that I was going to be a writer; rivers in my work often have a lot of Coolongolook water in them. The metaphoric appropriateness of the flying fox, a nocturnal creature who sleeps upside down during the day and flies out for miles at night in search of "grown and native fruit", to the general situation of poets in this country has a compelling force for me. I examined this in a poem written in 1974 and entitled "The Flying-Fox Dreaming, Wingham Brush, NSW". That poem connects the metaphor with the ancient ritual and economic significance of the flying fox in my country. Along the Manning in pre-white days, there seems to have been a seasonal ecology of native figs, flying foxes and Aborigines. The fruit bats are very nearly my "dreaming", in the half-serious, half-joking way that Douglas Stewart identified his totem animal as the bandicoot while claiming David Campbell's was a big red fox. This is not quite so jocular as it looks, though it can be taken too seriously. I remember, from devouring back issues of *Oceania* in

The Human-Hair Thread

Fisher Library when I was a young student at Sydney, that people of the east coast tribes were supposed to discover their dreamings for themselves through a sort of waking revelation. I know of a parallel to this, from a very different region of Australia, in which a baby's aged initiate relative discerns its dreaming for it. In a poem called "Lalai", translated by Andrew Huntley from a prose version by the anthropologist Michael Silverstein and published in *Poetry Australia* (no. 58, 1976), the Worora elder Sam Woolagoodjah says:

> In its own Wunger place
> A spirit waits for birth —
> "Today, I saw who the child really is —"
>
> That is how a man
> Learns to know his child.
>
> Namaaraalee made him,
> No one else,
> No one.
> But not all things are straight
> in this day.
>
> As I looked at the water
> Of Bundaalunaa
> She appeared to me:
> I understood suddenly
> The life in our baby —
> Her name is Dragon Fly.

Without pressing the point farther than it will go, I know I would be most reluctant ever to hurt a flying fox. The same poem also speculates about a possible origin for *tjúrunga*, the sacred objects in which ancestral spirits inhere; a dead and shrivelled flying fox is spoken of as "becoming a clenched oval stone". But this is guess, based on little more than the way dead things in a dry country are apt to shrivel and even become mummified in the sun, and it may apply more to the Centre than to the coast.

I suppose the next poem of mine, after the cattle cycle, in which a major Aboriginal component appears is one with the very long title "Thinking About Aboriginal Land Rights, I Visit The Farm I Will Not Inherit", written in 1972. This sonnet describes how the bush would reoccupy and obliterate our old farm, and how the potentials for such an obliteration lie everywhere in the landscape. It does not overtly refer to our having lost the farm — my father was too hurt and proud to buy it when his father didn't leave it to him, and so his brother bought it and gave it to his own son, who eventually evicted Dad from it — but rather counteracts a feeling of dispossession by talking about dimensions, intimacies, knowledge of the place which dispossession cannot touch. The speaker is thus in a rather Aboriginal position, vis-à-vis the usurper, and this is underlined by his becoming in effect a totem ancestor in the last line; like the figures in the legends, "I go into the earth near the hay shed for thousands of tears".

The human-hair thread thickens as we approach the present. In another, much longer poem written in 1973 after a tour in Western Australia the previous year, and entitled "Cycling in the Lake Country" (the Wordsworthian echo is not without mischievous intent), there are several allusions to Aboriginal matters, and the Aboriginal presence is pervasive throughout the poem. It is most explicit in Sections 2 and 6, though Section 8 has a reference to the sacred song associated with Ilbálintja Soak, a bandicoot totem site in Central Australia. In the special poetic language used only for sacred verses, the bandicoot initiates chant the words of the great sire Károra describing his *pmára kútata* or "everlasting home" (cf. Sam Woolagoodjah's *Wunger* place) at Ilbálintja: again and again, he refers to the rings of soil and clay and stone revealed in the soak as the water dries up in drought time:

> The crimson soil is grating under the heel;
> The white creek sand is grating under the heel.
>
> White creek sand!
> Impenetrable hollow!
>
> White limestone band!
> Impenetrable hollow!
>
> Rich yellow soil!
> Impenetrable hollow!
>
> Red and orange soil!
> Impenetrable hollow!
>
> Plain studded with whitewoods!
> Impenetrable hollow!
>
> White salt lake!
> Impenetrable hollow!

When I was looking for a way to describe the successive tide-lines left by water drying up in limestone doline-lakes well south of Kambalda, this was the obvious allusion. It seals, as it were, the description which precedes it, and helps to sustain the sense of Aboriginal presence.

In the second section of this long poem, which is based on an imaginary bicycle trip from about Leonora south to the sea at

The Human-Hair Thread

Esperance, there is a reference to the Central Australian belief that sacred quatrains and couplets (called *tjúrunga rétnja* or "tjurunga-names" in Aranda; each is regarded as a compound epithet by which the initiate addresses and invokes his spirit ancestor) have no human authors; they were composed by the great sires themselves as they did their deeds of creation, wandering over the country and pausing at various spots to rest and perhaps to dance and shake off thousands of tiny feathers from their ceremonial body decorations. These feathers became the spirits of their myriad progeny, and when their human incarnations shake off their showers of down in ceremonial performances, the totem species are renewed again and made to multiply. This process is described in the poem, which then goes on, in its allusive impressionist way, to invoke one of the most riveting of all Aboriginal ceremonies, the Northern Aranda circumcision rite, and make contemporary sense of it. I am conscious here of falling into the old trap of overdependence on Aranda tradition, but this was the way the poem unfolded itself to me, and I gather that initiation ceremonies all over the desert regions of our continent tend to be very much more severe than those in the gentler country; Aranda initiates had to undergo circumcision, subincision and even sometimes the tearing off of one or more fingernails: no wonder they referred contemptuously to coastal men as *wía*, or boys! Perhaps the Aranda ceremony is not too much out of place in the context of the Western Australian desert, though.

The ceremony is a very brutal one, and appears to revolve around the theme of violence, particularly sexual violence and the tension between the sexes. In the timeless creative age, a large party of *lákabára* hawk men were travelling over the country devouring quails on the wing, when they heard the sound of a shield being beaten on the ground and saw a number of female wallaby ancestors, many of them deformed, preparing to circumcise their boys with burning brands of bark. This utterly infuriated the hawk men, who flew down, assuming the form of men, and killed the women. Then, with angry violence, they circumcised the boys themselves with stone knives, after which they released the wallaby men from a ritual ban of silence, flew up into the air and continued on their way. This may well be mythologised history, too, but we have no way of checking that. What is certain is that ever since, the ceremony of circumcision, called *atuélama* (to make a man), *látnua ultákama* (to cut off the prepuce) or, most suggestively, *pára ultákama* (to cut off the penis), has been carried out among the Northern Aranda with great roughness and violence, reproducing the fury and cruel joy of the hawk men. By contrast, the rite of subincision, splitting the urethra, is carried out in a context of rather idyllic verses, some, of which have a comic, teasing note. In tribes farther to the north and west, the Rainbow Serpent replaces the hawk men in the story, and the women are not killed, but merely told that this is the new ritual, to replace *ordeal* by fire.

When I was writing the poem, it seemed to me that the circumcision rite had a significance not unlike that which it has in the Book of Exodus, a sacrifice of a part to propitiate forces which might otherwise demand the whole. Or, perhaps, remembering the idiom *pára ultákama*, it might have a suggestion that the prepuce is "enough". Of course, if the theory held by some anthropologists that circumcision was introduced by Moslem fishermen from Macassar in recent centuries and then spread inland from the northern coast is well founded, then the connection with Exodus and ancient Semitic practice becomes a direct one. Many Aboriginal self-mutilating acts have an element of propitiatory sacrifice in them; one offers one's blood and one's pain to satisfy harsh demands which might otherwise become exorbitant. Central Australian people still gash their heads and bodies after a death to demonstrate their grief and their innocence of murder; without such demonstrations, the dead person's relations might come and kill them. In our own culture, the instinct and need for sacrifice, the whole complex of motive and pattern in it, were for a long time resolved and discharged through the sacrifice of Christ on the Cross, as re-enacted every day in the Mass. For many people, especially intellectuals, this is no longer acceptable however, and they are forced to face the question again, willy nilly, and either work their way through it afresh or face destruction by it. As a parallel to my poem, it may be instructive to look at one of the quatrains in David Campbell's superb "Kuring-gai Rock Carvings" sequence:

> The kangaroo has a spear in his side. It was here
> Young men were initiated,
> Tied to a burning tree. Today
> Where are such cooling pools of water?

Well, Christians could tell him — but many white people will now not look our way. I may have been disputing with David in this passage of my poem, though I can't remember now whether the argument was conscious or not. It is relevant to mention here, though, as the media never do, that recent census figures show a very pronounced movement of Aboriginal Australians into the Christian churches; suddenly, Aboriginal Christianity is one of the great growth areas of our faith, on this continent.

In the sixth section of "Cycling in the Lake Country", I use the figure of Lionel Brockman, a West Australian Aborigine who twice escaped from Fremantle Gaol and took to the bush with his family, sparking off the most intensive manhunts in the State's history. This part of the poem does not bring in any specifically traditional material, apart from a slightly tongue-in-cheek allusion to shape-shifting as a method of concealment, but talks about Australian vernacular culture and the need to rid oneself of bossy *gubba* attitudes if one is ever to achieve the humility and the silence necessary to understand Australia and belong deeply to it. The Aboriginal slang word *gubba*, supposedly derived from *governor*, means a white Australian, particularly one who always knows better and wants to push people around. This leads on to the consideration of the true, latent Australian republic in the following section, and the need for much patient listening in order to discern that republic among the faint, shy, ironical or harshly intransigent indications. The whole poem contains a great deal of reference, and relates all of its points to the landscapes in which it is progressively located. It was one of the poems in which I worked out many of my beliefs about Australian civilisation and the opposition between our derivative "high" culture and our more distinctive "vernacular" cultures. I am more often a meditative than a lyrical poet, and the organising principle of this, like many others of my poems, was the meditation. It is a whole meditation with colloquy and all.

An even more intensely meditative poem which contains hardly any specific references to Aboriginal culture, traditional or modern, but which is nonetheless relevant here is "The Returnees", composed in 1975. It is relevant because, as part of its working, it attempts to come to terms with the common ground of human experience on this continent, the ground of perception and influence from which Aboriginal and white reactions to the country necessarily spring. The discovery of this common ground is done in terms of *sound*, the sort of thing filmmakers call "wild sound", which is to say that low, aggregate susurrus which emanates from living landscape and which has to be put on the sound track of any outdoor film; if it were not there the audience would probably not be able to put their finger on what was wrong, but its absence would probably unsettle them. Down beneath consciousness, we know that nature is never wholly silent, and we are apt to be awed when it approaches silence, but disturbed when total silence supervenes. The poem catches:

> a lifelong sound
>
> on everything, that low fly-humming
> melismatic untedious endless
> note that a drone-pipe-plus-chants or

>   (shielding our eyes, rocking the river)
>
>   a ballad — some ballads — catch, the one
>   some paintings and many yarners summon,
>   the ground-note here of unsnubbing art

If I had to find epithets for this partly synaesthetic signature-note of the Australian countryside, I would probably fumble with phrases like "beautiful monotony" or "belonging subtlety" or some such. I hear it very clearly in Aboriginal music and chant, a humming intricately enwoven with rhythmic liquid notes of the clap sticks and with undulating high-pitched, rather nasalised notes that rise and fade, echoing bird cries and the sharps and flats of midsummer blowflies. At least, this is how it has come to me, hearing it on recordings and also at odd times in Central Australia and the north west. That peculiar pitch of Aboriginal men's singing, somewhere between a man's voice and a woman's, has long fascinated me. It is the high-pitched light voice of the figure ancient alchemists called the Hermaphrodite, something we might expect in a religion involving the priesthood of all (male) believers. This is of a piece with the strange custom of subincision among the desert tribes, by which initiates are given a sort of mock vagina while remaining male. We achieve the same image of the hermaphrodite by making priests remain celibate, and having them celebrate the sacred mysteries in an ambiguous quasi-feminine garb. It is a very deep and necessary thing: a priest, to perform his rites properly, must stand in a difficult balance between the sexes, resolving the primal tension at the heart of all our dualities.

It is more than a decade since I first read R. M. Berndt's translation of the great Wonguri-Mandjikai Song Cycle of the Moon Bone. It stunned me when I first read it, and it may well be the greatest poem ever composed in Australia. Of course, it isn't *one* poem, but a cycle of traditional couplets in a sort of telegraphese verbal shorthand meant to be filled out by music and dance, rendered into long, syntactically complete lines by Professor Berndt, celebrating the life of the people and animals around Arnhem Bay in north-eastern Arnhem Land just before the start of the monsoon season:

>   In here towards the shade, in this Place, in the shadow
>   of the paperbarks.
>   Sitting there in rows, those Wonguri-Mandjikai people,
>   paperbarks along like a cloud.
>   Living on cycad-nut bread, sitting there with white-
>   stained fingers,
>   Sitting there resting, those people of the Sandfly clan...

> Sitting there like mist, at that place of the Dugong, and
> of the Dugong's Entrails...
> Sitting resting there in the place of the Dugong...
> In that place of the Moonlight Clay Pans, and at the
> place of the Dugong...

After the prescriptive despairs and alienations of Western literature, which are so often merely matters of class identification, it is good to immerse oneself in this great peaceful poem, with its total acceptance of an intimately known and coherent world. Some may find its Edenic calm almost frightening, for it calls so much human effort and history into question, and presents an idyll wholly opposed to and perhaps impossible in a crowded technological civilisation. Again, it expresses that total harmony and communication of all living creatures which we remember from fairy tales, but which we resist in adulthood because it carries the dangerous nostalgia of Paradise:

> At that place of the Dugong, of the Tree-Limbs-Rubbing-
> Together, and of the Evening Star
> Where the lily-root claypan is...
> Where the cockatoos play, at that place of the Dugong...
> Flapping their wings they flew down, crying, "We saw the
> people!"
> There they are always living, those clans of the white
> cockatoo...
> And there is the Shag woman, and there her clan:
> Birds, trampling the lily foliage, eating the soft round
> roots!

Judith Rodriguez puts the matter well, in a book review in *Contempa* (no. 2/4, 1977):

Is it a sickness of sophistication to long for that "Always there" which occurs through the... ritual cycles, to find in that universalising imagery of climactic annual ritual chant something that makes our own sacramental feast of blood and flesh and our own uses of sex seem secondhand, tawdry and difficult to live by? Certainly in the Aboriginal rituals there is an assurance inaccessible to us; and our civilisation has made it inaccessible to the very people who told it to Ronald Berndt at Yirrkala in 1947.

And yet I would venture to disagree, not only about our own sacramental feast (and I have an abhorrence anyway for our modern uses of sex), but also about the alleged inaccessibility of that assurance. It is perhaps an inaccessibility that is most marked for intellectuals. I know some other white Australians who possess this assurance almost in its purity, in terms that are their own. And it is not a sickness to long for that "Always there", but a real health of the spirit; it is sickness to reject it. One of the triumphs of Berndt's translation is that it renders the Aboriginal poetry into a language deeply in tune with the best Australian vernacular speech, and reveals affinities. The tone, as well as the images, is profoundly familiar. It has perhaps been the tragedy, the sickness, of poetry here that it has so rarely caught precisely that tone, and that our audiences have been trained not to expect it from us.

Around Christmas 1975, I conceived the idea of writing a cycle of poems in the style and metre of Berndt's translation of the Moon Bone Cycle. As I thought about it, I realised it would be necessary to incorporate in it elements from all three main Australian cultures, Aboriginal, rural and urban. But I would arrange them in their order of distinctiveness, with the senior culture setting the tone and controlling the movement of the poem. What I was after was an enactment of a longed-for fusion of all three cultures, a fusion which, as yet perhaps, can only exist in art, or in blessed moments when power and ideology are absent. The poem would necessarily celebrate my own spirit country, the one region I know well enough to dare comparison with the Arnhem Landers. In the final stanza of a poem called "The Gallery", I had made what was in effect a trial flight, teaching myself to handle the rhythm and spirit of the Moon Bone Cycle. Fairly soon, I lighted on a device by which the projected poem could be launched and ordered: this was the annual exodus of many urban Australians to the country and the seaside resorts, people, many of them only a generation or two away from the farms, or even less, going back to their ancestral places in a kind of unacknowledged spiritual walkabout, looking for their country in order to draw sustenance from it. Or newcomers looking for the real Australia. Or people going to seek unadmitted communion with the sea, with the bush and the mountains, recovering, in ways which might look tawdry to the moralising sophisticated eye, some fragments of ancient festivity and adventure.

The poem took about six weeks to write, in two bursts approximately a month apart; the hiatus came, I remember, between Sections 6 and 7. It may be relevant to examine each of the sections in turn — there are thirteen of these, as in the Moon Bone Cycle. Section 1 starts by evoking the southern limits of the region and the different styles, interests and ways of speech of small-town people and country people, then moves into a description of the preparations being made for the return of those who have gone away to live in the cities and finally enumerates some of the legendary, and in one case suggestively notorious, associations of their ancestral region. In Section 2, the Pacific Highway in peak holiday

The Human-Hair Thread

time is described ironically in terms of a great fiery but all-giving Rainbow Snake writhing over the country and throwing out deadly little offshoots of excitement into the districts up back roads. Section 3 begins the process of rediscovery of intimacy with landscape and familiar creatures, though there is some residual violence in it. Names of creatures begin to be capitalised, in a way recalling the capitalised substantives in the first section; a sort of affectionate, quasi-totemic empathy is suggested by this, a kind of casual sacredness in well-known things. The process of recovery continues in Section 4, with a growing renewal of powers of observation in the returnees. Section 5 broaches the subject of ancestors. This is a purely white matter; Aboriginal religion, with its reincarnationist schema and its taboo on mentioning the dead, is quite at variance with white reverence for particular, successive ancestors. In the poem, though, the particular pioneer ancestors are, as it were, given the aura of the great ancestral sires of the Central Australian sacred sites, and the timelessness of these founding ancestors is stressed as against their successivity, so there is convergence. Premature judgment of them in modern terms they never heard of is rebuked — one may not preach without a sacrifice — but jokes are permitted, because of the affectionate intimacy they evince. Communion with the dead, of a slyly laconic sort, is established by recalling their *words* and the values behind them through the image of their great animal, the horse. Section 6 celebrates genuine popular pleasures of which the conservation-minded might disapprove, but the vigour, the beauty and the meaning of those sports is discerned because judgment is put aside in favour of *looking*, without prejudices. Non-judgmental looking, if you like. In Section 7, there is an unobtrusive mingling of memory and perception which makes it possible in the end to discern a pattern of human work and settlement going beyond the ambit of one person's sight. Section 8 is almost pure celebration, though it is bound together by the image of blood exacted from all the inhabitants of the forest by one creature's need of it. Blood is a condition of reproduction for mosquitoes, and by inference for other creatures as well. In Section 9, a human type perhaps especially prominent in the New World in recent times, though it isn't confined to the New World, is examined and presented through its characteristic words, the *tjúrunga rétnja* of its values, and the section ends in a sardonic antinomy, with the working men watching boys, new recruits to their non-privileged world, "who think hard work a test, and boys who think it is not a test". You can't win in that game except through real maturity and personal independence. Section 10 is again almost unalloyed celebration, of places and habits of the ibis, with peripheral human figures tentatively rediscovering "things about themselves, and about the ibis". Section 11 continues the celebration of places, and describes the almost accidental acquisition of memory and significance by children; the children are learning ancestral things (and communing with them through the act of eating the fruit) which will inform their sense of the world and of their country, and make it just a bit harder for them to become thoroughly alienated or effectively colonial. You might say they are absorbing the accidents of nationality. The very long twelfth section evokes place and season and the great rhythms of the day and the weather. Its central insight is the one about abandoned things "thronged with spirits". We will come back to this in a moment. Section 13, of course, is the poem's finale, and links the evoked region with the heavens, with what I call the Great Imagery of the stars. The region is *placed* in the universe, and the whole experience of the Holiday, the walkabout quest, is mapped and sealed for the people who now have to go back to their other life. The Southern Cross is evoked emblematically, at each end of the section, and is described in intimately colloquial terms echoing the loving intimacy of the Aboriginal treatment of the Evening Star in the Moon Bone Cycle and the vernacular ease and tang of the most characteristic white Australian style of speech.

Apart from quality, my poem cycle differs from its great model in two main ways. It is progressive, in a loose sort of way, while the Moon Bone Cycle is static and accretive, and it contains irony and social comment, though these are always presented in contexts which have the power to overcome or at least soften them. It would have been treason to the facts of modern Australian life if all conflict, all edginess, had been left out, and only a sugary picture of too-easy reconciliation allowed to remain. Again, there is a time element in my poem, because our white cultures *are* time cultures, and because one of the great secular religions of Australia is worship of the past and of that which has been made harmless and poignant with the passage of time. Abandoned things, whether in folk museums or compendia of obsolete slang, are thronged with spirits for us. Sadly, it is perhaps a measure of the acculturation of the Aborigines, a process in which black radicalism may be just another stage, that we now sentimentalise them in much the same way. For good and ill, one of the chief bearers of our new secular Shinto in recent years has been the conservationist movement. Great tributes have to be paid to that movement for, in particular, implanting the Aboriginal concept of the sacredness of the land and of one's native region in the minds of many Australians. This has come about largely as a by-product of the agitation for Aboriginal land rights — and has begun provoking some white country people to start thinking about *their* land rights, rights to live in places which have formed and continue to nurture their spirit. Where this is merely an attempt to trump the Aborigines, it is to be deplored, but it does point to the inequity of, as it were, releasing one section of our population from the ordinary laws of economics while letting the rest continue to suffer the effects of these. We need to think about the applicability of the principle to all of our people.

In a lecture given to the English Association at Sydney University on 25 May 1973, David Malouf writes:

> It is only through Caliban that we get this sense of the richness of the island, its tumbling fecundity. His capacity to name things, and by naming evoke them, is a different sort of magic from Prospero's but no less powerful and real. It might remind us of the extraordinary way our own Aborigines have possessed the land in their minds, through folkstories, taboos, song cycles, and made it part of the very fabric of their living as we never can.

My contention is that of course "we" can, and some of us do possess the land imaginatively in very much the Aboriginal way. We have recently been awed by the discovery that the Aborigines have been here for thirty or forty thousand years, or even longer, but I think too much is often made of this. Forty thousand years are not very different from a few hundred, if your culture has not, through genealogy, developed a sense of the progression of time and thus made history possible. Aboriginal "history" is poetic, a matter of significant moments rather than of development. To make it historical in our sense requires an imposition of Western thinking.

In art, in my writing, my abiding interest is in integrations, in convergences. I want my poems to be more than just National Parks of sentimental preservation, useful as the National Parks are as holding operations in the modern age. What I am after is a spiritual change that would make them unnecessary. And I discern the best hope for it in convergence of the sort I've been talking about. In Australian civilisation, I would contend, convergence between black and white is a fact, a subtle process, hard to discern often, and hard to produce evidence for. Just now, too, it lacks the force of fashion to drive it; the fashion is all for divisiveness now. Yet the Jindyworobak poets were on the right track, in a way; their concept of *environmental value*, of the slow moulding of all people within a continent or region towards the natural human form which that continent or region demands, that is a real process. Once or twice, perhaps more often, I have been able to capture a sense of that process in verse. From the earliest days, with few real exceptions I can think of (Thomas Keneally is partly one; Xavier Herbert is another), white Australian writers have written about Aborigines as figures *other* than themselves, as objects almost, figures to be described with perhaps very great sympathy, but figures existing over against the writer and his world. Identification with them has been sporadic, fashionable only during a particular period, and has lately been attempted mainly at the level of polemic, which can be exploitative, as well as pointlessly divisive. In particular, urban writing has tended to work over against almost *all* kinds of Australians who do not share a certain derivative "educated" sensibility, and to use Aborigines as a stick to beat the Ockers with.

It is true that ease with Australian imagery has become much more noticeable in our poetry in the last few years. But it is not true to claim, as some do, that the whole question of acceptance of Australia by poets has been resolved and is now old hat. The attitudes, the orthodoxy, of alienation work too powerfully on us for that. It's what I was saying to Lionel Brockman in the Lake Country poem: you, as a primal embodiment of essential Australia, are right to reject people like me. The takeover smell, the gubba smell, is still strong on us, because modernist orthodoxy has changed art from being Culture (which is bad enough) to being *a* culture, an enclave of borrowed despairs over against our fellow Australians. I am deprived of my natural audience by the stain of association; for now, and perhaps all my life, I have to live with that and try not to let it distort my work.

I'm out to break that gubba-ism, though. I am grateful beyond measure to the makers and interpreters of traditional Aboriginal poetry and song for many things, not least for showing me a deeply familiar world in which art is not estranged, but is a vital source of health for all the members of a community, and even goes magically beyond the human community, ensuring proper treatment of the natural world by its dominant member-species. Aboriginal art has given me a resort of reference and native strength, a truly Australian base to draw on against the constant importation of Western decays and idiocies and class consciousness. If the lore-which-is-law has a weakness, it is in its too-rigid separation of the sexes, and in its secrecy, though that has clearly been a strength as well, in times of violent conquest. The parallelisms, the convergences here are fascinating, especially as regards separation of the sexes. This separation seems to have been particularly rigid in Central Australia: the Northern Aranda circumcision story may refer to a historic moment in the past in which the ritual separation was begun, or accentuated. In my region, spiritual adventures, usually under the cloak of alcohol, were a male preserve, while women were expected to preserve a certain fairly narrow Puritan respectability. Venturing was for men: women were supposed to embody stability. Among Aborigines in eastern Australia, women have often found solace in conversion to Christianity, while men, deprived of the flights and intricacies of their religious preserve, have suffered a crippling inner collapse — and it is the same with white men deprived by fashion of their military and work-ethic themes and scorned for their decency and lack of education. In times of conquest, or repudiation, it is possible that while women suffer more, men lose more.

With responsible scholars like Berndt, Strehlow and some others, one may be sure one is not reproducing anything which should not be published. Strehlow, in particular, was entrusted with the Aranda sacred verses in order that he might preserve them against the day when the old culture died out, at least in its old pure form. At his death, he still held large amounts of material which cannot and should not be released until those who own it in the traditional sense are dead. I gather some mainly pictorial material did get out improperly, through what looks like naiveté about the international syndication links of popular magazines; this was the unfortunate *Stern* case. The elders of many tribes have made at least tacit provision for the storage of important material in white archives, knowing that assimilation and acculturation are facts; in many places, few if any young men are found fit or willing to embark on the lifelong arduous disciplines of traditional ritual instruction.

It is to the credit of the Jindyworobak poets that they were the first white artists to try to make assimilation a two-way street. Convergence is a better word here, though; assimilation carries too deep a stain of conquest, of expecting the Aborigines to make all the accommodations while white people make none. The Jindies represent a creolising impulse in our culture which may be constant, though faint just now and inhibited by a temporary ascendancy of separationist rhetorics. I suspect that creolisation and separatism are complementary impulses which will persist in our society for centuries, each having its alternating periods of dominance. Perhaps ironically, the present phase of confrontation has led to an emphasis on and an enrichment of the idea of the sacred in Australia, at a time when religious concepts were supposed to be in decline. Even those interested in using the Aboriginal struggle as a stalking-horse against the wider social order were constrained to talk about sacred things, and keep alive a term they would otherwise wish to see disappear.

My guess is that creolising convergences will have their next run when the Land Rights phase has obtained whatever proportion of its mostly quite moderate claims the practical politics of the nation allow it. It should be remembered, of course, that the Jindyworobaks were not solely concerned with the resources of

Aboriginal culture; they sought recognition for all genuinely Australian traditions, including such suppressed ones as Barossa German. The movement did start in South Australia after all. In a way, they were our first multiculturalists, long before we imported the Ethnic idea wholus-bolus from Canada and the United States. In much the same way, the Australia First movement some of them were peripherally involved with was arguably a forerunner, a generation early, of one very major strand of the anti-Vietnam campaign. With hindsight, it is possible to see both impulses as having implicit republican content. And of course some of the Jindies were out-and-out republicans.

My affinity with Aboriginal art and thought is only partly elective, and goes on into convergences I have yet to explore. The ground of integration, of convergence, is rocky and ill-mapped; sooner or later, I will have to give some blood for dancing there. What I hope I may have done so far is to promote, and revive, the use of Aboriginal themes and imagery in Australian poetry. Although mistakes and distortions are probably inevitable — and may indeed be fruitful in artistic terms — I hope I have got my borrowings mostly right, and done some justice to our greatest autochthonous tradition. It may be proper for me to close by quoting from Strehlow again, daringly, though I see myself mainly as a precursor; on page 729 of *Songs of Central Australia*, he writes:

It is my belief that when the strong web of future Australian verse comes to be woven, probably some of its strands will be found to be poetic threads spun on the Stone Age hair-spindles of Central Australia.

Meanjin 4/1977

Cole of the Funny Picture Book

Cole of the Book Arcade: A Biography of E. W. Cole by Cole Turnley (Cole Publications, 1974)

In its heyday in the last few decades of the nineteenth century, Cole's Book Arcade had over a million books on its shelves. A host of supporting attractions included a monkey house, a band to supply music, a tea salon, a bazaar complete with Indian hawkers and an Ornament Exhibition billed as "the prettiest sight in Australia". Best of all, it was the policy of the Arcade that anyone might read the stock to his heart's content without being asked to buy. Clearly a folk university, and an autodidact's paradise! There was nothing like the Arcade anywhere else, and it was the heart and pride of Melbourne during the boom years and the nineties depression alike. It was also a very personal creation, and depended for its life on the wonderfully humane, eccentric and moralising spirit of its founder.

Within ten years of his death in 1918, the great Arcade was gone, and only the unique Cole's Funny Picture Books survived as its memorial, being "among the oldest, oddest and most deeply rooted of Australian institutions" as the poet Randolph Stow has described them, and a publishing phenomenon with few parallels. Never out of print since Cole's own day, they have sold over three million copies.

Edward William Cole was born in the village of Woodchurch, near Tenterden in Kent, on 4 January 1832. His father, a farm labourer named Amos Cole, died when Edward was three or four years old, and the boy's mother subsequently married a man called John Watson, a strict Wesleyan but a kindly man, who always treated Edward and his brother Richard as though they were his own children, and taught them to read from the family Bible before sending them to the village school. Here, Edward came under the influence of a schoolmaster who was something of a freethinker and who introduced the boy to astronomy. Reproved sternly by his stepfather when he voiced doubts about the Biblical story of creation, Cole nevertheless grew up with an independent and questioning mind.

Given his half of the forty sovereigns the boys' father had left them, he considered joining his elder brother on the Californian goldfields, but fear of crossing the ocean caused him to seek his fortune in London instead. There he hawked sandwiches, almost starved, very nearly took the Queen's Shilling — he was a quarter of an inch too short and was told by the recruiting sergeant to "come back when you're not so tired and slumped-like" — and finally emigrated, first to South Africa, then to Australia.

Melbourne, when young Cole landed there, was a raw frontier town in the grip of gold fever. Cole and a mate went to the Forest Creek diggings, where the mate died of a combination of typhoid and dysentery known in those days as Colonial Fever. Alone again, as he preferred to be — all his life, Cole was happiest, he said, in "the company of one" — the ex-digger found he could earn more by selling lemonade to the miners than with his pick and shovel, and thus set up the first of the stalls which he was to run and out of which, more than a decade later, the Book Arcade was to grow.

A many-minded, thoughtful and energetic man, Cole combined his business ventures with a programme of omnivorous reading, devouring especially anything he could get on the great religions of the world. He became a syncretist, convinced of the validity and value of all the great religious traditions, and the earliest of his many attempts at educating the public in tolerance and the broader view was a pamphlet entitled "The Real Place in History of Jesus and Paul", which he brought out in 1867. Then, and on the many subsequent occasions on which he trotted it out, this pamphlet, like most of his other serious philosophical writings, only achieved any substantial circulation when the author gave it away for nothing.

From the quotations which his grandson Cole Turnley scatters through his affectionate and very well-written biography, one can see why. For the most part, though the ideas aren't all bad, the tone is naive, sentimental and preachy, too much so even for an age almost as preachy as our own. The style is all wrong for intellectual readers, too programmatic and simplistic by half, while some of Cole's ideas may have seemed too much in advance of their time for the general reader. He did have the satisfaction, though, thirty-odd years after he had predicted it, of seeing heavier-than-air flight achieved.

Cole had a fervent belief in the coming federation of mankind, and supported the federation of the Australian colonies as a first step towards it. Accordingly, he was bitterly disappointed by the adoption of the White Australia policy, and fought against it in a stream of books and other writings, all to no avail. Many of Cole's serious concerns, his lifelong opposition to the evils of racism for example, left their deposits in the Funny Picture Books, but his yearning to be listened to and regarded as a thinker and man of letters, rather than merely a highly original merchandiser of books, went almost totally unsatisfied. Melbourne and Australia thought of Cole as perhaps the supreme eccentric of his time. They were delighted by the original things he did, and by the Book Arcade with its rainbows and its notions. They loved to recall the story of how Cole advertised for a wife, and got one, but they took less notice of his achievement in getting right through the Hungry Nineties without sacking any of his staff.

But I won't pre-empt all the good things in this book. It is, incidentally, very well produced, and a lesson to publishers in the art of producing illustrated books which *are* books and not merely coffee-table extravaganzas. The cover carries a reproduction of the cover of the first Funny Picture Book; only one very valuable specimen of this edition is now known to exist. As well as being a valuable contribution to Australiana, and quite the best biography I've read for a long time, the story of E. W. Cole would make an ideal Christmas present. That would be very much in his tradition — as is the book's very reasonable price.

Sydney Morning Herald, 30 November 1974

Of Phenicopters and Beccaficoes

The Pantropheon, or A History of Food and Its Preparation in Ancient Times by Alexis Soyer (Paddington Press, 1977)

The thing which strikes modern people, when we think about the eating habits of the ancient world, is the number of foodstuffs familiar to us which were unknown to the ancients. Imagine a world with no potatoes. And no tea, or coffee, or cocoa, or oranges, or sugar, or cauliflowers, or capsicums, or even any pumpkins or spinach. And no peanuts or tobacco either. Imagine Italy without the tomato. Or summer without watermelons.

The Classical peoples did, of course, have pretty well our whole range of meats, fish and poultry, excluding the turkey, and most of the grains, fruits and spices we know, as well as many of our modern vegetables. Some familiar things were not used nearly as freely as we might use them. Garlic was known, for example, but despised as soldiers' food, just as the Greeks scorned beans as food for lawyers. The poor subsisted on pretty monotonous fare; gruel was the Roman staple in pre-Classical times, being replaced by bread comparatively late. Crowds at the gladiatorial games feasted on cooked peas, and soldiers conquered the known world on a basic diet of hard *buccellatum* biscuit, onions and watered vinegar.

The ancients were deficient in stimulants (or comparatively free of them, if that is your preference). Distilled grain spirits were a later Celtic invention, and beer was an aberration which the cultured Egyptians shared with the barbarian tribes of northern Europe. Apart from wine, usually served with water, or else mixed with honey and all manner of spices, the Greeks had only poetry and conversation, plus perhaps the odd bit of pederasty, to enliven their banquets, and the Romans had only these plus cruelty and licence. Unless we count cannabis seed, which was sometimes served fried as a dessert. The author of the *Pantrophaeon* is rather disgusted by this:

That hemp should be spun and made into ropes, well and good, but to regale oneself with it after dinner, when the stomach is overloaded with

Of Phenicopters and Beccaficoes

food, and hardly moved from its lethargic quietude by the appearance of the most provoking viands that art can invent — what depravity! What strange perversion of the most simple elements of gastronomy!

Perhaps the ancients knew something which Soyer didn't.

As readers will have guessed from this quotation, if the name of Alexis Soyer hadn't already put them on the alert, this is not a contemporary book, but a reprint of an 1853 treatise on the history of food and cuisine in ancient times.

Alexis Soyer was a talented, dashing, delightfully vain Frenchman who, as well as reigning supreme as the master chef of London's Reform Club, also organised food relief for the starving during the great Irish famines. With Florence Nightingale, he reorganised the catering system of military hospitals during the Crimean War. His grand breakfast for two thousand people at Gwydyr House in 1838 long remained a legend, as did his *banquet de luxe* for Ibrahim Pasha and a hundred and fifty guests on 1 July 1846. The breadth of his reading, and his wealth of Classical knowledge, are astounding. The ease of his High Victorian prose is a delight, too: though French by birth and training, he wrote this and most of his other books in English, and his style is almost entirely free of Gallicisms.

M. Soyer's history is craftsmanlike, in his own rather than the academic sense, and probably the better for it. He begins with a short account of ancient agriculture, then moves on through a detailed discussion of ingredients, to methods of preparation, preservation and cooking, to culminate in descriptions of meals, service, tables, eating habits and the like. At times, his writing has a delightful straight-faced quality, as when he recounts how shepherds used to cook eggs by whirling them around rapidly in their slings, the cooking being done by the heat of friction with the air.

Reading the book, one gets the impression that Roman banquets were in some ways rather like modern Chinese and South-East Asian ones. Courses consisted of dozens of dishes placed on the table together, with little concern for gradations, and many of the dishes served would probably seem to us a bit like the sweet-and-sour ones of Southern Chinese cuisine. Sugar ("honey of reeds") was a rare import from the East, used almost solely in medicine, but honey was apt to be used in almost everything, even the meat dishes.

Many dishes, too, may have tasted rather like those of South-East Asia, because of the Romans' fondness for *garum*, a condiment made of fermented fish and brine that sounds very like the *ngoc mam* sauce of Vietnam. *Garum* was likely to be added to almost anything, rather as some moderns add tomato sauce. In that age of no refrigeration, too, many foods came in pickled or preserved form. One great difference from East Asian cookery, of course, was the use made of milk and cheese. Butter, on the other hand, was a rarity pretty well confined to medical preparations.

The author has some hard things to say about the *nouveau riche* Romans' habit of scouring the world for rare and expensive delicacies — the fatty tongues of flamingoes, or phenicopters as he calls them, were a particular favourite — and he disapproves of their frequent gluttony. Of course, they only ate one main meal a day, usually in the evening, but after reading about some of their blowouts it comes as no surprise to learn that they went in for digestive salts. Food was eaten mainly with the fingers, one's own or those of slaves, though spoons were used for eggs and shellfish. Despite the breads and honey the ancients ate, it is clear from the recipes and menus given that the diet of even the richest Greeks and Romans was basically healthier than our own, lower on carbohydrates and higher in protein and roughage. If there is one fancy dish I would like to see resurrected, perhaps only once, from the days of Apicius and Macrobius, it would be the little fig-pecker birds, or beccaficoes, roasted and served in a jacket of fine sauce inside an egg.

Unlike some of his noble and mercantile patrons, Soyer seems to have had a real concern for the poor of his day. He does not fail to mention the horror of ancient slavery, when a magnate could fatten his conger eels for the table by throwing live slaves to them, and there is a very dry passage in the introduction to this book which still bears thinking about:

The Greeks and Romans, egoists if ever there were any, supped for themselves and lived only to sup; our pleasures are ennobled by views more useful and more elevated. We often dine for the poor, and sometimes dance for the afflicted, the widow and the orphan.

Sydney Morning Herald, 3 December 1977

The Aboriginal Poet — An Ecological Niche

People Are Legends: Aboriginal Poems by Kevin Gilbert (University of Queensland Press, 1978); *Jagardoo: Poems from Aboriginal Australia* by Jack Davis. Drawings by Harold Thomas (Methuen of Australia, 1978)

In her introduction to Jack Davis's second collection of verse, Judith Wright has written:

It would be wise of white Australians to give (these poems) an attentive and thoughtful hearing, for many reasons — not least for the debt we owe to ourselves as well as to the Aboriginal people, a debt we cannot redeem by any Budget allocations, for it is a human debt.

This is profoundly true, and deserves to stand as a final justification for both books under review. I have acknowledged the debt publicly more than once, but it would be undignified for me to labour the point when I am going to have to say some hard things about black writers who attempt to write poetry in English.

For a number of reasons, both humane and merely fashionable, a section of the white Australian reading public wants there to be at least a few good Aboriginal poets whom they can point to, admire and take up. Since as yet there are none, premature acclaim has been accorded to some people who are really little more than publicists. The impulse is respectably liberal but enormously patronising. We are in effect setting a lower standard for black writers, and thus demonstrating that we respect neither them nor poetry.

It is worth noting that neither of these books carries any acknowledgments for magazine publication of the work they contain. Their authors haven't come through the normal routes where you have to satisfy editors (and where, be it said, most editors would have been delighted to help them with advice on technique and necessary poetic standards). Their books simply appear out of nowhere, rather as liberal curios.

When a truly first-rate Aboriginal poet does appear in Australia, he or she will surely be one who has evaded, or gone beyond, the corruptions of premature white praise, of easy, stereotyped indignation and disguised careerism, the "leader of our people" syndrome. He or she will very likely be a lonely person, rejected in some measure by both "sides", but able nonetheless to bring genuine honour to the unluckiest group of Australians, honour worthy of their suffering. And worthy, too, of Aboriginal achievement in the traditional or semi-traditional arts of painting, song-poetry and the dance.

I have spelt out the specifications for the future Great Aboriginal Poet at some length because it is still just possible that Kevin Gilbert could one day fill them. At forty-five, he isn't too old to continue developing. He has come a long way already, through some frightful country. He is intelligent, passionately concerned, loyal to the very poorest of his people, and has an ear for many different rhythms and registers of language. Against fearful odds, he has managed to educate himself, and can write clear, vigorous prose of no little profundity.

He has great understanding of people, at least of Aboriginal people, and can create dramatic *personae* who are effective mouthpieces for points of view. And he has the candour to make them say some hard things to his own folk; the biting humour of Granny Koori is a case in point. That, and the compassionate, dignified poem "The Contemporary Aboriginal", are probably the best-realised pieces of his collection. He has flashes of real verbal wit, as in the vernacular "Advance Australia Fair":

> Their Captain Cook, alias Captain Kidd
> Took *all* of Australia off us
> No bother about stealin' no fuss
> Why can't we have some of our land?
> Takes it out of nobody's hand
> Millions of miles of "Crown Reserve"
> They've got a thievin' bloody nerve!

In the last poem in the book, entitled "True", he also gropes interestingly towards a real tightness of intellectual argument, and we suddenly no longer hear the activist making declarations, but the nascent poet wrestling with complexity in a way which, if not successful this time, at least points in the direction of a real deepening in his aspirations.

Over against his strengths, Gilbert has a number of weaknesses which will need to be combated as his discipline grows. There is no real observation in his work, for one thing. The details of black degradation and privation are there, but they are pretty well always the expected ones, familiar now, and lacking real surprise. They aren't worked on in an artistic way and made memorable. We don't really feel or see the bag humpies, or the riverbank camps, or the

The Aboriginal Poet — An Ecological Niche

flagons; they shame us in a conventional way, but never really pierce our marrow.

The urgent speed of his anger also allows him to be content, too often, with forced rhymes and poorly scanning lines, and a certain carelessness or uncertainty about levels of language betrays him into old-hat poeticisms such as "neath" and "pen this letter" when he is trying to be most serious. Worst of all, he confuses vehemence with poetic intensity. Unlike many radical versifiers, he has things to be vehement about, but poetry will not be forced.

It's really a matter, I suppose, of trusting poetry. A great many Australians fail at poetry because they don't really trust it. They try to use it as a shortened, pithy form of journalism, with the energy coming from the external subject matter rather than from its imaginative transformation within the poem.

Of course, learning to think poetically, as Mr Gilbert seems to be doing in the last poem of his collection, has dangers for the committed. They have to begin facing the depths of things, and risking what may be a precarious and bitterly won identity. In the case of Aboriginal poets, I imagine that one of the things they'll have to wrestle with is their people's real and only recently rejected biculturalism, the guilty, dismissed, but still-potent white ancestors within them, the passionately denied fathers.

If I have concentrated on Kevin Gilbert, it is because his journalism and other prose, as much as anything in this book, lead me to entertain real hopes for him as a writer. The noted West Australian playwright Jack Davis, for his part, is an obviously decent and gentle man who has rendered good service to his people, not least through his editorship of the magazine *Identity*, but he scarcely exists as a poet. He does write on themes other than the Aboriginal plight, some of the time, but almost nowhere does he generate any poetic excitement. In a book of cheepings, he strikes only one clear note of song; Judith Wright also mentions this one, in her very generous introduction to his book. It's in the catalogue-poem titled "I Love":

> A full moon's golden edge
> Above the range,
> The call of mopoke
> And the frogs of April...

The whole poem is simple and peaceful like that, and comes from a time before a current and perhaps temporarily necessary divisiveness between two sorts of Australians.

Sydney Morning Herald, 7 October 1978

The Year of Living Dangerously

The Year of Living Dangerously by C. J. Koch (Nelson, 1978)

For most Australians of past generations, South Asia, by which I mean roughly India, Sri Lanka, Malaya and the then Dutch East Indies, was a band of mysterious darkness lying between their safe colonial world and the cool green spaces of ancestral Europe. In more recent times, the mental darkness has been made physical for tens of thousands of travellers by airline schedules which always seem to take one through tropical Asia at night. The band of darkness becomes a bleary-eyed half-world of hallucinatory airports sweltering in the heat of midnight.

This darkness is a pervasive presence in C. J. Koch's splendid new novel. It is the tropical darkness of Conrad or Graham Greene, the spiritual night in which Western souls are brought to strange extremes. More deeply it is Kali-Yuga, the Dark Age of Hindu mythology, the night of the fearsome goddess Durga, the dancer in the cemetery. Of course, thousands of Australians have also sampled the daylight realities of our near north, and Koch's novel does not hide from the flat equatorial glare. But nearly all of its most significant moments occur at night, away from the sun, by street light, airport lights, hotel candlelight or the dim oil lamps of the Jakarta slums.

And yet it is in no way an obscure book; everywhere, it glows with the lucidity of very mature art. It is a profound and beautiful book, symphonic in its structure and recurrences; in a time when many Australian books strive to be smart and cool, it is instinct with deep feeling. At the same time, it is a first-rate read, and tells its momentous story with a style and pace few recent novels I've seen can rival. It goes miles beyond the average international thriller by, say, a Len Deighton or a John le Carré, and on the way it beats them at their own game.

Every Merdeka Day, in the huge Jakarta Sports Stadium, it was the custom of the late President Sukarno to give his ecstatic followers an inspirational name by which the coming year would be known. Now it is 1965, the Year of Living Dangerously. As the

Indonesian economy collapses and no more money can be borrowed abroad for the monuments and other grandiose symbols of nationhood, Sukarno has taken his country out of the United Nations, instituted confrontation with Malaysia, and is in effect cocking a snook at the whole world.

He has created a frenzied revolutionary theatre for his people, in which slogans and acronyms are locked in heady conflict. Crush Malaysia! Down with Nekolim!

The few Western journalists permitted to stay in Jakarta hide their white faces in the Hotel Indonesia's air-conditioned Wayang bar when off duty, living on camaraderie and excitement, swapping Sukarno stories.

One man in the Wayang Club has a sympathy with Sukarno which goes beyond media analysis and yarn-swapping. He is the Chinese-Australian cinecameraman Billy Kwan, a borderline dwarf four-feet-six tall, a brilliant eccentric with the gift, given to saints and freaks, of being able to cast aside his dignity and play the merry fool to men of no vision. Beneath his fooleries and theories, Kwan is a man of passionate depth, who sees himself as condemned to live through others. He identifies with two men in the novel, with Sukarno and with the handsome, brilliantly competent correspondent Guy Hamilton, who works for Australian radio and TV.

In this novel of dualities, both are ambiguous, divided figures, like Kwan himself. Hamilton is secretly torn, in a way that has a long tradition in Australian writing, between English origins and an Australian upbringing. Sukarno, the god-king and liberator of his country, is a man born of a Balinese Hindu mother and a Moslem father, a Javanese aristocrat of the *priyayi* class who idolises the proletariat and the Marhaen, his term for the small farmers of Java, and is idolised in return.

As the year sweeps on towards the terrible climax of 30 September, the night of the PKI coup and the military and Moslem countercoup which followed, both of his heroes fail Kwan. The man of surrogates is finally driven to act, in person and alone. He resolves to reach Sukarno, to assassinate him or save him — it almost amounts to the same thing. The dictator has lost the impossible balance he was trying to hold between the disparate forces of the nation, and is falling away from his own poetic vision of Marhaenism into the hands of the Marxists, while out in the countryside the Moslem peasantry seethe with hatred of the PKI gangs who seize their property and spit on their God. "They are like dogs," a Moslem village elder tells Hamilton, "they have no souls." It is a presage of massacre.

In a novel that is also about tragic imbalance and the loss of balance, the author never loses his own equilibrium. Billy Kwan

Persistence in Folly

sees that the PKI, in embracing exclusively material goals, have become the enemies of tradition and the spirit. "But the spirit doesn't die, of course," he tells Hamilton at their final meeting, "it just becomes a monster."

Underlying the whole novel there is a substratum of myth in which Billy Kwan moves easily, and which the others stumble over without awareness. As Kwan sees it, everything in the tragic slide of Indonesia that year has its parallel in the ancient Javanese shadow-play, the Wayang, which retells the Hindu epics known in Java long before the Moslem missionaries came. The whole book is built, very unobtrusively, on the tripartite structure of the great Pandava cycle and the immemorial conflict, far older than Western political terminology, between the Wayang of the Left and the Wayang of the Right, in which the Wayang of the Left, the enemies of the gods, finally run amok and are destroyed by the Wayang of the Right.

Having narrowly escaped death at the hands of PKI marchers in Central Java, Hamilton encounters the Wayang in a remote village, and senses its great significance for the first time. He sees it almost as a video machine from an unknown civilisation.

From then on, he begins to awaken and grow in awareness, and in the end, through grievous loss, he achieves a measure of wisdom and the ability to love. It is, we are deftly reminded, the last year of the astrological cycle, the year before the witches' year of 1966, the double-six, and already Vietnam is opening doors in the West through which a host of frenzies will come. It is the last year of an older, more formal and reticent world, and perhaps that is why The Year of Living Dangerously now seems so oddly long ago and far away. It is a year in which many things were prefigured for us. Superbly and minutely researched by an author who has been a broadcaster and has worked for UNESCO in Java, the book touches history at many points, but nowhere with greater depth and unease than there.

Sydney Morning Herald, 21 October 1978

Bruce Dawe

Sometimes Gladness: Collected Poems, 1954-1978, by Bruce Dawe (Longman Cheshire, 1979)

Writing in the American magazine *Rocky Mountain Review* (Spring 1978), David Headon says of Bruce Dawe that "his widespread success can be attributed to his bringing the poem out of the universities back to the people".

There's a lot of truth in this, though the universities remain a powerful backstop even for work such as Dawe's, with its wonderfully modulated command of vernacular language and concerns. All the same, for non-academic readers who will tackle poetry, Dawe's poems reflect, and reflect wisely on, the common experience of urban and suburban Australia. They are often genuinely in touch, and more open to a participatory compassion and acceptance than most recent Australian writing, with its lumpenmandarin disdain for the common life of Australian people.

Along with the strong, distinctive voice, it is probably this which gives his work its real popularity. Dawe's books sell better than almost any other books of verse in Australia, and his work has been set for study all over the country.

At its weakest, Dawe's work has the faults of its virtues. It can approach the topical "smoko" recitation or the loosely versified preaching-to-the-converted that goes with peasant prints and guitars, but just a little way beyond that it can flower attractively into a sort of arch tribal celebrativeness that is finally on the side of love rather than of disdain:

> When children are born in Victoria
> they are wrapped in the club-colours, laid in
>   beribboned cots,
> having already begun a lifetime's barracking.
>
> Carn, they cry, Carn... feebly at first
> while parents playfully tussle with them
> for possession of a rusk: Ah, he's a little Tiger!
>   (And they are...)
>   (Life-cycle)

Persistence in Folly

At its highest and purest, Dawe's poetry achieves an elegiac singing mode that is both indigenous and very powerful. You strike this in, say, "Homecoming", which is already beginning to look like the only really distinguished Australian poem about Vietnam, or in the beautiful "Elegy for Drowned Children":

> What does he do with them all, the old king:
> Having such a shining haul of boys in his sure net.
> How does he keep them happy, lead them to forget
> The world above, the aching air, birds, spring?
>
> • • •
>
> Unless he loved them deeply how could he withstand
> The voices of parents calling, calling like birds by the
>   water's edge,
> By swimming pool, sand-bar, river-bank, rocky
>   ledge,
> The little heaps of clothes, the futures carefully
>   planned?

It is always a delight to hear Dawe read his poems aloud, in his mock-episcopal cadence; he is probably the best reader among Australian poets. The voice comes unfailingly off the page, too, working with and intricately against the rhythms of common speech and lofty rhetoric alike.

Because of the continuous demand for Dawe's work, Cheshire has now issued a volume of his collected poems, designed to update and supersede his earlier selected volume, *Condolences of the Season*, which has been in print since 1971. The new book reprints most of the poems in the earlier selection, and adds a good many new pieces. Nearly all of Dawe's best poems reappear, except for "Somewhere Friendly", a poem about the Resurrection which has the freshness and indigenous quirkiness of a good primitive painting, and is an old favourite of mine.

In general, it is the religious poems which tend to have been dropped from the new collection, whether from motives of strict judgment, waning faith or academic respectability it would be improper to speculate. The new book isn't arranged chronologically, but under twelve fairly broad headings related to subject matter and concerns. Each section has one of the famous fake quotations as its epigraph.

There is, however, a chronological index at the back and this, rather sadly, reveals that very few of the best Dawe poems are recent. Apart from a biting Chestertonian rebuke to the Soviet trusty-poet Voznesensky and a bitter tilt at a now-rescinded recognition by an earlier Australian Government of the Soviet takeover of the Baltic States — our Governments must be unique in the world for their readiness to lick spittle even *before* they're asked — there is really nothing much of interest later than 1970.

Most of Dawe's trivial pieces, topical hits at Queensland, Bjelke-Petersen and the like, date from his years as an academic at the Institute of Advanced Education in Toowoomba, the Provincial City he evoked so movingly if despairingly in the superb poem of that name he wrote in 1970. Toowoomba is perhaps a long way from the Melbourne of his younger years, and perhaps the academy has known how to play a waiting game. Lacking the international readership his work certainly deserves, even as nationally successful a poet as Dawe can't hope to live and support a family on royalties alone, and Academe can at least provide security of income and work that isn't all drudgery. It does subtly enforce conformities, though, and I would be deeply sorry if Dawe's great gift has desiccated there, because I have always enjoyed his work and admired it. He is surely one of the best three or four poets we have had in this country.

Sydney Morning Herald, 3 February 1979

The Greater Metroland Anthology

The Penguin Book of English Verse edited by John Hayward (Allen Lane, 1979)

In the twenty-three years since it was first published, the *Penguin Book of English Verse* has established itself as one of the great beginners' anthologies, read and dog-eared by lovers of poetry everywhere; there is probably no more popular introduction to the core tradition of English poetry. It has also established itself as one of *the* great textbooks for poetry's large captive public; it is prescribed year after year by schools and university English departments from Abidjan to Zamboanga. I have no idea how many times it has been reprinted, since the book itself doesn't say, but several dozen times would be no wild guess. Now Allen Lane have brought it out in a handsome hardback edition at a price which, considering the riches of its content and today's bookshop prices, is not really excessive. All the same, a lot has happened in over two decades, and it is fair to ask whether even a great standard anthology can continue to be reprinted and reprinted without any change or any updating.

For one thing, it now carries a flavour of cultural imperialism, and a compromised form of cultural imperialism at that. It is *not*, after all, a book of purely English poetry, at least not after the mid-nineteenth century, but a book of English and American poetry; the other great metropolitan centre of literary power has had to be admitted and its productions included. Lacking similar prestige and pull, if not comparable quality, the other English-speaking nations remain unrepresented. Students in those countries using this book inevitably get the impression that even the best of their countrymen aren't worthy to be considered among the tops.

The very special cachet which Penguin books still confer cannot fail to give students at least some sense of a high table at which only the master poets are invited to dine. English teachers, many of them, perhaps most of them, go out into the classrooms with this imputed hierarchy in the back of their minds, and either propagate it outright or in some way betray the fact that deep down they believe it. And so another culturally colonised generation is formed, of people slightly but crucially damaged in their confidence and self-respect.

To be fair, when the book first came out, studies in what has come to be called Commonwealth literature had scarcely begun anywhere. The teaching of any mere colonial literature would have been unthinkable in the United Kingdom. The situation has changed a lot since 1956, however. Not only are the writers of the former colonies, first the black ones, then the rest, now being studied in literally dozens of universities all over the world, but the climate of thinking has begun to change too. Writers and at least some readers outside the English-language dual monarchy are beginning to question the prestige of authors who, however they may appear to dissent from the ruling values of London and New York (or Huddersfield and Marin County, for that matter), are yet exalted above equally good or better writers by the disguised nationalisms and resulting powerful publicity machines of the metropolitan powers. And exalted too, particularly in the case of America, by forces at once cruder and more subtle still; it is not far-fetched to say that the prestige of all artistic productions emanating from that country today is powerfully if invisibly underwritten by the existence of Wall Street and the Polaris submarine.

Again, continuing to take this hard but not unfair line, it would be possible to argue that the 1956 Penguin book, continually reissued, serves as a device which sets the mental climate for, and so helps to legitimise, the cold-blooded commercial domination of the book market in the rest of the English-speaking world by British and American publishers. Their books pour into our countries, and almost none of ours are allowed to flow out; if they are exported, they will not, in general, be reviewed or distributed in the United States or Great Britain, and all sorts of iniquitous agreements exist to perpetuate the closed-shop system, though it is fair to add that non-metropolitan publishing houses with bridgeheads in London and New York are often extremely sluggish about extending them. They are unable, with very rare exceptions, to attract first-rate local staff, and are in any event themselves hypnotised by obeisances to the centres they have managed to penetrate. It's the same brain-wash: the "inferiority" of writing from the smaller English-speaking nations is a self-fulfilling prophecy which is *enforced*, so that our people and theirs will continue to believe it.

The original editor of the Penguin book, John Hayward, is now dead, and it would be a delicate matter, in any revision of the book, to modify his selections. It would also be a pity, since, for the period before the present century, they are generally excellent.

A lot of changes and excisions could be made in the twentieth-century part of the book, though, and room could easily be made for a dozen or so of the best poets from outside the London-New York axis; the banal Bridges and the equally mediocre Edward Arlington Robinson could easily be dropped altogether, for example, to accommodate, say, Slessor and Judith Wright, de la Mare could readily be pruned to accommodate James Baxter. Edith Sitwell might easily yield her space to William Plomer, the brilliant South African who even, for heaven's sake, lived and published in England, and thus should be exempt from the metropolitan bias against "colonial" publishing and literary life.

Again, the book's bindings would probably stand the extra twenty pages or so which it would take to represent the good metropolitan poets of the past two decades. In 1956, it was fair enough to stop at Dylan Thomas; now, to achieve a similar contemporary relevance, it would probably have to come up to Seamus Heaney. With such updating, and a proper recognition of the fact that literature in English has for fifty or more years been polycentric and world-wide, this could once again be one of the great anthologies and the best poetry textbook going.

Sydney Morning Herald, 14 April 1979

The Big Loose Poems that Rule Us

The Origin of Table Manners: Introduction to a Science of Mythology, Volume 3, by Claude Levi-Strauss. Translated from the French by John and Doreen Weightman (Jonathan Cape, 1979)

Large synthesising theories, of the sort attempted by writers such as Freud, Darwin or Marx, are in many ways similar to large works of art. They are like huge poems, with analogous massings of observed detail, big recurring themes and daring leaps of insight. It is probably best to see them this way — certainly it is infinitely less dangerous than regarding them as revelations which explain the world and justify action; that is the tyrannical and often brutal path of ideology. If we consider the large theories as quasi-artistic constructs, we have a right to expect of them that they will bring about something like artistic suspension of disbelief; I've never yet met with one which wholly did this for me, though Darwin came close for a good while. I suspect that Levi-Strauss may be, or may eventually be, in the class of the great theorisers named above, but fairly often in this book I found myself questioning his leaps of interpretation and asking: Is this really what that particular myth is about? Is this parallel between two different myths from widely separated places really valid? Maybe, maybe not...

Also, I was worried a bit by his very heavy reliance on North and South American myths, to the near exclusion of mythological material from the other continents. Granted, South America has been the scene of most of his own very extensive field work, but surely it is a bit premature to attempt a general synthesis of myth and its place in human mental and social life without considering relevant material from the whole world. We don't know yet whether basic similarity of all human groups around the world is a matter of fact or of ideology, at bottom. It may be something we postulate, or anyway exaggerate, to protect us against the very real horrors of racism.

On the other hand, Levi-Strauss' postulations are fascinating, if intricate, and represent an intellectual feast of a high order, both for those professionally concerned with mythology and for the general reader who has the stamina to face just over five hundred pages of unfamiliar matter and close reasoning.

And the subject itself is enormously important. It is fair to say that everywhere outside the quasi-rationalist enclave which Western man has so recently created, the elaboration of myths has been perhaps *the* great human endeavour, since it is through them that man has attempted to order and make sense of the world and to live in a civilised, balanced way in that world. And, of course, this same use of myth still goes on in a disguised way within the Western enclave, too.

Myth is man's primal philosophical system, and the one which sees all things as interrelated; it is possible that man's oldest great intellectual synthesis is still the most seminal one ever made: this is the law which is often expressed in the occultist formulation: *That which is above is like that which is below*. This is, in a way, the central underlying tenet of the mythic world view, and is the basis for our seeing God in the likeness of a dove or, to take a less familiar example, the basis on which a Brazilian Indian man refrains from chewing his food noisily and so offending the Sun, that savage figure who is so liable to bring down drought on his crops. In more temperate parts, of course, he might well act in ways which his people would consider "rough" and uncouth, in order to show fellowship with the rough, masculine Sun; he would thereby take on some of its power, and it would take encouragement from him to do its work of warming the world and promoting growth. In the latter society, of course, there would tend to be countervailing myths as well, to restrain the man and the Sun from too much disruptive wildness; the man might be obliged to refrain at set times from eating roasted or grilled meat, the food of hunters in the wilds, and to eat boiled meat, the food of women in camp and thus of domesticity and necessary social restraint. Boiling takes more equipment than grilling or roasting, and thus presupposes a more sedentary style of living as well as a more technologically advanced one. Eating boiled food appeases the feminine Moon.

Every society in the world has its code of "table" manners, even if, as in most cases, it has no tables. Continually relating myth to social custom (*which came first, the custom or the myth?* is a chicken-and-egg question to which the sensible answer is "both", because they're aspects of each other) and to the facts of nature and human physiology and psychology, Levi-Strauss sees myth as forming wherever there are poles of tension between opposites, between masculine and feminine for instance, or between wildness and restraint, or violence and social stability. His is a pervasively dualist view, and pretty convincing overall, in the way these large

The Big Loose Poems that Rule Us

prose-poetries are when they are well done, though we can argue with his interpretation of particular cases.

In this third volume of his ongoing study, he goes beyond the task of bringing to light the hidden logic behind mythic thought, and discerns an ethic behind it as well. This is the ethic which "puts the world before life, life before man, and respect for others before self-interest" — in other words, which stresses, as the myths do, the interrelatedness of all things, and enjoins a responsible attitude towards all things in the light of that realisation. It has probably never been more necessary, as he points out at the end of the book, to proclaim that others, other species, indeed the world itself, must not be treated as *things*, but rather as *beings*, toward whom we need to act with decency and discretion. Of course, it is hard for people who have grown up in the rationalist world view to do this at all naturally; some try, in various well-meant but fairly artificial ways, while their societies are still getting on with the job of finishing off the last remnants of cultures for which the mythic view *is* the natural one.

In sounding a warning note here, I think he makes a small but significant error. He writes:

It remains to be seen whether man's victory over his powerlessness, when carried to a state out of all proportion to the objectives with which he was satisfied during the previous millennia of his history, will not lead back to unreason.

This is a very real danger, but I think we have to object to the word "back". Unreason is not a way "back" to the mythic order, but rather a modern phenomenon which parodies that order; it is the world of cult and fake primitivism, of romanticism and rebellion, and has at its heart an ambition and a hysteria of desperation very foreign to the civilising objectives of traditional myth. Nazism, the Jonestown horror and a host of other examples may well suggest that in fact unreason is the greatest threat to mankind that now exists.

The cure for it, however, is almost certainly not larger doses of desiccating rationality. Bad, corrupt mythology has to be combated with good, civilising, balancing mythology. And that has survived in very real ways in those highest distillations of the mythic heritage, the great religions.

Sydney Morning Herald, 12 May 1979

Isaac Rosenberg

The Collected Works of Isaac Rosenberg: Poetry, Prose, Letters, Paintings and Drawings edited by Ian Parsons (Chatto and Windus, 1979)

There's a piece of perhaps hardboiled writers' folklore, borne out surprisingly often, that if you've managed to build and keep a reputation in your lifetime, it is bound to fade after your death and only start to rise again, if it ever does, some fifty or sixty years later. Fifty years, of course, is the period an author remains in copyright after his death, but it also seems to be approximately the turnover rate for literary sensibility, the time it takes for a dominant tone to pass into history and be seen objectively. Of course, there are cases in which your period of obscurity will last much longer; John Donne was on the outer with critics for more than 250 years. And with poets who die young, especially those who die "relevant" deaths, deaths related to the great concerns of their time, the pattern is apt to be rather different. Love, and the group loyalty of those who were in the battle with the dead one, play a part in such cases. Pity, sentiment, guilt, anger and their political derivatives can enter the picture too, and a reputation can grow up almost as a defiant substitute for the life the author was prevented from living out. In a tragic way, such a reputation can also be made into a substitute for the development which might have made him or her into a major writer. In the years since Issac Rosenberg's death on the Western Front in April 1918, his reputation has grown steadily — and yet it too has undergone a sixty-year spurt. No less than three biographies appeared in 1975, and there have been recent efforts to put him up as the greatest of the lost English poets of the First World War. A Penguin anthology of the War poets, edited by John Silkin, gives Rosenberg pride of place over Owen, Sassoon, Blunden, Graves and all the rest. I think these efforts are misplaced, if honourable, and that they might well embarrass the man himself, if he could hear of them.

It is notable, though also prone to politicising overemphasis, that Rosenberg was almost alone among the significant English poets of the First World War in not being an officer. It meant that he lacked

Isaac Rosenberg

the secure, relatively comfortable background of the others, and that he suffered the full misery of barrack-room brutishness. At the front, his life was probably only marginally more miserable and inconducive to writing than theirs; it is hard to know what difference having some ascribed dignity and having none at all makes when all are in Hell together. It probably makes some, but Rosenberg never harps on the point. His real torment came before this. As an undersized man and a Jew to boot, he appears to have found his first months in the Army almost unendurable. Ian Parsons, who has sensitively edited this complete and probably definitive collection of Rosenberg's writings, recommends that the surviving letters be read through from start to finish, and it is a deeply moving experience. Almost the only time Rosenberg complains or approaches despair is during the period of his training in the so-called Bantam battalion of the Suffolk regiment, among down-and-outs, illiterates and ticket-of-leave men; the Bantam battalion consisted of men so small and weedy they would never have been accepted for the Army in less desperate times. The really tragic thing about Rosenberg's war service is, of course, that he only joined the Army because he was chronically broke; he wanted to help his family by allotting half his weekly seven shillings to them. Men in the AIF at the same period got five shillings a day. He hated war, though he seems to have accepted the current attitudes to Germany and the Kaiser fairly uncritically; he did at least one piece of Jingo versifying in 1914 ("The Dead Heroes") and a few more later on. He found himself drawn into the holocaust by sheer poverty, and several letters survive in which he can be seen resisting the temptation of dreadful but easily available "employment". The Rosenbergs, huddled in the slums of London's East End along with so many other Jewish rufugees from the Russian empire, had never broken out of the cycle of destitution and dependence on their people's communal charities. In his efforts to make a living as a painter-poet (or was it poet-painter?), their son never broke the cycle either; it says a great deal for his courage and endurance that he tried, and a lot for Jewish community spirit and kindness to talent that money was found for his training at the Slade School of Art and for some of his later needs. A few of his letters, from the period before he joined up in October 1915, are clearly begging letters and duty letters to patrons, if you read between the lines; they are cheerful and dignified, however, never arrogant or cringing.

Probably the only good thing the war did for Rosenberg was that it resolved his indecision over whether to concentrate on painting or on poetry; poems can be scribbled with a pencil stub on scrap paper in a dugout, but painting under such conditions is impossible. A few small sketches survive from his war service, but all of his relatively few surviving paintings date from before he went into the Army. Several are reproduced in Ian Parsons' book, but I do not feel able to judge their worth; I know from experience that there's no such thing as a reproduction of a painting. The art critic Maurice de Sausmarez wrote of them that they had "a quality that is intensely personal and suggests the probable direction of a later development. This quality is not easy to characterise, but includes a simplification that moves towards compression of experience rather than towards the schematic, a design which is not arbitrarily imposed as in some of Stanley Spencer's work, but is distilled and inseparable from the content. The symbol always retains the sensuousness of the original experience and he mistrusts an art that uses 'symbols of symbols'."

This is also a very good description of what is best in his poetry. To cite just one example, here is the second stanza of "Midsummer Frost", a poem written in 1914 but revised several times before its publication in the following year:

> See, from the fire-fountained noon there creep
> Lazy yellow ardours towards pale evening,
> To thread dark and vain fire
> Over my unsens'd heart,
> Dead heart, no urgent summer can reach.
> Hidden as a root from air or a star from day;
> A frozen pool whereon mirth dances;
> Where the shining boys would fish.

Beneath all the fag-ends of a worn-out poetical diction, there is something alive in this, a genuine imagination finding terms for inner experience, re-creating it in images rather than in formulae. The image of the heart "hidden as a root from air or a star from day" is pure Rosenberg, alive and infinitely more daring than the tame decorums of most contemporary Georgian poetry; it foreshadows the beautiful image, used in two of his poems written in 1917 ("Soldier: Twentieth Century" and "Girl to Soldier on Leave") of a figure hidden like "a word in the brain's ways". As a whole, "Midsummer Frost" is a failure; the first two stanzas are fascinating, with the real grip and involute strangeness of poetry, the rest of the poem loses tension, loses focus, loses itself in unresolved verbiage. As so often happens, the sense of a powerful, evolving personal style peters out almost as soon as it is created. The poet obviously detected this himself and wrestled with it; time after time, the useful notes which the editor supplies with very many of the poems and fragments record repeated rewritings, recastings, pleas for advice or comment from the half-dozen or

Isaac Rosenberg

more people to whom he would send his drafts and who served as his sounding-boards. In what is really quite a small output if we remember that he was writing seriously for twelve or thirteen years before his untimely death at the age of twenty-eight we see poem after poem marred by the scheme, the arbitrarily imposed design, the retreat into received sentiment, archaism, pallid atmospherics:

> Have we sailed and have we wandered,
> Still beyond, the hills are blue.
> Have we spent and have we squandered,
> What's before us still is new.

That is from "Have We Sailed and Have We Wandered" (1914). It doesn't get better in the remaining two stanzas; the jingling rhyme and metre do all the poet's thinking for him. What is more heartening is the wide variety of attempted forms to be found in the same smallish output. There is even a small impressionist sketch from 1915 that has something of the vivid freshness of a Welsh englyn or a Japanese tanka:

> Green thoughts are
> Ice block on a barrow
> Gleaming in July.
> A little boy with bare feet
> And jewels at his nose stands by.

It is interesting to note that, apart from the very early and unsuccessful "Ballad of Whitechapel", this is the only glimpse of East End life, perhaps of his own childhood, in Rosenberg's whole corpus.

It is also one of only seven or eight poems of Rosenberg's which I would consider complete, finished pieces. More even than most poets, he is a writer of starts, passages, middles, fragments, and more than most poets he has to be read in a spirit of retrieval, of sorting out the magical from the overcompressed, the off-key and the muddled. He has little sense of poetic logic, though he strove to master it. Even the best of his war poems, the four or five on which his reputation has grown, are shaky, with dead lines, patches of bathos and frequent tendencies to melodrama. In his most famous poem, "Dead Man's Dump", there are passages like:

> ...rusty stakes like sceptres old
> To stay the flood of brutish men
> Upon our brothers dear.

And there is the unfortunate description of the dead:

> They lie there huddled, friend and foeman,
> Man born of man, and born of woman,

which does seem rather hard on one side or the other. The whole conception of this poem, in my opinion, is essentially melodramatic; it is rescued only by precariously successful writing strung between some truly excellent bits, such as the well-known image of the death of soldiers:

> When the swift iron burning bee
> Drained the wild honey of their youth

or that other image of the war's stupendous charnel:

> Burnt black by strange decay,
> Their sinister faces lie
> The lid over each eye,
> The grass and coloured clay
> More motion have than they,
> Joined to the great sunk silences.

Melodrama of conception ruins several other poems of the war period altogether, poems such as "In the Trenches", "The Dying Soldier", "In War", and disastrous bathos wrecks the mock-portentous "The Immortals". "Break of Day in the Trenches" succeeds, shakily, because it attempts no very high flights, but really the only satisfyingly complete, all-of-a-piece war poems are two or three quite short ones, the successfully philosophical "A Worm Fed on the Heart of Corinth", "The Troop Ship" perhaps, though it is little more than an impression, and "August 1914", which is worth quoting in full:

> What in our lives is burnt
> In the fire of this?
> The heart's dear granary?
> The much we shall miss?
>
> Three lives hath one life —
> Iron, honey, gold.
> The gold, the honey gone —
> Left is the hard and cold.
>
> Iron are our lives
> Molten right through our youth.
> A burnt space through ripe fields,
> A fair mouth's broken tooth.

I am a little worried by the youth/tooth rhyme; Rosenberg is far from immune to the bad habit of inserting a word, or writing a whole line, for the sake of a rhyme, but, in view of the quality of the rest of the poem and the marvellous image of the ripe fields, the last line can probably be allowed to pass muster. The famous

"Returning, We Hear the Larks" has a more serious weakness in its ending, an image about girl's hair which has not been properly worked out and integrated in the poem; we see that it is a Medusa image, but it has been left conventional and disjointed, not tautened into poetry. This is a great pity, because the conception of the poem is sound and original, and the balancing of joy and deadly threat summons up a vivid sense of a moment in the nightmare life of the trenches, a moment when an unexpected grace comes out of the natural world at dawn and seems to bless stumbling, tired men full of profound relief at still being alive.

Given the circumstances under which Rosenberg wrote his war poems, my strictures may seem harsh; I doubt I'd have done half as well, in his place. I also understand the problems of the slow-developing kind of poet, the poet who experiments widely in order to find his way. There is ample evidence, in the letters, that Rosenberg regarded it as essential to get poems and concepts down and fixed, even in an imperfect way; shaping and refining could come later, after the war. Writing to Laurence Binyon in autumn 1916, he says:

I am determined that war, with all its powers for devastation, shall not master my poeting; that is, if I am lucky enough to come through all right, I will not leave a corner of my consciousness covered up, but saturate myself with the strange and extraordinary new conditions of life, and it will all refine itself into poetry later on.

Similarly, writing to Edward (later Sir Edward) Marsh in May 1917, he says:

I liked your criticism of "Dead mans dump". Mr Binyon has often sermonised lengthily over my working on two different principles in the same thing and I know how it spoils the unity of a poem. But if I couldn't before, I can now, I am sure, plead the absolute necessity of fixing an idea before it is lost, because of the situation it is conceived in.

It is legitimate, I suppose, to wonder how much faith Rosenberg thought he could invest in the prospect of a calm life after the war in which all of its horrors and depths could be refined into great art, and how much he was driven by the reality of terrible danger to get something down on paper, even if patchy and imperfect, something to stand against extinction. Like many of us, he was half in love with the big-poem-yet-to-be-written, and conscious of the provisional nature of nearly all actual poems. It takes time, perhaps a lifetime, to see what is lasting and timeless in one's own work and what isn't, to realise that the great project is *in there,* wound through the texture of what one has done. Rosenberg didn't have that sort of time; he died with youth's belief in an available future, profoundly shaken perhaps, but still necessary to his thinking about his art. If he is sometimes praised nowadays rather in the spirit of the process theory of poetry, the poem as a mimesis of disorder rather than a wrestling with it to discover deeper order, I think that is anachronistic and rather corrupt, an attempt to recruit him to modernist, revolutionary purposes he never espoused and probably never heard of. It is probable that, if he had survived, he would have become a very important poet indeed, perhaps more important than any of the other English poets of the war generation, but it is also likely that his unsureness and lack of an instinctive sense of poetic design would have plagued him for many more years. Despite everything, I do believe his best passages point to a distinctive power in him which might have allowed English poetry to renew itself in a native way through his development. This may be what attracts English critics and poets to his cause, a wish that English poetry had been able to cross over into the modern era in its own terms, without the alien and wrenching effects of Eliot's and Pound's Franco-American modernism, that powerful but suspect strain which English poets have aped and resisted ever since.

But this is a nostalgia for national prestige in art, and resentment at relegation: it's about the Empire. In the long run, Rosenberg might have made the transition to peace better than Wilfred Owen, and might have found more to say. His wide range of experimentation with different modes and subjects before the war suggests it. Compared with the classic, coherent war poems which Owen achieved, however, his look patchy and tentative, and we are forced into valuing potential above performance if we place him above Owen. I think it is more justifiable to see him as ultimately superior to the rest, even Graves. Given a longer run, I'm pretty sure he would have left Graves far behind.

Ian Parsons mourns the lost potential of Rosenberg, but does not stretch it into speculative polemic. He has the more modest purpose of showing that his subject should not be thought of simply as a poet of the war, but as one who achieved distinctive and lasting things in the prewar period, things quite different from and in advance of what most of his Georgian contemporaries were doing. There is some merit in this claim, in that he certainly *tried* many quite distinctive things, poems about a female godhead, about a dead and rotting god, about gigantic, quasi-Blakean figures, and there is the rather fervidly erotic "Night", which reads like a tussle with a deep and potent anima. There are many traces of this figure in his other poems, and we could start what the Germans call *culture-historical* hares if we began to speculate on its significance.

Isaac Rosenberg

To grow too involved in a poet's half-realised or unrealised themes, though, is to court the academic preference for ideas above poetry, that ambitious vice which has been the curse of criticism in this century. In my opinion, the nearest thing to a satisfyingly worked-out poem from Rosenberg's prewar period is the delicate "In Half Delight of Shy Delight", in which the young girl is seen "still plaiting her men-unruffled curls"

> She walks so delicately grave
> As lovely as her unroofed fancies
> Of love's far-linked dances
> In waters of soft night they lave
> Through measureless expanses.

That is the true dancing measure. For an Australian reader, the comparison with Shaw Neilson is probably irresistible. A slighter poem from the same period which achieves simplicity without slipping into trite tum-te tum is "A Bird Trilling its Gay Heart Out". Otherwise, we are once again left with fragments and retrievals.

From the letters, it is clear that Rosenberg carried with him into his wartime period a great many continuities and poetic interests from the past; he probably never thought of the war as his prime theme, in the way that Owen did. The letters show that he held on, naturally enough, to a lot of poetic coggage which he would have had to discard if he had survived; in particular, he remained interested in his huge, fragmentary and nearly unreadable "Moses", a sort of historico-mythical verse play on which he worked for years. An extract from this, the "Ah Kolue" speech, was the only poem of Rosenberg's which ever appeared in Marsh's annual *Georgian Poetry* anthology. It is hard to escape the feeling that, faithful as he was to his Jewish identity and heritage, the Hebrew tradition (got at second hand, since he did not read Hebrew) was never a very fruitful source for his poetry, though he dipped his bucket there many times, and was planning an epic or verse play on Judas Maccabaeus for the postwar period; a lot of his experience of war, and a lot of his thinking about it, was to have gone into this project. I have a feeling he would have met with a good deal of frustration, if he had lived to attempt this. The garment might not have fitted the body. His Hebraic poems always have a worked-up, costume-drama feel to them. He was, after all, a modern Jew, admittedly only a generation away from the *stetl*, but drawing nearly all of his cultural sustenance from English society and English art. His contribution, and it is a real and precious one, is to English poetry. His tragedy was part of a greater tragedy of

Western man whose dimensions no one in his time could discern; he helped us to feel and imagine something of its inwardness. To that extent, he helped to bring our age into consciousness of itself.

Quadrant, March 1980
Reprinted in *Twentieth Century Literary Criticism*
edited by Dennis Poupard
(Gale Research Co., Detroit, 1984)

The Bonnie Disproportion

It is probable that something under one-tenth of all Australians are of predominantly Scottish extraction. I call these people the Scots Australians, though not all of them might approve of the title. In my own family, the term used was always the older form "Scotch". John Kenneth Galbraith, in his delightful book about the Scots settlers in Ontario, *The Non-Potable Scotch*, reports the same usage, adding that "Scots" was considered a bit precious there. It seems to be the preferred form nowadays, though, if only to distinguish the people from the whisky. In family contexts, ingrained habit will probably lead me to speak of the Scotch, and being Scotch, keeping Scots Australian for the pukka, generalising parts of my treatise.

Apart from the tenth who are Scottish in the main line or lines of their ancestry, a great many other Australians, of course, would have a substantial Scottish admixture, whether they were conscious of it or not. This is where things get shaky. Given the facts of intermarriage in a new country, separating out the different ethnic strands can be a task at once intricate and gross. Opting for one ethnic tradition, usually that of the father's line and the surname, tends to downgrade the female side of one's ancestry. If anything undercuts the present vogue for ethnic consciousness, especially amongst Old Australians (perhaps it wasn't primarily meant for us) it is the question of the slighted mothers. I've been a publicist for the ethnic thing myself, so it behoves me to say that.

The Scots, along with the Jews, have probably been the great ethnic success story in Australian history. Some Irish Australian friends of mine once demanded to know what the Scots, as compared with the Irish, had achieved in Australia. "Well," I replied, "we own it." The enormous number of Scots and Scottish descendants, in proportion to our share of the population, who have been leaders in commerce, in politics, in education, in military matters and in the pastoral industry is pretty well known, even in the absence of any really comprehensive and respectable study of the Scottish part in Australian history. Which is an amazing lack, when you think about it. Even though Australian politics has sometimes seemed a perpetual struggle between one Irish and two Scots parties, it has been the Irish who have attracted the historians and the explainers of our nation's culture. The Irish have been more visible, and more tragic, though there is a sadness at the heart of Scottish success which might yield much to a scholar prepared to probe deeply. And this sadness may also have a bit to do with my first surprising claim, namely, that another field in which we have been active and successful in a measure way out of proportion to our numbers is poetry. Just under one-tenth of Australia's population has so far produced between a fifth and a quarter of the country's poets. Ethnic satisfaction quite aside, this is a mystery, and a breach of stereotype, which I am concerned to understand. And it leads into other mysteries which are anything but comfortable.

Figures and numerical proportions, however approximate, are apt to seem coarsely managerial when applied to literary achievement, though there's also a dash of castle-snobbery in our resistance to statistics in the context of art. I think my figures are pretty reliable, though, and point in an interesting direction; I'd better say here how I arrived at them. The figure for the proportion of Australians having a predominantly Scottish background is derived from the Census question regarding religious affiliation. Until the mid-seventies, when the Uniting Church arose to muddy the picture, the main Christian denominations were still a fair guide to the ethnic background of most Australians. Catholics were rapidly diversifying, but Church of England was still a very reliable pointer to English origins, and Presbyterian overwhelmingly signified Scottish descent. As late as the Census of 1971, the last before the Uniting Church was formed, you could put together a pretty good estimate of the numbers of Scots Australians by taking the figure for Presbyterians, subtracting forty or fifty thousand from that to allow for Dutch, Swiss and Hungarian Calvinists, who tend to join the various Presbyterian churches here, and adding a much larger guesstimate number from the Not Stated and No Religion categories. The Scottish rationalist tradition, surviving in exile, ensures that there will be plenty of strong Calvinist atheists among the No Religion group.

It is harder to find a basis on which to attempt a decent guesstimate of Scots Australians who've followed less typical religious paths, the Scots Catholics (relatively few, in the earlier days of Scottish emigration, though the Catholic minority in Scotland itself now embraces nearly a quarter of the population) and Catholic converts, or those, usually Establishment Scots, who have become Anglican over the years, or those who have joined the smaller Protestant sects. I ended up awarding these less typical cases a

The Bonnie Disproportion

purely aleatory figure of twenty thousand; I had to get my Romish self in somehow! Using the 1971 Census figures, the whole procedure gave a total somewhere between 1,200,000 and 1,300,000, in a population of just under thirteen million. I doubt the proportion will have shifted much since, though it is hard to see how even this sort of rough calculation will be possible in future times. In the absence of a specifically ethnic question in future Censuses, which for many reasons would be a thoroughly bad idea, we have probably lost our only possible index of Scots Australian numbers. Names, even when you know your Scottish Macs from your Irish ones, are infinitely less reliable; indeed, they have got so thoroughly mixed around in the English-speaking world as to be hopelessly misleading, unless you happen to know a bit about each person bearing a particular surname. This was the basis on which I was able to use surnames in my survey of more than a dozen anthologies of Australian poetry, the survey which confirmed my long-held suspicion that the proportion of Scots Australians among our poets was freakishly high. Knowing at least a little about most of the writers whose names I encountered in the various collections, I could make a reasonably informed guess about their major ethnic heritage. And in many cases, I knew a lot about it. I was also able to include cases where a Scottish ancestry was masked by an untypical name. Two such cases were Peter Kocan and Judith Wright. When Clan McGregor was proscribed and forbidden the use of its name, in the early seventeenth century, one branch took the name of Wright; Judith is actually a proud clanswoman of Rob Roy himself! In Peter's case, I knew he was a Douglas; the name Kocan was that of his stepfather. Eschewing, for once and gratefully, all considerations of poetic quality, I simply looked at the names included in each anthology, and worked out the ratio of Scots ethnics as against the total number of names included. The proportion sometimes even exceeded twenty-five per cent. In two successive numbers of Philip Roberts' *Poet's Choice* (1972 and 1973), nine out of thirty poets included had predominantly Scottish ancestry. And in Douglas Stewart's recension of *The Wide Brown Land*, the ratio was twenty out of seventy-seven. The two *Penguin Books on Australian Verse* gave more typical proportions, fifteen out of sixty in the first edition and twenty-one out of ninety-four in Harry Heseltine's revamped edition. The proportion fell slightly below one-fifth in Bernard Hickey's Italian-English bilingual collection, *Da Slessor a Dransfield*, which had ten Scots ethnics out of fifty-two poets represented, but only fell markedly below it in Hall and Shapcott's *New Impulses in Australian Poetry*, where I could identify only two definite Scots Australians in a line-up of twenty-two authors. More recent collections of a modernist tendency generally yielded much higher and more typical ratios.

I felt confident enough in doing my ethnic breakdown of the various anthologies, because so far as I know no one had previously thought of doing such a crazy thing. I was convinced that even unconscious ethnic bias could be ruled out; to my knowledge the polemical intents of even the most programmatic editors have never exhibited an ethnic dimension. Not of precisely this sort, anyhow. The proportion of Scottish descendants amongst our poets surprised me first by being even higher than I had guessed it would be, and then by holding pretty constant all through this century; it was a good deal lower among the balladists of the nineteenth century and the early part of this one. In what was, I think, a very natural comparison to make, I found that the Irish ratio, high among the balladists and other poets of the last century, tailed off markedly around Federation and has tended ever since to hover around one-half to one-third of the Scots one. And this is in absolute terms; given the very much greater proportion of Irish descendants in the overall population, one would expect the contingent of Irish-descended poets to exceed the Scots by a wide margin. The two peoples are ancestrally linked by ties of blood and culture, though the linkages are ancient and complex, and are sometimes overstated, but a contrast of the sort I discovered clearly points to a major dissimilarity, not of native talent for heaven's sake, but perhaps of preferred cultural expression. I suspect that it may be significant that Irish Australian representation among the country's poets drops off at the period when the Labor Party was starting to gather widespread support. It is possible that the Labor movement, as well as their religion or in place of it, absorbed the souls of Australian Irish folk in ways for which our declining Calvinism and pragmatic mercantilist politics have offered no parallel. But it might be fruitful to examine other differences between the two groups as well.

The great link between the Irish and the Scots is, of course, the Gaelic language and culture, and in particular the common institution of the *fine* (pronounced, approximately, f*een*-ey), the extended clan family, which may yet prove the most durable legacy of the Gaelic past. Both countries were Gaelic kingdoms in the remote past, yet even when we look at all closely at this common fact, we begin to see wide differences. While Ireland enters recorded history as a country with a uniformly Gaelic culture, the space which gradually came to be known as Scotland was occupied, at the end of Roman rule in Britain, by at least three distinct peoples, the Britons of Strathclyde and the south who had known a slight degree of Roman domination, the Picts who had resisted Rome well enough to dissuade her from colonising their (to Roman eyes) unattractive regions in the north, and the *Scotti* or Irish Gaels who had recently established themselves in the Western Highlands. With the Teutonic invasions, a fourth people were added to the mosaic, as the Kingdom of Northumbria conquered all the south-eastern zone between Hadrian's Wall and the Firth of Forth.

The Gaelic kingdom of Dalriada conquered and began to absorb the Picts in the ninth century, and out of this conquest there arose the first "Scottish" kingdom, known as Alba, which remains the Gaelic name for Scotland to this day. It took Alba the best part of two hundred years to extend her sovereignty southwards to the present Anglo-Scottish border, and in the process she conquered the northern march of Northumbria whose Teutonic English language would eventually displace Gaelic as the dominant speech of the kingdom of Scots. There is evidence that Gaelic did penetrate for a time south of the Forth, and it did replace Welsh in the ancient British kingdom of Rheged, which became Ayrshire-Strathclyde, but the displacement of Gaelic by "Inglis" at the royal court probably began around the time of King Malcolm III Canmore (*Ceann mór*, the big-headed) and his Saxon Queen Margaret, in the middle of the eleventh century. Alba had, however, imparted a strongly Gaelic "set" to the whole society of the kingdom not so much through language perhaps — though the echo of Gaelic is pervasive in Scots speech even today, if you have an ear for it — but rather through institutions and modes of behaviour. Among these, the most powerful and long lasting seems to have been *finechas*, the feeling of kindred. The gradual retreat of the Gaelic language after Malcolm's time did nothing to hinder a remarkable fusing together of the disparate peoples into a new people, the Scots, who have kept a strong identity all down the centuries since, despite linguistic and other cleavages.

The Scots probably learned earlier than the Irish to think of themselves as one people whether they spoke Gaelic or English; in Ireland, until the English conquest hotted up under the Tudors, the Irish had always managed to assimilate incomers, Vikings, Normans, Welshmen and the rest, to their own language and culture; thereafter, the language and culture gradually became, and long remained, the prime bastion of oppressed Irishness. Probably right up until the collapse of the language in the period of the great potato famines after 1848, the Irish-speaking majority accepted as their own only those who belonged to their clans and their religion, and who shared in some measure the cup of their suffering. The bardic keepers of the old tradition, whose order survived until the early eighteenth century, would not have regarded Catholicism or sympathy as sufficient credentials for admittance to the by-then-underground continuities of the native culture. Even possession of a native name would have been no advantage, on its own; having the name without the language and the poverty put one at least to some degree in the odium of a renegade, a Quisling, a climber of the oppressor's social ladder. What the *Gall*, or foreigners, chose to call Irish was not necessarily what the Gael regarded as worthy of the name. It is fairly clear that the dynamics of this resistance to the oppressor's order, to the world-picture of the prison guard and the privileged man, are still a factor in Australian life today, with a certain salty egalitarian tribalism replacing the old tests of religion and culture and serving as their equivalent. In Ireland itself, it is very clear that some people still apply cultural tests as to what constitutes "true" Irishness, and are prepared to push the matter tragically far.

For many reasons, Scottish identity was never a contentious matter in any way or degree comparable with this. The Scottish nation was absorbed, in large measure, by the English; it was never the victim of brutal conquest (though that was tried several times in the Middle Ages) or centuries of merciless suppression. The dreadful harrying of the Gaelic Highlands after the Rising of 1745-46 is, of course, an exception, but the only one. Otherwise Scotland was incorporated, after the unfortunate union of the crowns in 1603, through economic pressure and cultural preponderance. When surrender of her national sovereignty in 1707 gained Scotland relief from English economic blockade and admission to economic opportunity in the growing English empire, Scots were allowed to keep their Scottishness as a consolation prize. After all, it threatened nothing; apart from Calvinist missionary work, there was no exclusively Scottish sphere of activity beyond the Scottish borders. Success outside Scotland was on terms set by the Predominant Pairtner or the other host countries of the Scots diaspora.

It is impossible to say to what degree something like the Gaelic clan system existed amongst the different peoples of Scotland before the kingdom of Scots came into being. The Brythonic kingdoms, being Celtic, may have had something similar, but the Picts appear to have had a system of tribes, probably matrilineal and totemic; we will probably never know much about their organisation and structure, though I think the persistence of certain recurring symbols in the heraldry of different groups of Scottish clans (the wildcat, the three stars and others) point to the origin of those clans from identifiable earlier tribes. The Northumbrians probably had nothing really comparable with the Gaelic system of *finechan* or kindreds. Quite early in Scottish history, however, we see the evolution outside the original area of Gaeldom of great territorial family groupings. The problem of powerful families was one which the Scottish kings never wholly solved. Some of them died trying. Well before the loss of sovereignty, lowland families in which Gaelic had probably never been spoken were behaving exactly like the Gaelic clans, and are fairly well justified nowadays in referring to themselves as clans in the Highland way; it isn't just modern hoopla invented by Sir Walter Scott. In the period of the Stewart kings (Stuart, the French spelling, is probably better reserved for the period of French exile and Jacobitism), we often encounter the term *interest* being used to refer to the territorial families, the Hamilton interest, the Huntly Gordon interest, the Atholl interest and so on. It should be remembered that, as late as 1746 in the Highlands and Islands, and generally earlier on, the chiefs of the local families, feudalised to some degree during the Middle Ages and later, possessed rights of judicature, of "pit and gallows", over their tenants and subjects. The kingdom was structured as a nexus of powerful families, whose power waxed, shifted and waned with the onrush of history. The family motto of the Bruces, *Fuimus* (We Were), is an excellent pointer to the experience of one such family, which once held the crown, but afterwards dwindled to comparative unimportance.

The common Irish and Scottish institution of the *fine*, the extended clan family, antedates feudalism by at least a thousand years and probably more (the Old Celtic form of the word is *vinja*, and must have referred to something comparable) and has survived in a real if subterranean and often-ignored way into modern times. Feudalism is a coloration it bore for several centuries, but has now almost sloughed off. It gave the two countries a terrific decentralised resilience to invasion, as well as an inherent tendency to division and petty warfare; Ireland survived and defeated the Vikings largely because there was never one centre, one stronghold whose capture would bring the whole culture undone. If the *finechan* weakened the two countries as nations in our sense, they also provided a resilient second line of defence for them as cultures. Their strongholds, each the residence of the patriarchal chief who was seen as the descendant or "Representer" of the perhaps legendary founder of the name, were centres of music, of poetry and storytelling, of style-setting innovation and the rituals of family unity. The chief's officers and tenants were his *clann*, a word which means nothing other than children, and consanguinity, real or theoretical, with him gave his subjects rights of appeal and criticism, often expressed most effectively in horatory song-poetry addressed to him by his bards. Chiefs were not by any means all-powerful, though their power tended to increase as the system became more feudalised. They were still subject, in the last resort, to the will of the clan, and there are cases of chiefs who were deposed or even killed by their clansfolk. John "Handsome Iain" Macdonald of Keppoch (floruit c.1498) was deposed by his clan for handing over a relative to the vengeance of the Mackintoshes. His descendants were thereafter known as *sliochd a'bhràthar bu shine* (the line of the elder brother) and were the forebears of the fierce Jacobite satirist John Macdonald, known in Gaelic as Iain Lom. Some bards very likely were toadies to their chiefs, but their position carried a very large measure of traditional dignity and indeed sacrosanctity, which made it possible for bards of character to look two ways, and serve the people as well as the chief.

In "Inglis" and Gaelic alike, the literature, that is poetry, which survived was preserved in family verse-books (*Duanairechan*), the greatest of these being the Bannatyne manuscript made in 1568 for the Stewart court. The tradition of manuscript books persisted in Scotland well into the era of printing, and was still dominant in the Highlands and Islands in the eighteenth century. As in Ireland, the bards and their more vernacular successors tended to be a conservative force, celebrating the lasting values of the society and the clan and keeping these ever before the eyes of the chief and his people. It is misleading to see these relationships in terms of modern polemic. This whole patriarchal power structure has long since vanished, but the essence of the *fine* system persists in clan societies and family associations found wherever the Scots and Irish have emigrated. These societies often appear rather sentimental and backward-looking, but there is something real contained in them, a sense of identity, of historic pride, of *finechas* or kindred transcending time and space. And transcending class, as well; as R. L. Stevenson wrote of a servant woman in "Weir of Hermiston":

...she is not necessarily destitute of the pride of birth, but is...a connection of her master's, and at least knows the legend of her own family, and may count kinship with some illustrious dead. For that is the mark of the Scot of all classes: that he stands in an attitude to the past unthinkable to Englishmen, and remembers and cherishes the memory of his forbears, good or bad; and there turns alive in him a sense of identity with the dead even to the twentieth generation... The power of ancestry on the character is not limited to the inheritance of cells.

There is a modern version of Scottish history, not wholly disinterested, which would depict the country as inherently and fatefully divided as between the Gaelic north and the non-Gaelic Lowlands. What Stevenson is describing, however, is pure *fine*, though the family involved is the Elliots, a Border name of Norman origin.

Antic pride of family, however poorly informed, is a sort of dormant social principle we carry with us, one which has the

The Bonnie Disproportion

potential of becoming real again in adapted forms whenever circumstances warrant it. I grew up in a place in which such a resuscitation of the system actually occurred, and in which the family nexus is still a moral and social reality existing and holding its own amongst other, competing systems of value. My experience may perhaps be anachronistic, in modern Australia, but it is far from unique. Many other country people, especially, could tell a similar story — and might well suspect that the very frequent downgrading or ignoring of the family-dynastic elements in our national life has something ideological in it.

Our family is Pictish in origin, one of a number of families stemming from the lowland area around the Moray Firth which have three stars as their prime heraldic charge; Brodie, Innes and Sutherland share this symbol with us. We may all once have been a single tribe distinguished from the Cat people (the term Clan Chattan still exists, though as a grouping of clans rather than a single family) or the Deer people by a tribal tattoo of stars; the Latin term *picti* means painted or tattooed, and we may have borne tattoo designs in much the same way as the Maori wear their *moko*. The name of our family is identical with that of the Firth, and its meaning is unknown but certainly pre-Indo-European. Scattered all over Scotland in the early Middle Ages, as a result of their resistance, the historian Ian Grimble believes, to the feudalising of the Gaelo-Pictish north by Queen Margaret's descendants on the Scottish throne, the Moraymen or Murrays acquired territorial holdings from the Central Highlands clear down to the eastern Borders. Some of their local centres of power remained small, others grew in importance, until by the eighteenth century there were two Dukes of the name in Britain, Their Graces of Atholl and Mansfield; that is a piece of swank no other family in Britain can match. Except that Hanoverian one.

Sovereignties and titles probably meant something, but not too much, to the struggling farm people around Jedburgh, Hawick, Denholm and other small towns in the eastern Borders in the middle of last century. The Murrays of the region were respected as a "good" family, but their strict Calvinism and Convenanter traditions must have militated against respect for worldly pomps, and the aristocracy by that late stage were mostly Anglicised and infinitely remoter from their kinfolk than they had ever been under the old kingdom. What was probably of much greater interest to the Border Murrays was their ramified interconnections with the other local families, the Veitches, Turnbulls, Scotts, Beatties, Eastons and Rutherfords, to all of whom we're related. When John Murray, farmer at Camptown near Hawick, Roxboroughshire, died in 1845, his widow Isabella decided to send four of her eldest sons and their nineteen-year-old sister Agnes to New South Wales to see what prospects existed there for the family. To ease them into the new country, the boys had the promise of jobs with the Australian Agricultural Company on arrival; their mother's cousin George Easton occupied the post of Overseer of Free Men at Stroud. If all went well with this arrangement she would follow with the five younger boys. This first party accordingly embarked under sail in the *Castle Eden* in 1848, and my great-great-grandfather Hugh Scott Murray and his wife Margaret Beattie had their first child on the voyage. The child was my great-grandfather John Allan, Johnnie of Bunyah, born according to tradition in the middle of a great storm in the Bay of Biscay. He lived up to that beginning later on, though always with great geniality. Agnes married a Gaelic-speaker from Inverness named Paterson, and their descendants are to be found all over the Manning-Myall region today. The boys all quickly secured parcels of land along the upper reaches of the wild Manning River, and in 1851 their mother arrived with the rest of the brothers. The rich flats of the upper Manning have been the heartland of the family ever since, though it has put out offshoots into all the districts around; Johnnie and his wife, also named Isabella, moved out to Bunyah in 1870 and took up land there, as did Uncles Jimmie and Tom. Another brother, Veitch, was more venturesome, and travelled all the way north to the Atherton Tableland to found his dynasty. Until my own generation, though, most of the Murrays stayed around the Manning, and remained in such close touch with each other and the other Scots of the region, the Lobbans, Eastons, MacKinnons, MacCraes, Patersons, Cowans, Wrights, Breckinridges and others, that it was only the grandchildren of the first-comers who regularly spoke with an Australian rather than a Border accent.

Following a very ancient pattern embedded in their civilisation, the Murrays installed themselves on separate farmsteads (land for selection was plentiful at a pound an acre, uncleared). These farms were worked by father, mother and all the children. Four years was the usual age for learning how to milk cows, and a child's day from then on began before sunrise with a backbreaking hour or two of milking, unless he was off on business with his father; my father, for instance, began helping his father to drove cattle to market at the age of seven, and was dealing in them on the latter's behalf at nine. Girls did their full share of the dairy work as well, and were excused only the heaviest and most dangerous jobs on the farms, grubbing stumps, ploughing, felling timber. Their household tasks of breadmaking and slinging the ponderous iron jam-pans and camp ovens on chains above the open fire were quite onerous enough, and unremitting.

The Bonnie Disproportion

The cultural life of these settlers had two main centres, the church (I never heard the form "kirk" when I was a child) and the house party. The Murrays belonged to the strict non-conforming Free Presbyterian sect of Calvinism, which survives to this day in small pockets right along the east coast of Australia, from Geelong and St Kilda to Sydney and the northern rivers and thence up into Queensland. It is the true heir of the Covenants, this small church, still heavily predestinarian and given to an effortful plainness of observance intended as a rebuke to all papistical idolatry and opulence. Churches are utterly unadorned, and the only music allowed in them is unaccompanied singing of the Psalms; hymns are mere human songs, and an organ would be the devil's kist o'whistles. And yet the services have no silence in them either, no mystery, no awe; they are dry theological lectures interspersed with extempore prayers and the Psalms of David in Metre.

A severely Puritan style of life is enjoined upon followers of this tradition. My great-grandfather's first cousin, Sir James Murray, of the *Oxford English Dictionary*, never entered a theatre in his life. Neither did any of the early Australian Murrays, for the good reason that such temptations to loose living simply didn't exist on the northern rivers in their day. They went along, the men anyway and the less fanatical womenfolk, to any travelling amusement that did come their way. The Wee Free faith had a tendency to turn some of my forebears into bigots and one-upping hypocrites, eager to score points over you by displaying greater rectitude and rebuking your laxity. Some of my relations are still like that, and I fear that my detestation of that whole religious tradition began early. A chance copy of Darwin's *Origin of the Species* that fell into my hands when I was nine helped me to escape the mental atmosphere, and my religious travels eventually led me to Catholicism and the Sacraments. In a way, predestinarian Calvinism is a sort of disguised Islam nominally within the Christian fold. Only God matters, and Christ's sacrifice is really a vain thing, because election to glory, or damnation to everlasting death, have been settled for each soul from all eternity, and no action of vice or virtue can change that. No one can deserve anything of God; grace is a free gift. And yet I have known some Free Kirk Presbyterians who were gifted with real grace, despite their theology. Our minister, the late Mr Malcolm Ramsay, who had the charge of Taree and district for many years, was a gentle, scholarly, rather saintly man whose delight was to read some Greek every day; he preached erudite theological sermons to bush congregations, but was also on hand in our times of trouble. He was a good pastor. In Scotland in earlier times justification and the assurance of election became almost obsessive themes, bulking far larger than they had in

Calvin's own writings. It is worth noting that in the Scottish Faust story, James Hogg's *Confessions of a Justified Sinner*, the devil does not have to tempt his victim at all; he merely appears to him in mufti and encourages him in his beliefs, to the point where he will commit patricide, matricide, any enormity. There was a terrific pull against this faith under the surface of my people's lives, but it left on many of them its marks of cruelty, moral snobbery, competitive holiness and wilful ignorance, the ignorance that dismisses all culture of the mind as worldly and unclean. In the absence of a Christian morality, we made do with pride plus something like what the Greeks called *Themis*, a sort of moral-aesthetic sense of propriety which is, I think, the true ancestress of the Right Thing and the Fair Go, and a close cousin of proportion. Enthusiasts in Australia make a bad tactical error when they offend against *Themis*. She is more ancient and more ruthless than they imagine.

The house parties in the old days tended to be weekend affairs, beginning on Friday (sometimes as early as Thursday) and ending God knew when the following week. My father remembers a pair of bearded elders striking matches at eleven of a summer's morning to determine if there were a frost; this was on the Tuesday or Wednesday after a big "*shivoo*" as these affairs were sometimes called. The word comes from *chez vous* "at your place" — a modern Irish equivalent might be "hooley", though that's often just a one-night party. I imagine the word is derived from *ceilidh*. The days were devoted to huge meals, picnics, horse sports and raising hell; the nights, except for the sabbath night, were for nonstop dancing to the piano, the fiddle, the accordion and occasionally the pipes. On the Sunday night, recitations and stories, and sometimes singing, were allowed. Many Australians have, away in the back of their memory, a feel for what is called in Gaelic *corracagailte*, which means a hearth fire when it has burned down to glowing coals late at night, and the deepest stories and the oldest, most profound traditions are brought out amid spellbound silence. It was our lens, that hearth, for looking back down the experience of our people right to the fields and attitudes of the Heroic age. A shadowy blind man sits by the glow and begins to chant an intricate cross-weave of syllables, and the blood freezes on the brink of understanding. Your very bones know the tune, but what do the words say? You may spend your life trying to find out.

Of all the non-church values the Murrays instilled in their children, the greatest was the one called not freedom but *independence*. It went with the separate farms, the houses standing at a dignified distance from each other in the valleys and on the hills. It went with self-containment and discretion about private matters: "Don't tell anyone how much you've got in the bank, boy.

Don't let old mother So-and-so pump you: she wants to know the ins and outs of a mag's arse." I still don't know what sort of a mag was meant. Independence went with making your own judgments about the worth of people and actions, and here moral snobbery was apt to raise its head. The key values were very much Burns' "Sense and Worth o'er all the earth": good sense, integrity and a certain nobility of demeanour were valued; weakness, childishness and lack of basic solidity were despised. There are few things colder than a Scots eye turned upon footling behaviour — unintentionally footling, that is; intentional leg-pulling foolishness is well understood and appreciated — and few phrases more withering than a Scot's laconic "I hear you", meaning that what you've said is not worth a response. It was a shame culture, rather than a moral culture; in my childhood, I would have heard the word "disgraceful" far more often than "wicked". A person could be good and still be an idiot, and the common phrase "he's a good poor bastard" was anything but a recommendation. There was a large dash of family pride in the judgment of behaviour: "Murrays don't do those sort of things. They're for them low-living people." A lot of this, I admit, persists in me; how could the son of Cecil Murray behave beneath his father's standard and shame the family? I was amused the other week when my eldest daughter was reported as saying airily at her school: "Murrays *never* misspell words!" A lot of them in fact do, but she doesn't.

In small communities, surveillance is unceasing; I have often told the story of my two aunts who had telescopes to scan the district for signs of pregnancy or other evidence of carryings on. A few old women, and old men for that matter, took a delight in loosing a sudden volley of reproof on the young, to disconcert them and make them submissive. By the time you decided that the whole thing was just a farrago, you had lost the initiative and been made to feel bad — a necessary preliminary to making you pliable. This was the more vicious side of the leg-pulling, straight-faced style of humour our people favoured. By the time I came along, the old bush predilection for the practical joke had pretty nearly passed away — thank God! — but in earlier generations many of the family had devoted fiendish ingenuity to working up schemes for gulling each other and any innocents within reach. For economy of means, it would be hard to beat my cousin Veitch (Bunyah Veitch, that is, not Killawarra Veitch or Queensland Veitch) who once bestrode a stick and happily rode it down through Bunyah to visit my uncle Sam. After a merry day or two of whisky and Burns, Veitch returned home without his mount, and asked his serious-minded farmhand to go over to Sam's and retrieve it for him. Sam shared the man's concern when the horse was not to be found, and solicitously suggested directions in which it might have wandered; the hapless employee spent the whole day searching paddock after paddock on foot. Towards evening, Sam consented to come and help him search. "God blast it, George, here he is still tied up to the fence where Veitch left him. I don't know what the boys can have been thinking of, to leave him without feed or water!" The man left Veitch's employ that same evening, at the top of his voice.

When I was a child, and to some extent still, the word "Scotch" had two meanings amongst my people: we were Scotch, and anyone who was careful with their money and goods was Scotch. Outright meanness was condemned; a cousin of mine was nicknamed Gandhi, because he was said to be too mean to feed himself. A certain largeness of gesture, especially in matters of hospitality, was respected; my great-grandfather was famous for keeping open house at Bunyah, entertaining dozens of guests at a time. He was never considered foolish because of that; there was a proper nobility of attitude in what he did. Losing his homestead in a card game, however, *was* excessive, and was hushed up fairly thoroughly; I only found out about it a few years ago, from an aged aunt who waxed loquacious late one night. Gift-giving was uncommon, and done, when it was done, with a certain perfunctoriness and lack of imagination, as a duty; a birthday would bring me several handkerchiefs, which would be passed on still wrapped to others having birthdays. I still have to be reminded to give presents; it was not a spontaneous thing with me — not that spontaneity was ever regarded as a virtue among Scots! Presents were mostly for children, and given at Christmas. That was expected, and my uncle who told his kids that Sandy Claus had been shot down by the Japanese and wouldn't be coming any more was considered a dreadful brute.

Some of the Murrays were cooperative souls, but it was far from unknown for others of them to charge their kinfolk money for helping out on the farm in emergencies; when important business obliged us to go away, we usually had to pay to have the cows milked. Conversely, I have often known relatives to offer money in return for a favour. That way, you buy off obligation and remain independent. Many of these things point backward, surely, to ancestral frugalities in a country that was rarely prosperous. And to something else: for our ancestors, opulence and high living were almost never a constant thing. They were part of *occasion*, of celebration and display. Few even among the clan nobles lived well all the time, and the poorer folk probably tasted fresh meat only once a year, when the surplus cattle were killed at the beginning of winter. Music, poetry and the other arts attained their full magnificence in the ambience of the *feast*. So did sports, so did

The Bonnie Disproportion

dalliance. The dream reiterated in hundreds of the bardic elegies and eulogies which have survived is that of the ever-opulent house and the ever-generous chief; it was probably always more the ideal than the reality. In Australia, poor settlers from the Gaelic world often found themselves quite prosperous, and suffered a painful inner struggle between ingrained peasant frugality and the stereotypes of noble open-handedness imprinted for centuries on the deep mind of their culture. Generosity and concessiveness were more common in that culture than kindness. Not that kindness was rare; however, I have seen, and experienced, tremendous kindness there — often disguised as the dourest sort of concessiveness.

Although the Gaelic language, in both of its forms, contains literally dozens of endearments, my Lowland forebears were apt to seem emotionally parsimonious. They had been through, and were often still in, the centuries of Puritanism, and distrusted demonstrativeness. Nothing, in fact, was valued more highly than deep feeling, but a consequent vigilance about the genuineness of that feeling — and surely such vigilance is still all-pervading in Australia — led to a tendency to regard all true emotion as too deep for words. Intimacy too was often conveyed, in a way which has become endemic among Australians, by signals rather than words, by small things like not using the formal *please* and *thank you* with people close to you; those words are for strangers. There is a world of warm emotional shading in Australian gruffness, if people will look for it. Control was highly valued, and loose, excitable gestures were thought insincere, as well as undignified. My own abhorrence of twittering, kissing hostesses has probably chilled many a warm heart, but that, as the Californians say, is where I'm coming from. A Scotsman might reserve his feelings for twenty years and discharge them all in one tearing shriek of joyous self-immolation as he leaped amongst the enemy with his bayonet. I've heard that same death-howl in a Glasgow pub brawl that burst out into the street in front of me once. There is an element of the visionary in it, a decision to crash boots and all into vengeance or significance, and damn the cost. The stereotype of the Celtic hothead is not without foundation, and can be a danger to beware in oneself. It may underlie the very strong disapproval of argument and dissention instilled in my people as children. Any community has reason to fear Kamikaze gestures of rage that may arise out of ordinary bickering. I was brought up to fear "rowing" and still find public disagreements exhausting and dangerous. Many of the older male Murrays of the Drinking generations went in for very loud choleric displays that terrorised their families.

One thing which "Scotch" never meant among my people was whisky; that was called by its name, and assumed to be Scotch;

Persistence in Folly

Irish whisky was unknown, and no one would drink Australian. It was the drink for solemn occasions, particularly those with some ancestral connection; it was invariably part of Old Year's Night, for example — the term Hogmanay was never used by my people up home. It was also, for men, the gateway to a world of owlish intensity and yearned-for significance. They would go on benders together, in which they recited and discussed Bobby Burns and Scottish things in befuddled terms for nights on end. My father's generation tended to abhor this ritual, partly because they had been forced so often in childhood to witness it and clean up after it. It was more a thing of my grandfather's generation, and the source of endless stories. Like the time Sam, Veitch and Grandfather, on about the third night of a spree, enticed their abstemious and rather henpecked neighbour Joe Lynch down from his house to the road and coaxed him into a strathspey-and-reels contest. "I'll whistle the tunes, Joe, and Sam here'll step you for a fiver." They danced Joe for hours, slipping whisky and rum into him under his guard, until he collapsed on his hands and knees in the mud of the road. "It's been terrible dry, Joe," cried Grandfather through the drizzle: "You're a good man, and we want you to pray for rain for us." Joe prayed loudly and disjointedly until he lapsed into incoherence and passed out. With befuddled concern for his welfare, and a healthy fear of his wife's wrath, they then shifted him into the gutter and tied a hurricane lamp to him with his pyjama cord, so that no one would run over him. "Must give the man a tail-light," they agreed, and drove off to look for more entertainment. Joe's wife discovered her sleeping spouse the next morning, and the Murrays did not travel that road again for some months.

Wives, of course, like all women, were utterly excluded from the drinking ritual; their permitted intoxication was religion, and if they didn't choose to go in for that, they were certainly expected to be respectable and dependable. A drinking wife was, if anything, even lower than an unfaithful one. The shamanism of distilled liquors was resented by the wives, though most resigned themselves to it somehow, and resented even more by that generation's sons, as they saw their inheritance going into the pub till, while they sat outside in the car or the sulky waiting to drive Dad home. Each man's "boys" were his labourers, often working for no wages beyond the promise that they would be given land and a "start".

I suppose what I have been describing is the common trap of ethnic consciousness. As the ancestral motherland recedes farther into the past, it becomes a dream, a fossilised style, a place of the wise dead. You have been taught to look to it for significance and depth, and yet it has become remote, a haunting tune recovered only in extremity, and then impossible to hold. My grandfather's generation was just at that distance from Scotland, in their lives. And they did not read, so they had no real way of refurbishing the fading image. Their grandparents probably had some grasp of the old Scots literary tradition, some familiarity, if only in an oral way, with the Border ballads and the great Scots poems, but the generation of drinkers up home had lost everything but Burns. They still understood, from childhood, the language of Burns' poems, though they did not really speak it or pass it on to their children. It is usually in the third generation that an immigrant group will suffer the wholesale loss of its language. After which the mind is apt to be haunted by the loom of words, a sense of a lost native idiom just below the horizon of the mind. Broad Scots — Lallans, if you like, surely a marvellous name for the language of the intoxicated — will produce this effect just as readily as Gaelic. Or German, or Arabic. I suspect that this phenomenon can, in odd cases, provoke the artistic urge in a person; there was a weird, undirected proto-poetry in the drinking Murrays' quest. And a hunger for cultural experience which their dour religion did not supply, any more than their bookless, almost schoolless region. Apart from the Bible, Scotland and the Bush were the only books they had, and neither was substantially on paper.

But we needn't become po-faced; I daresay the old fellows had a lot of fun, too. The family, both the majority still living on the lower north coast and the scattered members, is now well and truly over the hump of assimilation. Few definite traces of Scots custom or speech remain. We say "plat" for "plait", but that has become pretty well the standard Australian pronunciation. A trace of Scottish vowel quality remains when we pronounce words like "rinse" as "rense". Farmers call their cows' udders "elders", and the people of Bunyah say "gen" or "agen" where most Australians would say "by the time that": "Agen he gets here, I'll have the tractor fixed." Similarly, I have an impression that people from my district used to be almost as likely to say "I'll not" as "I won't" — the Scots pattern and the English one competed there. A trace of Gaelic phonetics is to be heard among some elder people when they say "srink" and "sred", for "shrink" and "shred"; the *sr*-cluster is, I believe, disappearing now even in Gaelic. Customs are in a comparable decline. It is probably a generation since any bridegroom has had his feet ceremonially washed by a senior male relative on his wedding day, and only some older people still avoid sleeping with their feet to the east. Few people in my generation even remember to put the adjective "poor" before the name of a dead person who was close to them; it was once almost an invariable title. Funerals are still the biggest social event in the region, though, and can easily draw crowds of four or five hundred. A week after I went to Kenneth Slessor's funeral in Sydney in 1971, which was attended by perhaps thirty people, I went to my cousin Hugh Murray's funeral at Krambach. Hughie, known in his lifetime as Johnnie Cope, drew eight hundred mourners to his interment. The wake is held afterwards, often at the pub or the club, and is called the sendoff. The contrast to be drawn here, I suppose, is between overt, conscious survivals of custom and unnoticed cultural continuities. The strength is now almost entirely in the latter.

In the last two generations, explicit clan feeling and the Scottish link has been preserved mainly by women, but the sense of "our lot" as a network of loyalty, of communications, of understanding and concern, that is common to all of us. In its Scottish and historical dimension, the *fine* is now a bit sentimentalised and bookish, but in its practical, local dimension it retains tremendous strength. Mine is the first generation to have enjoyed, or had a chance to enjoy, a decent formal education, and there has been keen understated rivalry between parents regarding the academic and worldly success of their children. All such successes are taken, however, as reflecting credit on the clan. And making up, in a sort of delegated way, for past deprivations and stunted lives. The clan gives you little encouragement to make your mark; after all, you should have enough gumption and independence to spur yourself along. It does, however, treasure and boast about your achievements when the world acknowledges them. So long as you haven't developed a swollen head; you are tested carefully and often on that score. You are reminded that of course any of the family would have done as well, if they'd been given the opportunity.

The clan — the word is used, usually jovially by menfolk, to refer not to the historical worldwide *fine* of the Murrays, but specifically to our branch of the family — is a superb and invaluable retreat from the asperities and alienations of the outside world; that is probably its chief value for the scattered members. It is a warm, but not cloyingly warm, nexus of familiarity; within it, you can talk easily to women, and even to young girls who would otherwise tend to regard any male approach as an Approach.

For people who stay in their home region, this extended-family aspect is probably satisfying enough. Conscious exploration of the historical dimension is an extra, brought on in my case by culture shock of the city and the university. It is a powerful sheet anchor for a threatened identity, to possess a blood tie, not genealogical in the linear feudal way but ramified and tribal in the Gaelic way, with a quirky assortment of noble and sometimes poignant figures inhabiting distant centuries: the Jacobite general Lord George Murray, the Marquis of Tullibardine who raised the Stuart standard in Glenfinnan in 1745, Sir James of the OED, the Marquise de la Trémouille who held out against Cromwell in her castle when all the rest of the British Isles had fallen to him, Lady Macbeth, whose name was Gruoch and who was a Gaelo-Pictish heretrix married to Macbeth for dynastic reasons, the first Duke of Atholl, who voted against the Union in 1707 and was narrowly dissuaded from raising a revolt when it passed the Old Parliament, the Countess of Airlie who was raped by Malcolm Fraser's ancestor Simon Lovat Fraser while his pipers played loudly to drown her screams... save for one, a roll-call of magnificent losers. No vulgar success there to shame a man's romanticism. Lexicography and lost causes, rather; things infinitely more germane to poetry. We rescued the lady of Airlie, by the way, and punished Lovat. Not half as severely as the Hanoverians fifty years later, though, when having tried to play off both sides in the Forty Five, he ended up on the wrong side and became, in his nineties, the last man in Britain to be hanged, drawn and quartered for high treason.

I have dilated on the inwardness of the *fine* and on my own experience, not merely as an indulgence, but also because my upbringing was perhaps more old-fashioned than that of many especially urban Scots Australians, and thus more in contrast with older social and psychological aspects of Scots settlement here. This has perforce meant that I have largely neglected the experience of wealthier and better-educated Scottish immigrants, people who rose fairly inevitably in colonial society because they brought with them the means of rising. I have also neglected those settlers, pastoral, mercantile or whatever who lacked education themselves but whose success, whether based on hard work or rapacity or luck, enabled them to buy position and education for their children and descendants. Scots did not typically come to the colonies as convicts, though some notable convicts were Scots; nor were they Catholic, so they were for the most part spared two heavy early disabilities. The four Scots universities and the excellent, relatively egalitarian Scottish secondary schools turned out a large number of well-educated people to whom Scotland itself offered no breadth of opportunity, but for whom the British Empire was a worldwide field for energy and enterprise. It is possible that the disproportion of Scots descendants among Australia's poets is merely a parallel case to the disproportionate numbers of them in, say, law or politics, and a result of nothing more than a high average of affluence and educational opportunity among Scots Australians in comparison with other ethnic groups here. It may be as mechanical as that, but I doubt it. I cannot think that the cool, individualistic Scottish version of the ancient Gaelic *fine* has had no effect — if only in promoting a sense of history in us and giving us a sense of

Persistence in Folly

more than ephemeral, rootless existence. Consciously developed as a personal myth, historical *finechas* can be almost as rich and strange as totemic descent from the original Platypus or the dreamtime Kangaroo. It can also be a valuable sheet anchor against a common modern tendency to downgrade all "biological" ties in favour of economic ones. Some of this effort is thoroughly worthwhile, of course; the sooner racism, for example, disappears from the world, the better. But the campaign can go too far, and promote a form of society in which the individual is not so much autonomous as atomised and helpless, available to be recruited and disposed of at will.

A personal connection with history, even if only vaguely examined, must surely have given many Scots Australians a feeling of greater weight and confidence, helping them to offset the common colonial sensation of insubstantiality, of being somehow less real than one's coevals in the metropolitan centres. Then, too, there is the old, serious regard which Scots have paid to poetry, above all other branches of literature, compounded in the past of respect for poets and their work and a readiness to read and judge the work. I find that most Scots Australians have now dropped this latter readiness, though thankfully they have at least kept the respect. An example of unnoticed cultural continuity, that, but unfortunately a truncated continuity. A third possible cause of the Bonnie Disproportion might well be the long-surviving Scottish delight in philosophical and theological disputation, a delight by no means confined to the formally well educated; this may have led some into quandaries of the mind and spirit that only poetry could express and assuage. I have not examined all of my Scots Australian poets to see whether any commonality of style or tone or poetic concern exists amongst them, but if anyone did survey them in search of a common denominator, I'll bet they'd find it lay somewhat in the direction of philosophical concern, mixed with verbal quirkiness, a measure of humour and patches of backward-looking yearning for a light once seen and now extinguished. Its greatest fault would probably be respectability of a poetically conservative sort. It might also frequently exhibit a measure of pedantry; the self-educated lad o'parts is a well-known Scots intellectual figure. James Murray and Hugh MacDiarmid, himself a Murray on his mother's side, are two examples out of many. James Hogg and the quarryman geologist Hugh Miller are two more.

The self-made scholar and the idiosyncratic self-made artist are variants of the self-made man, and it is possibly here that Scots Australians differ most markedly from at least a very visible and articulate group of Irish Australians. Amongst the latter group,

The Bonnie Disproportion

there is an historic distaste for the self-made man. And it is here that we step onto less genial ground, so let's talk about dragons. Amongst a number of dragons who live, Merlin-like, beneath the surface of Australian life, the green one and the blue one have a great deal in common, and yet they're often at loggerheads. The green one, having had a Catholic education, tends to be more familiar with concepts of charity and self-sacrifice for the group than does the Calvin-blue beast; the green dragon is also arguably more collectivist, and he has a different attitude to work. The blue dragon still clings to something of the old Puritan work ethic coupled with a severe blindness to the real sufferings of those who don't share that ethic, or who have "failed" its requirements. Much modern-day work is mere employment, of course, and close to a ritual activity, but the blue dragon is apt to be deadly serious even about treadmill-running. And to punish those who won't run, as well as those who can't. The green dragon is serious about it all in a slightly different way; he will insist, often, that you run on the treadmill, and stay among the treadmill runners, as an act of *solidarity*, of sharing the common lot — even though he knows it's all a charade. Or he will let you step off the treadmill, but only on condition that you pretend you haven't really abandoned the ranks of the croppy boys for alien privilege. Now, since the blue dragon tends to win the politics in Australia, while the green one wins the culture, this can be a matter of some discomfort for sons of the blue dragon who are engaged in the arts. They can find themselves expected to be "Characters", the permitted form of individualism in the Irish diaspora, rather than simply being themselves, and more oppressively they can find themselves subjected to demands for solidarity, for rhetorical attitudinising and for hectic, often baseless hopes which have their ancestral roots in the tragic past of Ireland.

Much of the above may sound like a deposit of class warfare, and there's some validity in that view, though I think all class-based analyses of society tend to be simplistic; ethnically based studies of history may be a useful corrective for them, though these obviously don't tell the whole story either. By what could be seen as an accident, but which is really related to a national tragedy of their own, Scottish settlers were amongst the first Europeans in Australia to interpose themselves between the convicts and the keepers. And that meant we were apt to be co-opted, and despised, by both groups. We were not so much the first Australian middle class as the first Australian "class" caught in the middle. It is undeniable, of course, that many Scots settlers here did, for reasons of moral snobbery, opportunism and the like, make common cause with the garrison gentry and the peculators. And some of the garrison gentry *were* Scots. We've been belaboured for all that. There is also a sense, though, in which we helped to *absorb* the garrison system and relegate it to the past; the first colonial ruler to see beyond the realities of the penal colony and begin the work of its relegation was, of course, the Gaelic speaker from Mull, Colonel Macquarie. In time, we helped to create new role models which a great many ex-convicts and Irish settlers were eager to follow — so far as long-lasting religious exclusivism on the part of Protestants here would permit. Many of our worst crimes, in this country, have been done in the name of religion. It has only really been possible to get something of a hearing for ideas of common Celtic identity since the loud static of the Reformation began to fade away. And of course in some places it hasn't been tuned out yet.

Parts of the style of Irish Australia are attractive to Scots Australians, stirring ancestral chords, but other parts of that style irritate us; this is something enthusiasts for the Celtic cause need to face squarely. It may be that some of the dissonance merely reflects the fact that our ancestral homeland is lost, while theirs is still a moral force to them, as it battles to save and restore itself. Their Jacobites won, in the end; ours lost. And this may be relevant to poetry, even among the descendants. Poetry has an enormous ancient prestige among both peoples, but in the Irish case, perhaps for the very reason that it was often the tough spine of an embattled civilisation, Irish poetry even in English has never really developed the idiosyncratic, sometimes cross-grained venturesomeness of Scots, or the readiness to deal with new realities. For an Irish parallel to Hugh MacDiarmid, you would have to look to prose writers, perhaps pre-eminently to James Joyce. As descendants of a people which sold itself out, or was sold out, under pressure, we lack a Kathleen Ni Houlihán, the all-loving, all-demanding mother-muse who permits only endless variations on the one immemorial sad tune. If suffering narrowed and concentrated Irish poetry, grief and anger opened Scots poetry out. The Irish balladists of the last century in Australia, from Frank the Poet Macnamara onward, were after all composing in translated Gaelic metres on Irish themes only lightly disguised by an Antipodean decor; they are still singing the sorrows of Ireland. By contrast, the Scotsman Adam Lindsay Gordon, and Paterson and Will Ogilvie more confidently after him, could respond to and celebrate a new way of life, with new possibilities, new energies. Of course, they did tend to make that life into something of an idyll.

I must avoid any appearance of unkindness to the Irish; my father's mother came of the Wexford Paynes. We do share a great deal with them, especially a passion for talking with the dead. The difference, though, and this is the secret sadness at the heart of Scottish success, is that our dead shame us. When the Whigs, the merchants and the Calvinist extremists voted to end Scotland's sovereignty, something was lost for which worldly achievement could never quite compensate the thoughtful Scot. The gold standard of his identity was debased, the pattern-book of his people's distinctive evolution was torn apart, and the pages could never be bound up correctly again. The dead were truer men than the living, closer to the heart of something very simple that had been given away. Gaining access to England, he lost the old contact with Europe. Gaining access to the British Empire, he gained the whole world — at the Biblical cost.

An anonymous contemporary pasquil on the Treaty of Union and the unrepresentative magnates who acceded to it conveys some of the fury felt by Scots of all classes at the loss of their country:

> Our Duiks were deills, our Marquesses were mad,
> Our Earls were evills, our Viscounts yet more bad,
> Our Lords were villains, and our Barons knaves
> Who with our boroughs did sell us for slaves.
>
> They sold the church, they sold the State and Nation,
> They sold their honour, name and reputation,
> They sold their birthright, peerages and places
> And now they leave the House with angrie faces.

It was inevitable that, more than mercenary soldiers, Scotland would now also export her peasantry, her scholars, her ambitious money men, her anachronistic Gaelic clansmen, her men and women of action; Scotland would never again be a whole world, capable of containing all of her people and meeting their needs. And that is at least an illusion a nation has to create, in order to function as a nation and focus an evolving human distinctiveness. Scottishness was a wounded and partial thing which, for all the efforts of her vernacular poets, Allan Ramsay, Fergusson, Burns, right down to MacDiarmid and his school in our own time, could never turn enough of her people, at home or in exile, away from what they saw as the economic and social realities of the world. "Reality" is a word with which Scots lacerate, or silence, their deeper selves. Poetry continued to be valued, if also often debased, because it was a thing connected with home and the values and unforgettable flavour of the lost nation; it was a *Scottish* endeavour, in contrast with most of the endeavours of exile and of modern times, which were things accomplished, often superbly, in alien terms and on the basis of alien values. Perhaps it is because of its ambiguous and painful importance to the exiles of the past that poetry has carried over, by a sort of inertia, into the time of the unconscious cultural continuities. That, too, might help to explain the disproportion we have been discussing, and its surprising persistence.

Much of the foregoing illustrates, I think, the elusiveness, the danger, the attraction and the decadence of ethnic consciousness. I was heavily exposed to the Scottish side of my inheritance because, when my parents married, my mother moved into the rural world of the Murrays from her native Newcastle, and I was born and grew up there. I was always in much less constant contact with her people, their Cornish-English background and their world of coal mining and heavy engineering. And the contact was weakened still further by her death late in my childhood. She had one last tremendous effect on my life, however, as it were from the grave; her strong wish that I should have as good an education as possible was faithfully honoured, to the point where I was financed at university longer than bare exam results might have seemed to justify. I was enabled to gain a real education, almost in spite of the system, and to begin to find myself as a writer. This, in turn, made it possible for me to appreciate and value my rural Scots Australian world, since there was no danger I would be trapped in its narrowness. I have lived in Scotland for a period, and explored it at a level a bit deeper, I think, than the romantic; when I was there, though, just after the failure of the Devolution referendum in 1979, I found the haggisry and the tartan trade more distasteful than ever, since the emptiness of heart and the cynical "realism" behind them had just been demonstrated. For all the tough, concentrated flavourfulness of style affected by many Scots, Edinburgh seemed more than ever the sham capital of a sham nation. And Whiggery did not seem to have changed its essence merely because it had adopted the intellectualising fake-airiness and fanatical chic of Transatlantic culture. And yet, when all has been said, Scotland is still the only overseas country in which I have never felt foreign.

Back home, I am probably one of the last of our lot to have felt, in a real way, some of the terrible gravity of the past; that won't persist beyond my generation at all, I suspect. My elder children love the old home region, and much of the life there, but they have mostly grown up in the cities. Besides, in the four generations prior to their own, they have no less than nine ancestral nationalities, nine ethnic traditions. The Scottish one probably won't emerge more strongly for them from that Babel of faint voices than, say, the Hungarian one or the Swiss one. Their only real option is to be Australians. Being Murrays won't now impede them in that; a couple of generations ago, it might well have been both a help and a hindrance. Now, if they are interested, they can approach the matter of origins and ethnic background in a spirit of study and perhaps use such studies to correct what Tom Keneally would call "Hanoverian" biases in the received thinking of our society. They are unlikely to suffer possession by the spirits of the restless dead.

Helix, 1/1980, and *Edinburgh Review*,
May 1981 (shorter versions). Expanded version
published Brennan Society Colloquium Papers,
Celts in Australia: Imagination & Identity, 1981

A Prose Diaspora

The Penguin Book of Hebrew Verse edited and translated by T. Carmi (Allen Lane, 1981)

When the late Professor E. V. Rieu founded the *Penguin Classics* series over thirty years ago with his translations of the *Iliad* and the *Odyssey*, he set what many poets have considered a bad precedent by rendering Homer's magnificent poetry into prose. He may have avoided the dangers of turning Homer into "exalted" verse in a worn-out Victorian manner and diction — the sort of thing which betrayed Gilbert Murray's translations — but he also evaded the difficult challenge of providing the modern reader with a fresh, vibrant English equivalent to Homer, one which would give the inner ear some direct echo of the majesty and pacing of the original, as Cecil Day Lewis did in his verse translations of Virgil. In a prosy age obsessed with matter at the expense of manner and spirit, he let down the poetic side.

This fault has persisted, with honourable exceptions, in the various Penguin translations and anthologies of non-English poetry ever since. Where the prose cribs merely accompany a presentation of the original texts, it's not so bad: if the originals are in a familiar script, as in, say, the *Penguin Book of Spanish Verse*, or the *Penguin Book of German Verse*, the prose versions at the foot of the page can be a doorway into a real enjoyment of the original poems, and a delightful aid to learning the language.

It takes a long time to learn to read an unfamiliar script fluently and naturally, however — I'm still slowed to the point of frustration by the texts in the *Penguin Book of Greek Verse* — and in such cases a prose rendering dumps the non-specialist reader between two stools: he can't "sound" the original at all confidently to get a sense of the metre and structure, and he can't get a feel of these from the translation either. All he has is brute primary meaning, fitfully deepened by footnotes perhaps, plus some loose idea of the level of the original and a ghost of its tone.

This is the great weakness of Professor Carmi's handsome new hardback *Penguin Book of Hebrew Verse*, and it almost ruins it.

A Prose Diaspora

What saves the book is the obviously superb quality of some of the poetry in it, as well as Carmi's excellent introductory material and biographical notes on the poets. Everyone recognises the supreme importance of the Hebrew tradition in the wider civilisation of mankind, and many will be familiar with its Biblical part. Carmi's anthology, however, surveys the whole three-thousand-year span of Hebrew poetry, and gives us a host of treasures from the two thousand years most of us know little or nothing about.

The oldest poem in the book is the Song of Deborah (Judges 5:1-31) which dates from around 1200 BC: the most recent is one by Dalia Ravikovitch, born on a kibbutz at Ramat-Gan in 1936. More amazing than the high antiquity of the tradition, though, is the fact that from slightly before Jesus' time right down to its revival as a national vernacular in our own day, Hebrew was used only for ritual and literary purposes, or as a *lingua franca* between scholars in the widely scattered communities of the diaspora. Folk life, everyday life, the speech of women and children, these went on in Aramaic and Greek, or, much later, in Yiddish or Ladino as well as the various native languages of the lands where Jews settled.

Like Latin, Hebrew was not so much a dead language as a noble princess who lived in books and sacred assemblies, spoke of exalted things and knew no slang. Yet she could be taught new styles. The *peytanim*, most of them cantors in the synagogues of the Near East and elsewhere, added their hymns and prefaces and verse ornaments to the liturgical readings of sacred scripture; Jewish poets in Moorish Spain adapted Arabic forms and cosmopolitan philosophies to the purposes of their lively Hebrew verse; the sonnet and *terza rima* were Hebraised in Italy; Yemenite Jews developed their tradition of song-poetry and the dance; modernising poets in eastern Europe last century turned away from the rigidities of their Talmudic tradition and began to fit the ancient language into modern moulds of thought; ironically, some of these even became regional poets praising the lands and cities from which the Holocaust would soon sweep them and their children.

It was not uncommon for Hebrew poetry in one part of the Jewish world to be centuries ahead of the development of another part. Underlying everything and forming the bedrock of unity was the heritage of Biblical Hebrew; even today, an Israeli poet has only to touch certain chords to set a whole complex of cultural memories vibrating. When Yehuda Amichai writes of the man under his vine speaking by field telephone to the man under his fig tree, a tension is immediately set up between the modern picture of military camouflage and the Biblical image of peace and contentment in one's homeland.

The armament of Biblical references and echoes has been a

strength and a test for Hebrew poets in all periods, used well and wittily by some, overused by others; like the weight of Classical Greece bearing down on later Greek poets, it has crushed the life and originality out of many of its poetic inheritors. A majority of the great number of religious poems in this book contain Biblical citations and echoes. A poem of the early fifteenth century has the beautiful but destitute Dinah objecting to an arranged marriage with an impotent old man: "Shall I in my youth...*lie with my forefathers?*" — a play on the Biblical phrase meaning to die.

In a visionary hymn dating from the third or fourth century AD, the Almighty addresses the angels around His throne:

Holy Beings, Holy Beings, who carry My throne of glory with whole heart and willing mind — blessed be the hour in which I created you: exalted be the zodiacal sign under which I fashioned you; radiant be the day on which you first occurred to Me. For you are the precious vessels that I prepared and perfected on that day. Now silence the voice of the heavenly beings I have made, so that I may listen to the voice of My children praying.

As we might expect from one of the world's great religious traditions, the book abounds with poems of worship and mystical illumination, as well as with Israel's long wrangle with its God. There is even a lengthy set of commandments issued to God by man, in return for the ten given to man through Moses on Mount Sinai. The score for obedience on both sides would, I guess, be about even.

Half in and half out of the religious category, there are some of the most pungent curses I have seen. A poem by Judah Al-Hazari (Spain, eleventh century) expresses the feelings of a man who has paid two thousand pieces of silver for a beautiful young bride, only to find when he lifts her veil after the wedding ceremony that he has been duped. It is a virtuoso performance.

Purely secular poems are less common before our own time, but are well represented by love poems and by erotic poems that *can't* be construed as referring to Israel's relations with the Lord, plus many aphoristic and occasional pieces. One pair of quatrains by Abraham ibn Ezra (Spain, eleventh century) seems to anticipate Australian idiom, with the poet complaining that his stars have ruined him, that if he dealt in candles the sun would never set, and if he dealt in shrouds no one would die as long as he lived. If it were raining gravy, I suppose, he'd have a fork.

Tragically, there are many poems of religious persecution and pogrom, some of them horrifying indeed. The one which moved me most, and illustrates the profound historical awareness of most Hebrew poets, was written by the great figure of the modern Hebrew revival, Chaim Nahman Bialik. It recalls the terror felt by

A Prose Diaspora

Jews during the great plague in medieval times: if there were no deaths in the ghetto, they would be blamed for the pestilence and slaughtered. When at last two of their number die of the disease, the relief of the community bursts forth in rejoicing.

There are many great poets represented in Carmi's collection, but for me the real discovery was the renowned scriptural scholar, astronomer, military commander and vizier to various kings in Moslem Spain, Samuel Hanagid, Samuel the Prince, whose dates are AD 993–1056. Perhaps the most perfect of Hanagid's poems in this collection is a song commemorating the solar and lunar eclipses which occurred within a month of each other in the year 1044.

Are you asleep, my friend? Rise and awake the dawn, look up to heaven. See, it is like a leopard's skin, all covered with spots. And see how the half moon, which should be full on this night, is as black as the mouth of an oven or the rim of a pot; like the face of a girl, half flushed and half in shadow.

Now look again, at this month's end, and see the sun almost engulfed by gloom. What little light remains upon its darkness is like a diadem on the head of a Negress. And the earth, as if in mourning for its sun, is like a woman disfigured by tears.

He who is master of might and beauty, He struck both his luminaries in the very same month. He covered the face of the moon with His terrestrial globe and blocked off the sun with His moon. All this was done by God, who does as He wishes with His works.

He darkened the light of day in midmorning, and the light of night at midnight, like a raging king who harasses all his lords in their own domains. First He struck the night light, and only later did He strike the light of day, like a king who gives a stupefying drink first to his maidservant and afterwards to his queen.

Sydney Morning Herald, 15 May 1981

Poetry and School

Poetry and education have a complex and sometimes uncomfortable relationship with each other. There is nothing in the school syllabus more important than poetry, and yet it is not a thing which sits comfortably with the requirements of study, analysis and examination. It isn't really at home in the classroom. Poetry is a somewhat solitary art, and its essence is contemplative wisdom, which likes to live and move at its own pace. Both contemplation and wisdom are apt to fly out the window, too, when the atmosphere inside is one of pressure or competition. There are students who come to dislike poetry because they see it as an imposed thing associated with school. A fashion for somewhat shallow and automatic rebelliousness encourages this, of course, but such students do command some sympathy. They have at least caught on to the fact that informed enjoyment of poetry is not common in the broader society they also inhabit. They may have noticed "cultural" stuff like poetry being used to snub certain classes of people, to serve as weapons in a mean form of class warfare. They may even have taken their own incomprehension of poetry as a stage in the process by which society grades and relegates its members, and rejected the thing that seemed to reject them.

In all of this, they're partly right. For much of this century, for reasons connected with artistic modernism and an increasingly policitised cult of the avant garde, poetry has been more than usually estranged from the wider public it has had in other periods of history. It's not wholly the fault of poetry, of course; to keep going at what has become a frantic and shifty pace, our society has often chosen to live, as it were, behind its own back, deliberately ignoring or trivialising the hard insights which poetry brings. Educational establishments have had to serve as a sort of National Park in which poetry could survive, if often at the cost of mutating into rather forced and wilful shapes. There are signs that this situation is easing now, but we need not be prematurely reassured. The sheer economics of art — the capital costs of poetry may be no more than pens and paper, but poets have to live — are such that it

Poetry and School

is very prone to become dependent on successive elites and their tastes and preoccupations. Once, poetry had to play the courtier to kings and nobles; lately, it has had to pay some court to educators and the new intellectual classes in society. Indeed, some poets now see themselves as intellectuals, a claim on privilege which obscures the far older dignity of our vocation.

On the other hand, the fact that poetry may not be appreciated by one's neighbours or one's gang is no argument against poetry! Conformity is no argument for or against anything, and there is usually a good deal of concealed incomprehension, fear and shame in even the breeziest rejection of art. Again, acceptance of relegation without a fight is surely rather weak, however snarly we may pretend to get about it; it is no triumph to collaborate with our imagined relegators, nor to take the first relegation as final. The fact that we don't like or haven't understood a poem doesn't mean, always, that it has failed; we may have failed the test it set us. This is rather awful when we have exams to face, but in the longer perspective of our life it doesn't matter nearly as much. We are always free to come back to the poem later, when a degree of personal independence has been achieved and we can afford to be more receptive. A good poem is very much its own thing, and we need to be pretty much our own person to deal with that. We shouldn't be panicked, either, if a poem doesn't yield all of its significance at once; if it is a truly first-rate poem, it will go on giving out freshness and delight — it may be sombre and terrible delight — over a great many readings. Art can even be defined as containment of the inexhaustible within disciplined limits. A poem may only begin to work for us after a number of readings, and years after we have read it, we may find that it applies with dazzling precision to circumstances and events we wouldn't have dreamed of relating it to when we first read it.

There is a tendency these days for people who do accept poetry, or at any rate who take it up, to try to mobilise it, to make it "exciting" and "relevant", to make it serve causes and purposes. Poetry will go a little way in this direction, but not too far. Quite soon, the poetry falls away, and we are left with some sort of versified pamphlet or journalism-in-lines, with the energy coming not from within the work but from the ephemeral concerns it is on about or the current attitudes it reflects. Such work tends to date quickly and disappear, however exciting it may have seemed when it was first published. Western society is the first in history to have been heavily permeated with journalism, and our society's yen for excitement is only paralleled, probably, by that of the crowds who flocked to the arena in Rome. The kinds of excitement we have been trained to accept, however, and the insatiable desire itself, are fundamentally alien to art, though it may use them as subject matter. What the journalistic mind reveals about itself most often, when it deals with art, is that it doesn't really think art on its own is *enough*. In this, it resembles the sort of critical mind which really prefers the prose commentary to the poem. Both kinds of people look for outside references and dimensions to legitimise and *complete* the work of art — and yet art itself, good art, is one of the few truly sufficient things on Earth. It satisfies because it contains its own well-rounded completeness. Ordinary journalistic excitement stimulates us, but it also divides us and leaves us wanting more of the same; art stimulates us, too, but it integrates things and enacts their completeness in fresh ways, thus promoting completeness in us, when we absorb it.

In going round to many schools and colleges and even universities, I have found that there seems to be a point at which students quite suddenly "get" poetry, when, to use an old-fashioned word, they twig what it's all about. Before that point, most things are puzzling and obscure and a bit threatening; after it, things fall into place with surprising speed. Everything seems to *follow* now, where everything was drudging incomprehension before. I'm not a teacher, and I don't know how to bring this insight about. A teacher who does know and can bring it about is worth his or her weight in fine platinum. I had two such, at Taree High, and I've met some others. My own lasting flash of insight, which came as late as my final year at high school, came in a dual context of *relevance* and *delight*. When I was shown poetry written in my own time, or near enough to it, and written in an engrossingly alive language, I began for the first time to get interested. And when I was shown such poetry written in my own country about things I knew or was interested in, the magic happened. Suddenly, a delight in words and in the fine details and processes of things, interests which had always been with me, had some sort of correlative outside my own head. I had been timidly feeling my way towards art, but a poor hand with the brush and a relative lack of interest in plot or character would probably have made all that abortive — now, however, I had found an art form in which detail and patterning and the significance of things were central, and where words rather than mucky disobedient paint were the medium. I leaned headlong into this new revelation, fell head over heels, and came up writing verse. After some years of absorbing large amounts of other people's poetry, and burning heaps of my own stuff, I began writing some poems worth keeping. I am still learning the disciplines and flexibilities of my craft, and the fascination has remained inexhaustible.

The moment of catching on to what poetry is needn't provoke

Poetry and School

the extreme reaction of becoming a poet, and in most cases it obviously doesn't, but I do suspect that that core of illumination is the very heart and centre of education, and may be the effect the whole machine is ultimately designed to produce. And to service, after it has happened. The deep reason why art fits uncomfortably into schools is that it is a bigger thing than school, and can replace it. It is itself the lasting school of mankind, in which the best and most durable wisdom of civilisations is distilled and laid down for succeeding generations to contemplate. Poetry has been regarded, in the past, as the senior art form — certainly it and its cousin song are by far the oldest forms of literature. One reason for this very high regard lies in the fact that it uses language, the most characteristic and complex attribute of human beings. In poetry, language can be used at something like full stretch, with all its resources of nuance and overtone and quasi-musical resonance, and also with all its daylight resources of precision and the capacity to catch the sheer *this*-ness of things in ways which make them unforgettable. If we view poetry this way it ceases to be a suspect refugee sheltering in schools and intellectual magazines, and becomes the whole point of schooling. We begin to suspect that if we manage to get through school without coming to terms with poetry, we have failed school and are not yet really educated. It doesn't matter what distinctions we may have gained, or how high we may subsequently rise in the world. Indeed it may be a curse to the world if we do rise high in it. To be civilised, you don't have to be genteel or pretentious or trendy; far from it. But you do have to have got the point. The point is a free, rich, contemplative integration, renewed all the time in delight and called wisdom. That is what good art is continually about.

Preface to *Poems for Senior Students*
edited by John Palmer (William Brooks & Co., 1980)

Centering the Language

The Macquarie Dictionary: Editor-in-Chief A. Delbridge (Macquarie Library, 1981)

Barring disasters between now and Christmas, it is probable that the most historic event to take place in our country this year will have been the publication of a hefty but by no means unmanageable green-covered book. This is the *Macquarie Dictionary*, the fruit of ten years' painstaking lexicographical work, and it is not going too far to describe the appearance of this book as a discreetly republican occasion.

Just as the *Oxford English Dictionary*, the venerable OED, defines and presents words from a primarily British standpoint, and *Webster* from an American one, the *Macquarie Dictionary* bases its definitions, its pronunciations and its view of the English language squarely on the facts of usage here; the Australian meaning of the word, if it's the most common meaning the word has in Australia, is given first.

This isn't just another collection of Australianisms, valuable as some of those have been, but a comprehensive and scholarly dictionary which is quite obviously set to become an institution. Within twelve months, I predict, it will be completely unremarkable and natural to hear people say: Look it up in the *Macquarie*.

Some people, here as well as abroad, may be surprised to learn that Australian English goes beyond slang and the heavy pungencies of Bazza Mackenzie, but if they examine the matter for a little while they will realise that there are thousands of words and expressions, completely unslangy ones, that are either peculiar to Australia or which have meanings in Australia quite different from their meanings elsewhere. Examples of terms peculiar to this country would include family court, bouncinette, clothes hoist, anabranch, bridging finance, dawn service, beanbag, topnotch, land rights, disposals store, walkathon, electric jug, blue-rinse, rotary hoe, green ban, home unit — it's hard to know where to stop, and the *Macquarie* contains more such items than any other dictionary.

The case is similar with words that exist elsewhere but have distinctively Australian significances here: arbitration, informal (vote), selector, whaler, station, yard, terrace, flat, lay-by. If you need a quick blushful lesson in this matter of Australian usage versus usage elsewhere, just try going into a stationery shop in Britain and asking for some Durex. Here the word means transparent sticky tape, but in the United Kingdom its primary meaning is a rubber contraceptive. I've tripped up on this one, and so have thousands of other Australians abroad.

Another area in which some people still doubt the validity of Australian English, or even regret its existence, is that of pronunciation. We are not yet free of the colonial habit of apologising for the way we sound, or else exaggerating our accent out of intransigence. The executive editor of the new dictionary, Susan Butler, tells how, when the project was with Jacaranda Press, she used to have ding-dong arguments with Brisbane taxidrivers who thought it a great insult to be regarded as speaking something other than Oxford English; they seemed to think Australian English meant an obscene way of talking. It was as if we all lived in a great continent-wide conspiracy, speaking a kind of shirtsleeve English most of the time, but ever ready to put on the dog, or try to, when the occasion seemed to warrant it.

The fact is that Australian is a dialect of English which has grown up in this country in response to our particular history and linguistic needs; it is remarkable in having a basically uniform pronunciation over a wider geographical area than any other dialect on earth. Apart from some very slight variations in vowel quality in Adelaide and on the Bass Strait islands — many people from outside South Australia will have noticed how Adelaide women, in particular, pronounce words like "now" almost as "nigh" — the sounds we make are essentially similar from Cairns to Fremantle. Within this overall dialect, the *Macquarie Dictionary* distinguishes four forms of pronunciation, Broad, General, Cultivated and Modified Australian. When I studied phonetics at Sydney University under Professor Arthur Delbridge, the editor-in-chief of the new dictionary, we heard of Broad and Educated forms (Broad and Flash, as some commentators have preferred to call them), but the classification has both widened and grown subtler since then.

Scholars don't quite like to call these forms levels, though there is sometimes a touch of class differentiation about them. Broad Australian is the form in which vowels and diphthongs have their most strongly marked Australian flavour, and in this form you tend to get more slurring and running of words together; these latter processes are more politely called assimilation and elision, in the technical terminology of linguists.

Cultivated Australian, on the other hand, is the prestige form of our national dialect, and approaches the quality of other prestige forms of English, the sorts of English spoken by educated people in New York or London or Johannesburg. In all the prestige forms of English, local features of accent and intonation are reduced, while not being eliminated altogether, and speech tends to be fluent and lacking in clumsiness.

Most Australians, of course, speak General Australian, which lies between the extremes of Broad and Cultivated, and we all tend to slide back and forth between the two according to our mood, our company, the effect we want to create and so on. I've often been amused by what I call Labor Intellectuals' English, where special effects are got by combining a highly educated vocabulary with a very broad, salty pronunciation and idiom. This is not quite the same thing as John Singleton English, sometimes called Synthetic Ocker, though the difference is largely a matter of style and attitudes.

Modified Australian is a catch-all name given to various attempts to sound more cultivated than Cultivated; a better name might have been La-de-dah. You tend to hear this form in the mouths of some politicians who have studied abroad, as well as in, say, the fashion departments of large stores: Would Modom cyur to step this wey? Another name for this sort of thing might be His Master's Voice English, though that term is clearly too frivolous for a scholarly work. I tend to include in my category of HMV English the various American-derived forms as well, things like Wooloomoolo Yank, a sociolect heard on commercial radio, and Tamworth Bluegrass, a nasal accent with wrongly placed r's used locally for singing Country-and-Western songs. This latter, in turn, is fairly close to the internationally received Dixie-flavoured accent of rock singers. I'm not sure whether the *Macquarie*'s category of Modified Australian includes these.

Although the *Macquarie Dictionary* sets out pronunciations, in International Phonetic Association symbols, for every word it contains, neither in point of pronunciation nor usage is it interested in saying what is "proper". If there are two common Australian pronunciations of a word, it will give both, with the more usual or widespread one first; in the case of castle, for instance, the pronunciation which rhymes with parcel is given first, followed by the one that rhymes with hassle. The latter of these tends to be the more common pronunciation south of, roughly, the Murrumbidgee.

In this and other ways, the *Macquarie* follows very strictly the modern preference for descriptive over prescriptive dictionaries, and is at an opposite extreme from, say, the dictionaries sanctioned by the French Académie, which seek to regulate the French language and keep it free from *barbarismes* such as *le weekend*.

The *Macquarie* tries to record the facts of English speech in Australia and abroad without any bias at all; if a word is or has been in use, it qualifies for inclusion. Thus all of the dreaded four-letter words and their derivatives appear; if this turns you on, off you go and have a perv. (For some reason, the *Macquarie* gives the spelling of that word without the final -e as its main form, though the form perve is given as a secondary and presumably less common spelling.) One gathers it was not always easy for the editors and compilers to maintain their value-free approach. Some of them hated having to include the offensive terms of racial and ethnic prejudice, words such as dago and ding and gubber, and there were fierce arguments over *ocker* before the present balanced set of definitions was arrived at.

What is more remarkable about the new dictionary than its permissiveness, however, is its range and the sheer amount of vocabulary it fits into its single volume. Words as contemporary as ayatollah and Zimbabwe are in, along with short-lived ancient slang words such as onkus and the beautiful ugly words of science: siphonostele, pycnometer, byte.

In both pronunciation and lexis, which is the technical term for words and their meanings, the *Macquarie Dictionary* bases itself on the English language spoken by those born in Australia and New Zealand, or whose speech has assimilated itself to that of such native speakers. It lists over one thousand distinctive items of vocabulary from New Zealand, not only familiar Maori names for trees and the like, but also words such as hoot (money), bach or batch (in the sense of a weekend cottage) and health stamp; this is fair enough, as New Zealand English is historically an offshoot of Australian.

The *Macquarie* has some etymological content, but I'm inclined to think it might as well have had none, since what does appear is often so sketchy as to be useless or downright misleading. It's little use giving the ultimate origin of a word if you're not going to follow through with some sort of an account of its history and the changes it has undergone. This is provided for some words, but not for most. The humble dunny, for example, is said to derive its name from British dialect forms such as dunnakin and dunnaken, meaning a receptacle for dunna or dung, but we're not told which dialects were involved, nor on which side of the world the word was shortened, nor when. I've heard the word dunny used in Scotland as recently as this year, but whether this was a reimportation from Australia no one seemed to know; some Scots, though, thought it was a word that had always been around in Scotland, in their lifetimes, and some roundly claimed it was the ordinary Scottish term for a toilet.

One fairly prescriptive thing which the *Macquarie Dictionary* can't help doing is to establish the spelling of some words which have hardly seen print before; nerd, for example, looks as if it's going to be spelt that way, rather than nurd. The only such spelling which worried me in the book was that of the adjective shonkie: surely that is a shonky rendition, compared with the one ending in -y.

A dictionary is an ongoing thing, though, and in a sense can never be completed, as language never ceases changing and growing. Tiny points such as these are bound to be attended to in the next edition, along with all the new technical terms, slang, political jargon and the rest which will have been added to Australian and worldwide English by then. The research and editorial work of the *Macquarie Dictionary* does not stop now just because the first version of the book is out: it has even generated its own publishing concern, under Hamlyn's former general manager Kevin Weldon, who took over production of the million-dollar project after it had passed out of the hands of Jacaranda Press and found a home in a cottage within the grounds of Macquarie University.

In the somewhat nomadic years it has been in preparation, the dictionary has relied not only on officially appointed consultants to furnish it with vocabulary — prison slang, for example, was provided by the Resurgents, a prisoners' debating society at Parramatta gaol — nor has it placed its entire reliance on written sources, though a prodigious quantity of those has been scanned; it has also accepted unsolicited suggestions, words and lists of words, queer local usages and bits of jargon from all sorts of volunteers interested enough to proffer them.

All purchasers of the dictionary, I should add, automatically become members of the *Macquarie Dictionary* Society, entitled to receive its free newsletter and welcome to provide any and all relevant information for inclusion in future editions. That invitation is, in fact, a general one, and I can testify to the polite and considerate treatment which contributors get. After-sales service is, of course, a native Australian expression; in this case, it will be most beneficial if it works both ways.

As well as everything else, the *Macquarie* is illustrated with many hundreds of small line drawings scattered over its 2049 pages; my favourite was that delicious crustacean the Balmain bug, which looked, drawn from above, like a weak-eyed and rather indignant Pharaoh with a bulbous nose. The drawings and diagrams aren't

Centering the Language

included to amuse us, though; they contain a wealth of information which accompanying definitions can't always convey.

If I finish up by saying that this new dictionary is a ripper (not a ring-ripper, since that expression fails to appear in it) it is very largely because of the dignity it confers on our form of English. It does this in part by showing how much larger and richer our dialect is than many had thought, in part by gently but firmly shifting our linguistic perception, so that our entire language is henceforth centered for us, not thousands of miles away, but here where we live.

Sydney Morning Herald, 3 October 1981

Starting from Central Railway — A Bush View of Sydney

Sydney's Central Station has been getting a million-dollar facelift lately. The huge country terminus, that great hall known to generations of taxidrivers as The Steam, has actually been seeing steam again for the first time in years, and sandblasters, too. Men have stripped away the soot and grime and petrified vomit of many decades, putting in new quarry tile flooring and semicircles of tough red plastic seating. You could almost forget that this grim enormous station is the gateway of culture shock for the country poor, the portal through which pass the uprooted and the dispossessed.

It is not merely the bright dreams and holiday anticipations which pour into Sydney on the country trains. Those come mostly by car, nowadays, or by plane; I gather even the wide-eyed guests of the Far-West Children's Health Scheme are usually flown to Sydney now. The ancient bush trains are the realm of schoolchildren and other non-drivers partly, but they're also what they always were under the surface — a realm of the depressed and the lost. They carry the broken-down stationhand retreating to the city to find an easier job, the shy Aboriginal girl with the cardboard suitcase and the address of her aunt in Redfern, the single mother with the frightened face and upset baby setting off to housekeep for an unimaginable lonely widower living up a long gravel road in the hills of regrowth scrub. If there is a Third World in New South Wales, one of the places to look for it is on the country services of the State Rail Authority.

The rural Third World, for everywhere it is essentially a rural thing, is not really to be found in the parks and sandstone arcades above which Central rears its floodlit ziggurat of height. The lower depths of that shadowy region contain mostly the derelict urban poor, not all of them old nowadays. But even twenty years ago the punch-drunk prelim fighters from Rushcutters Bay rarely dished out their four-bob servings of stew and peas in the Hole in the Wall cafe to uprooted bush types. Those were more likely to be met within the laminex cafes up on Railway Square, or dreaming in front of gun shops.

Starting from Central Railway — A Bush View of Sydney

If they lacked an address to go to in the suburbs, an old mate or a married daughter, they weren't usually to be found sleeping in the park across Eddy Avenue, not since the last great Depression anyway. They sought shelter in the cheap hotels and remaining residentials towards the city or in neighbouring Surry Hills, the sort of places where Henry Lawson's Mr Smellingscheck passed his time of quiet purgatory.

And in the People's Palace, you met the guarded country wives with hair drawn tight as a prayerbook's binding, women who could have afforded better but whom lives of reflex frugality had made psychologically incapable of seeking more than minimal comfort. For the Third World of the ex-countryfolk is often a matter as much of psychology as of poverty, real though the poverty may be. It is the world of the uprooted dairyman who has not, after three weeks in Sydney, got further from Central than the first dangerous rapids of George Street as it whirls into existence past Kings disposals store. It is the world of people unplugged from all of their connections, from the kinships and local knowledge which are their culture, and are now lodged in their minds like the language of an abolished nation. And it is the world of those two bush children who, not long after I came to Sydney in the late fifties, died trying to navigate back to Central from a tentative trip down town. Used to the logic of landmarks and remembered routes, rather than of street names, they set out to walk back along the tracks of the underground rail loop and were run over by a train in the darkness and killed. I have never forgotten them, or laughed at their silly story.

Years later I heard it again, from two young Gurindji men down from Wattie Creek, in the Northern Territory; they had followed the railway lines home after a party on the north side, but their line didn't take them through any tunnels, and they had survived. In the same way, if you have understood this story, it was years before I bothered to put names to the principal streets of the city. I simply learned where everything was, on that ridge.

The day those bush children were killed, they had probably visited the harbour. That's what people do when they come to Sydney. Beyond even its slowly declining function as a port, that is what the harbour is for, to be stunningly beautiful and uplift the spirit, to carry ferries and yachts, to reward enterprise and success, to be sold off in inexhaustible inches of postcard and estate agent's distant view.

The city and the harbour, and maybe the Cross, *are* Sydney to international tourists and bush ethnics alike, and no reminders that the bulk of the people in the Sydney conurbation now live nearer to Parramatta than to Sydney's historic core can change the fact. Let the electoral redistributors worry about that. It's like the fact that, because of the glasshouse effect of all its man-made heat, Sydney is a displaced island of subtropical climate, in which species of trees and flowers can be grown whose true habitat is hundreds of miles farther north. That, too, is a datum for enthusiasts, of which I'm one, in this case. I frankly love the paradise-garden aspect of much of Sydney, and the way unorganised private plantings of exotic trees and shrubs merge into the long fingers of native bush which penetrate the suburbs along the drowned river valleys and ancient rock-walled creeks. This mingling of urban settlement and natural bush is one of the truly distinctive features of Australian cities, and it began in Sydney. Some of my north coast relatives, of course, are horrified by the bushfire risk — they know that humans cannot safely live in the Australian forest — and it took me years to see beauty in the wiry sandstone scrub.

When I first came to Sydney, neither the Opera House nor high-rise buildings had yet appeared; it was still the packed five-storey city, which I can only revisit nowadays by staying up to watch reruns of "The Siege of Pinchgut" on late-night television. I was captivated by the city, but like everyone else I went to live in the suburbs. Despised and reviled, those Sydney suburbs are the prototype which set the pattern of post-conquest settlement in Australia, defeating the best that the planners of other towns and cities could do.

Few even of our country towns are distinctive, at least on the surface; if they aren't dying, they have become detached suburbs of Sydney. The pattern was set when the working people of Sydney began to break out of their terraces in search of the same privilege which available space had given their betters, a separate house on a private allotment. Distinctiveness in our other capital cities, too, has become a matter of minor and preserved details, stone houses, brushwood fences, houses on stilts, or else is confined to a small urban core surrounded by suburbs of Sydney. It is the greatest influence the Mother City has had, and the one with which our intellectuals find it hardest to come to any sort of humane terms, for it is vernacular of the people.

Despite recent image-making which presents Sydney as a sort of infinitely more aware and fashionable Surfers Paradise, the city and its people are not invariably informal. Outward appearances have changed, though, in the direction of climatic sanity. When I came to the city, businessmen still wore dark suits in the summer heat, and women and schoolgirls still commonly wore gloves. People at the only university which Sydney then possessed recalled the days, not long past, when students had been required under the

Starting from Central Railway — A Bush View of Sydney

by-laws to stand to attention when the carillon chimed out in memory of fallen servicemen.

The first member of the academic staff to wear jeans in working hours was Doctor, now Professor, Bernard Martin, in 1958. He had just joined the English Department from angry young Oxford, and we thought him profoundly dashing. It was not until 1962 that the first undergraduate regularly attended the university barefoot; his name was Philip Chambers. By then, though, the years of the Bohemian Occupation were beginning, and it was hard to tell what was Sydney style and what was international. One feature of the new spirit which dovetailed well with Sydney's own traditions was a certain knowingness, initially rather classy, which we called Sophistication when it first came in with Rowe Street and espresso bars.

Sydney's own sophistication was always more democratic, a matter of references to Tommo's two-up school or the dread marksmanship of police sergeant Ray Kelly. Crime only hurt, and became distinctly unfunny, when you got too close to it. It didn't much matter whether gossip about the Big Boys of Sydney crime was accurate; it was a sort of signature tune of the city which had invented the word *bludger* and was just starting to use the word *hoon*, successive terms for the same occupation. Crime has been a native theme since the day Governor Phillip founded the first South Seas Gulag, and whole governments here have worn a glowering snap-brimmed racetrack air, an atmosphere of marked cards and standovers which the city has deplored and enjoyed since before Chicago was thought of. It's tragic that narcotics ever came in to turn the comedy jagged and ugly. The dance of the pratfalling Police Commissioners is a never-failing public entertainment, but who needed the drugs, in a State whose Government had discovered, in the poker machine, a means of taxing the residents of all the other States as well as its own people?

Apart from minor Good Things such as plentiful harbourside restaurants (at last) and bookshops and cinemas staying open on Sunday, two laudable developments of the past decade or so in Sydney have been the coming of trees to the Western Suburbs — people growing them are no longer, I believe, told to "Garn live on the North Shore where yer belong!" — and the movement of people back into the city proper. Without committed full-time inhabitants, a city centre gradually becomes what country people, with that humbly unconscious lordliness which so irritates the middle classes, think any city or town is: a show, a place of supplies and novelties, a sort of red-light district apart from and rather beneath the ordinary. The city is a place where you put up with the shallow smartness, the go-getting and the childishly short attention-span of the inhabitants in return for interest and diversion. And maybe some profit. Also, as cover, as a place of sexual and other variety, it is a place where country people are freed from community and thus from a sense of consequences.

No one who has ever done rural work regards urban work as quite real; it is a disguised holiday, and urbanites, modern people, seem to him the enviable denizens of Holiday City. And so alongside the common modern sense that real life is always somewhere else, which is itself a potent producer of Third World phenomena, there is this extra Australian feeling that the good life is something we're getting away with, a con we're succeeding at because we aren't mugs. If this is corrosive of self-respect, we can blame ex-bush people and bush-minded transients for it, as well as speculators and oldtime lags made good. Like the suburbs, it is historically a legacy of Sydney to the nation.

Sydney Morning Herald, 31 January 1981

Notes on the Writing of a Novel Sequence

Quite literally I wrote *The Boys who Stole the Funeral* in order to find out what happened in it. I had the beginnings of a story, that is to say, a situation and some characters, and I wanted to see how it and they would develop. I'd written portraits, pieces of action, even crowd scenes, but never characters, and I was curious to discover how it felt to create figures who would stand up, move off and assume a life of their own. Oddly, perhaps, I never doubted that I could work this magic. What I didn't yet know was how imperious characters can become, how they will reject out of hand some line of action you propose for them, and take another. I also didn't know as yet how hard it would be to give them up at the end of the book and put them to sleep again. For more than a year after I'd finished *The Boys*, they kept popping back into my mind, wanting to move on into a further book and more adventures. Indeed, they haven't stopped yet.

At the outset, all I had was an incident in which two young men in Sydney steal an old country man's body from a suburban undertaker's and ferry it up the north coast for burial. This notion came to me in about July 1977. I knew that the old man was an ex-serviceman, probably a veteran of the First World War, and that he'd been something of a rolling stone in his lifetime, until he fetched up in his last years in a converted back shed belonging to some distant relations. I did not yet have a motivation for the theft of his body; all I knew was that the reasons for this had to be good ones, in no way frivolous. None of this was based on any actual incident; the truth of it, which I felt strongly, was wholly fictional. Knowing that the question of the boys' motive would find its own answer if I waited, I mused about the possible meanings of such a journey, and its relation to the serious value which is attached to funerals in the Australian rural culture from which I come; it's not unusual for a funeral Up Home to attract seven or eight hundred people wishing to pay their last respects. I thought, too, about the vital importance for many Aborigines of returning a person's remains to their particular spirit country so that their soul may be reincarnated when a pregnant woman passes nearby; the spirit of a person buried in a strange place is lost, dwindling away in homeless misery. And I worked on some formal problems I'll describe in a moment.

After a couple of months, the necessary breakthrough came. I was talking to a friend who serves on the New South Wales Prices Commission, and that body had just done a survey of the undertaking trade. "How much would it cost," I asked, "to have an undertaker arrange a funeral in which the corpse had to be transported from Sydney up to such-and-such a place in the mountains behind the north coast?" An approximate figure was named, and I was delighted. I had my motivation! The old Digger's family, not considering that funerals warranted any very large expense, weren't prepared to honour his wishes and bury him in his native district. They wouldn't put up the money, so the one young relative who had been close to him in his last years would have to act decisively and fast, and go right outside everyone's conventions. Getting him back inside these when necessary would be a fascinating problem to solve further on in the story. First, though, there would be the theft, and the bizarre journey.

At around the same time, in about September 1977, I also solved the other problem which had been standing in my way, that of the form and structure of the book. I wanted to reclaim the narrative for poetry, to recapture ground which the senior literary form had begun losing to the novel as early as the end of the seventeenth century, and which it had decidedly lost to film and TV in the twentieth. But how to do it? Every time I started to write the story in continuous verse, with a single metre or a varied one, it broke down almost at once. Something was wrong, and I can't write anything until I've established some sort of formal base for it. If I were a Scottish piper, I would say that I need an *urlar* or base-tune before I can begin weaving variations. Need focuses receptivity, though, and the answer came through a glimpse of pattern, rather than through any verbal models. John Forbes lent me a book of sonnets by a New York poet whose name I'm afraid I've rather ungratefully forgotten, and while I was only mildly interested in the poems themselves, their arrangement on the book's pages, two on the left, two on the right, gave me a picture of the form and the density of verse I needed, and how to organise it, which is to say, really, how to *time* it. Also, I'd always liked the sonnet, and had written single ones and sequences. It had always seemed to me a very "natural" form, concise enough to restrain sloppiness, roomy enough to accommodate almost any content. With its containment and its one or more internal *volte* or turns, it seemed an ideal conjunction of discipline and freedom. And there was nothing to prevent its serving as an analogue of a "take" in film, or a scene on

Notes on the Writing of a Novel Sequence

stage, or even as a short chapter or section of a chapter in a novel. It could be entire in itself, or it could serve as a unit in building up larger patterns, or be the means of cutting back and forth between different foci of action, and there was ample room within fourteen lines for both action and meditation...The possibilities were not only adequate to my purpose, but inexhaustible. I tried a couple — and the story was away and running, moving at a rapid underlying speed but containing all the stillness, the timeless pointing quality which poetry reconciles with movement better than any other art can, which I knew my narrative also needed. It moved, but it didn't blur; everything could be in motion and yet *held*, in ways which tend to look artificial and literary in prose narratives. I found, too, that I could have amplitude without crowding but also without the heavy explanatory quality you get in all but the very best prose. I could have everything, in short, that the novel, the drama and the film could provide, without losing poetry. I just had to keep on discovering the potentials of the structure I'd set up.

A colleague of mine, a prose novelist, says that the best book is the one you chuckle over as you write it. I had a lot of that quiet, intense joy over the next fourteen months. I was freer than I'd ever been from the grey, conformingly non-conformist consensus tone of modern poetry whether it's written in Wigan or Wichita or Wollongong, and I was further than ever from acquiescence in its received class values, or from playing little timid variations on them within a permitted range. It was so damn good to be away from Modern Literature at last, and working deeper and deeper into a native voice, or voices. Writing *The Boys* was the best fun I've had from poetry, and I long to tackle a project of similar or even bigger dimensions again some day. For that, though, I have to wait till the right idea comes along. Using, essentially, the storytelling methods I unconsciously learned from my father in my childhood — Dad is a man whose culture is almost wholly oral and musical, and he is a truly gifted spinner of stories — I didn't plot *The Boys* in advance at all, but simply wrote it from the beginning to the end and then stopped. With the characters having plenty of say in my decisions, I constructed each scene, each moment, each departure pretty well as I came to it. I only remember a couple of occasions on which I had slightly to shift the placement of a sonnet, and only one (number 24) had to be discarded and rewritten differently. Of course, there were some passages which had to be refined painstakingly into shape, as for example when Clarrie Dunn is describing life in the trenches, before shifting abruptly to the story about the woman who gave him the white feather in Bond Street (Sonnet 52). It took a while to get the precise tone for his image of barbed wire "like singed guts in the wind". The white feather incident didn't have to be invented, however; that actually happened to one of my mother's brothers, a gunner on HMAS *Sydney*, when he was on shore leave in Melbourne after helping to sink the German raider *Emden*. Another device which came to me with a sense of inevitability and naturalness as soon as I started writing the story was that of giving each character a "signature", some peculiarity of speech or punctuation or rhythm which would make it immediately clear who was speaking. Or thinking.

There is probably little more I can usefully tell about my motives and methods in respect of *The Boys*, at least in the absence of specific questioning, and it's probably not for me to enter too deeply into wider evaluations of it or commentary on it. One thing it isn't, I would claim, is any sort of Catholic thesis-novel. That would have been to reduce the eternal Church which is based on Divine revelation to something approaching what is pejoratively called Literature in the poem, which is to say, repeated attempts by man to force meaning on the world and seal it with literal human sacrifice. Experience, Catholic Christianity and what I discover by writing poems are my three prime guides to reality, and they guided me in the writing of *The Boys* as they guide all of my work. In the poem, the Church is not a cause, but a touchstone for judging causes, just as one's mind and spirit are touchstones for judging the Church. If there was any sort of meta-artistic concern in the book, it is probably for the despised and relegated country poor, the people I come from and belong to, and to whom I dedicate everything I may achieve. And I guess that, here, I don't finally mean only Australian country people, but all who have to put up with this world's Pilates and Pharisees.

Australasian Catholic Record, July 1981.

Some Religious Stuff I Know About Australia

Most people would agree, perhaps after some dispute about terminology, that something like a religious dimension exists in every human being. Some might want to call it a dimension of wonder, of quest, of value, of ultimate significance or the like. Some have denied its reality altogether, but I think the weight of human experience and, to beg a few questions perhaps, of perceived human behaviour is against them. Modern students of religion, and modern proponents of what we may call natural religious systems, tend to differ from upholders of at least some traditional religions in suggesting that religious activity arises from a human perception of phenomena, whether in the world at large or within the person. They think of it as a human response to the beauty, horror, mystery or incongruity of the world, or to some emotional need within us. The Christian and also I think the Jew and the Moslem, though their terminologies would be different, would rather assert that it is a response to the activity of God's Spirit working within us at a depth usually too great for direct sensory perception; it impinges on our consciousness most directly, perhaps, at the point we call the conscience, though some modern schools attempt to explain that away as internalised social conditioning and the like, and perhaps what we regard as our conscience may include some of that. The attempt, the wish really, to dispose of the divine element in conscience is interesting in another way, however. Christian theology teaches that the love of God, like the rejection of Him, arises from the will rather than the emotions. It is a decision of acceptance, of Assent, in Cardinal Newman's term. We choose to love God because He has touched us in some way; as Scripture says, "we love Him because He first loved us". And we can only come to an understanding of the real things of religion through our acceptance of the subtle, persistent lifelong offer of Itself which the Spirit makes to every human being.

In the second chapter of his first letter to the infant church in Corinth, St Paul says, in the Jerusalem Bible translation, "an unspiritual person is one who does not accept anything of the Spirit of God: he sees it all as nonsense; it is beyond his understanding because it can only be understood by means of the Spirit. A spiritual man, on the other hand, is able to judge the value of everything, and his own value is not to be judged by other men." This does not signify a haughty refusal to be judged, but merely points out that the person who lacks some share in the mind of God as acquired by accepting His Spirit can't accurately evaluate the insights (or, as an unfriendly critic might say, the claims to insight) of one who has such a share. The Spirit, we say, works upon and awakens to life something in us which is like Itself and may indeed be, or perhaps become, a part of Itself. Christ has told us that no one comes to God except through Him, and in past centuries many Christians have taken this to mean that no one who wasn't a Christian could be "saved", that is, come to an adequate response to the activity of the Spirit working on their inmost life. A more modern understanding, though it isn't wholly modern, of this saying of Christ's would be that Christ is That through which such an adequate response happens whether the person responding knows His name or not. St Paul's statement quoted above doesn't deny the possibility of degrees of acceptance of the Spirit; something that is little more than, or no more than, a vague yearning to "make sense of it all" may be the beginnings of a spirituality we would have to recognise. Such early stages can be perilous, but perhaps not more so than later ones; the religious dimension in man is quite possibly the most dangerous thing on earth. A great deal of history, and perhaps pre-eminently a great deal in the terrible history of this century, supports such a contention. We cannot deny our inmost nature; as Christopher Koch says in his novel *The Year of Living Dangerously*: "The spirit doesn't die, of course; it turns into a monster."

Since the spiritual dimension universally exists in human beings, it has to be dealt with by them in some way or other; a sacramentally minded Christian would say that it has to be fed. It can be wrongly fed, though, with dreadful results for the world. God's Spirit may stir our soul and then not be allowed to enlighten it. In this chapter, I want to talk about some of the ways, "natural" ways if you like, in which Australians attempt to feed it, apart from the means of mediation offered by the churches. Some of the responses I'll be describing are innocent and wholesome ones, others are less so. And some are quite simply frightful, if not usually as spectacularly so here as in some other countries. They may be the more insidious for that, insofar as our fairly orderly social polity protects us from their more obviously horrifying implications. They are thus less commonly recognised for what

Some Religious Stuff I Know About Australia

they are and so allowed to persist. An example of what I mean would be human sacrifice.

Wait on! Human sacrifice? Surely that's an archaic horror that survives only very marginally in a few Third World groups that anthropologists write about? Surely the holocausts of this century in what we call "our" civilisation can only be called human sacrifices in a very metaphoric sort of way? Surely there's a distinction to be made here between the literal and the metaphorical? My answer is, there may be, but I don't know of one watertight enough to prevent the blood from seeping through it. When I hear someone say, as I did yet again the other day, that this country needs a war to restore and cement its sense of community, I recognise that as a call to literal human sacrifice, to be performed for one of the classic archaic reasons. When I am told that thousands of Australian men died in the First World War so as to prove their country's worth to the world and make it "come of age", I don't know whether that was in fact their motive (I strongly doubt it), but I see the assertion as one which makes their death into a post facto human sacrifice, and accepts it as such. And this despite not only the Enlightenment we used to praise as our deliverance from such archaic nonsenses, but also despite the much earlier action of Christ in consciously taking the whole deeply ancient human motif of sacrifice on Himself and as it were completing and sealing it, so that henceforth we might refer the whole complex impulse to His action and never again enact it literally on a living victim. The position of the Catholic and Orthodox sacrament of the Eucharist is interesting here, as lying midway between the literal and the metaphorical, as a sort of middle term which maintains a vital tension between the two; this is an essential feature of the sacramental dimension, I think. A much harder implication of Jesus' action, of course, is that sacrifice, including human sacrifice, is as it were wrong but not erroneous. It suggests that it is an inherent tendency in human behaviour, as universal as we observe, say, ritual to be. It could not be dismissed, as rationalism would later attempt to dismiss it; it had to be *resolved*, and the very act of its resolution then kept alive.

With the decline of traditional Christian observance, things formerly bound have a way of being loosed again on mankind; after the mass suicide of Jim Jones' followers in Guyana a couple of years ago, it is surely much harder than it may have seemed before to say that man evolves beyond highly developed religion. In perhaps a majority of cases, he falls out of it backwards, back down into archaic practices (nonetheless archaic for their modern veneer) and quandaries which had long since been resolved. In a poem I wrote a year or so ago, I put it this way, adding a codicil to something Chesterton once said: *Those who lose belief in God will not only believe in anything; they will bring blood offerings to it.*

Of course, not all quasi-religious practices in Australia or elsewhere are as dire as this. After the above long but necessary preface, let's look at a few, with headings to prevent my trying to say everything at once.

Strine Shinto

In the native religion of Japan, deity (*kami*), sometimes individualised into deities of a polytheistic sort, is held to be present in all sorts of existing objects, in certain mirrors, wells, rocks, swords, mountains, in special shrines and the like. These bearers of immanent divinity are called *shintai* ("god-bodies") or *mitamashiro* ("divine-soul-objects") and can even be living beings, such as the Emperor, and reverence is due to them. It appears to be a formalisation, surviving surprisingly long in a developed form, of a pretty widespread early response of man to intimations of the Spirit's presence. In the West, Wordsworthian romanticism, the "sense of something far more deeply interfused" in things is a modern analogue, and ancient analogues abound in the major and minor observances of the Greeks, Romans and others. Something similar is obviously also at work at times in Catholic and Orthodox veneration of icons, despite repeated warnings by the clergy that the spiritual realities are represented by the devotional object, not immanent in it. We, and God, put the value into the object; it isn't inherently in it.

Speaking metaphorically, but not perhaps entirely so, it is possible to say that every people has its own peculiar form of Shinto, not perhaps as developed as the Japanese form, but consisting in all those intimately familiar, common properties and distinctive features in which what is felt to be the spirit or soul of that people somehow resides. Australia is no exception here; we have our familiar landmarks, such as Ayers Rock, the Murray River, the Barrier Reef, Sydney's Bridge and Opera House, our distinctive animals, among which the kangaroo and the kookaburra carry perhaps the warmest freight of identification, gum trees, sheep stations, even such products of man's genius as pavlova, distinctive idiom and Australian Rules football. Some of our venerated sites and objects have the National Trust as their priesthood, others have conservationists and park wardens to be their guardians and supervise their rites. In many country towns, as well as the war memorial, there will be a special shrine, often tended by old people and open only at erratic times, called the Folk

Museum. This will contain the memorabilia of the community, mingling documents, portraits, and objects of real historical interest with quaint stuff which the museum has had to accept and display on what I call the O'Hennessy Principle: refuse some prized piece of junk offered by one of the O'Hennessys, or any other long-established local family, and the whole clan will become the enemy of your enterprise. A great deal of writing in our magazines and even more notably in the features pages of our newspapers consists of anxious sub-theological debate about the relative fitness of different sites, objects and even products to be counted among the Sacred Treasures of the nation, and this debate has grown ever more vociferous with the passage of the decades. War memorials rise, are devalued by many, are reinstated by some as at least acceptably campy, then genuinely begin to regain prestige; the terrace house is despised as a slum, then it is painted by Sali Herman, discovered as indigenous vernacular architecture and begins its long reign as an icon to be admired and possessed.

As in any late-colonial society, it is possible to be shamefaced or dismissive about any of the enshrined symbols of identity, and to miss the real love which they may half covertly bear. In Australia, though, a couple of further developments occur. First, there is a broad general consensus about which symbols are to be treated seriously at pretty well all times — no one slings off about the Barrier Reef, and only a few subcultures now eschew a fundamental respect for Aboriginal things — and which of them may be more or less affectionately sent up. Second, a class of what we may call clown-icons has arisen whose rites are always and characteristically derisive: tomato sauce, the meat pie (though I've always thought that one something of a journalistic ring-in), blowflies, gladioli, exaggeratedly grim country cafes which close for lunch and regard sauce with the steak and eggs as a Christmas treat or an indulgence of the epicene, suburban respectabilities, early-model Holden cars — with varying degrees of good taste, Barry Humphries has made himself perhaps the high priest of the derision cult. This institution of the clown-icon is comparatively rare in other countries; I have struck analogues of it in the Celtic lands, especially Wales, but it is hard to imagine in, say, France or China. It may be more highly developed in Australia than anywhere else, and has a complexity and restraint often missing from, say, the rather indiscriminate nihilism of Goon Show-Monty Python humour. There is far less fatigue and angry despair at its heart, and less childishness.

The ability to laugh at venerated things, and at awesome and deadly things — remember the Anzac Book, and the infantrymen advancing into battle in North Africa singing "We're off to see the Wizard, the wonderful Wizard of Oz" — may, in time, prove to be

one of Australia's great gifts to mankind. It is, at bottom, a
spiritual laughter, a mirth that puts tragedy, futility and vanity
alike in their place. It was one of the things that led me back to
Christianity, when I heard my Catholic friends making affectionate
fun of sacred matters in their religion, intoning *Dominoes and
biscuits*. It was something I had never encountered in the deeply
puritan Free Kirk Presbyterianism of my childhood, except perhaps
when my father slyly used the word "religious" to mean glum,
long-faced dreariness of demeanour. "Righto, stop grinning now;
look religious!" The rites of derision in our native Shinto only
become ugly when they take on a flavour of class warfare, of
putting the supposedly ignorant and boorish folk back in their
place; this is what mars much of Humphries' work; perhaps he is
not yet, even after many years of developing his art, fully aware of
its priestly nature. I have sometimes been tempted to oversimplify
the matter as follows: if America, then France and the other
countries which followed her example of revolt against feudal
hierarchy, are the bourgeois revolution, Australia is perhaps the
proletarian evolution, and what develops from that fact may be
more productive for mankind than what develops from the effort
to suppress or disguise it. We began as the poor who were sent
away, to England's South Sea Gulag, and our continent was settled
largely by the poor who got away. Our immigration policies since
the Second World War have, if not usually for altruistic reasons,
tended to continue the pattern, importing the broken middle classes
of Communised countries certainly, but importing in even greater
numbers the town and village poor of Europe with a short-term
view to using them as factory fodder. The more important effect of
their coming, however, will probably be to enrich and further
diversify Australia's vernacular culture; this is already happening.
If one of the great marks of our vernacular culture is its wise and
subtly ramified levity — I once wrote that we are most colonial
when serious — that is because it has been fed by underground
traditions of working people's irony and fantastical peasant wit
that existed for centuries under the surface of respectable Upper
culture abroad. Here these things emerge into the daylight and
grow, and the clown-icon is one of their first fruits.

It is probable that many Australians now spend more of their
spiritual energy on the quest for national and communal identity
than on any other theme. This is not surprising, in a country just
far enough in time from its initial settlement for the themes its
people brought from their original homes to have faded and
become unreal in the minds of their descendants. If it looks at times
like the nationalism of older countries, I think that is a superficial
view. A new people's efforts to find itself are, I think, a cleaner

Some Religious Stuff I Know About Australia

thing than aggrandising National Interest, that idol for whom so many millions of human beings have been sacrificed in this century. Of course, any nation is a semicriminal conspiracy — but there is a sense in which finding some new vision, or new style, some new tune for the world to enjoy and maybe whistle, is a necessary work of atonement for stealing a continent and living well from the theft. If we don't make something worthwhile for mankind out of our conquest here, we are little more than thieves living on spoils. If the churches have so far taken no great part in this work of atonement, that is perhaps natural and not wholly to be deplored; they supply the terms in which we can identify our situation, but their ministry is finally not local and particular so much as a corrective to the local and the particular. Christianity was brought into being out of a particular tradition through an act done "for all men, so that sins might be forgiven". It is universal in its intent, and our best, if not always effectual, defence against the idolatries of nationalism; this is perhaps not always remembered by denominations which hang up battle flags in their churches and take sides in wartime.

Christianity can coexist with a good deal of Shinto, particularly perhaps a Shinto tempered by humour, because the two are about different spiritual concerns. The sort of Shinto I am talking about is almost obsessed by style, by manners, but it has nothing to say about Last Things. On the other hand, it does fit in, in a way which ought to interest Christians, with the oldest spiritual traditions existing in Australia in its celebration, now formal, now casually familiar, of special sites and objects and particularised animals held in emblematic, partially mythologised poses of contemplation. The Aborigines accorded this kind of veneration only to natural phenomena — they didn't, for example, venerate their spears or their digging sticks, and their *tjúrunga* were held by them to be not objects at all, but the actual bodies of the great creative ancestors — but Australians of overseas ancestry have added human monuments of all sorts to the list of what a Catholic might call the "sacramentals" of identity, while still reserving their most serious regard for the natural features of "our" fragment of the primordial Gondwanaland continent. This convergence is suggestive, I think, and may be enormously productive. We have come to the sense, which the Aborigines had before us, that after all human frenzies and efforts there remains the great land. As George Johnston wrote, nothing human has yet happened in Australia which stands out above the continent itself. We know in our bones that the land is mightier than we are, and its vast indifference can drive us to frenzies of desecration and revenge. We know, deep down, that the land does not finally permit of imported attitudes that would make it simply a resource, a thing; it has broken too many of us who tried to make such attitudes fit it. Unlike North America, it is not a vaster repeat performance of primeval Europe, a new Northern Hemisphere continent with familiar soils and seasons into which a liberal variation on inherited European consciousness might be transplanted with prospects of vast success. It is something other, with different laws.

Another and perhaps by now related convergence arose initially from fortuity: the continent to which the rejects of Great Britain were sent turned out to be one in which the native people were egalitarian in their way of life to a degree beyond the imagination of privilege and even of earlier liberalism; it must have been of some effect, even if only a barely noticed one, on the colonists that the new land offered no ancient indigenous models of hierarchy at all. The solitary ego could be at once as vast as the horizon and as unimportant as a straw of windblown grass. Fences were a desperate spiritual necessity, and yet kept failing to hold. We still punish the Aborigines for the fear and the temptation this sets up in us. It was an insult to all our notions of productive work and getting ahead, that they could be so seemingly destitute and yet at the same time lords of infinite space: "The Natives are unfitted for anything," cried an exasperated early commentator, "except to be gentlemen." In every generation, men especially have felt this temptation to drift away and camp out along the creeks forever. It was only by hiding from the continent, in homesteads and towns and cities, that the colonists could feel comfortable with their traditional, imported ways of life. God, in Australia, is a vast blue and pale-gold and red-brown landscape, and his votaries wear ragged shorts and share his sense of humour. Space, like peace, is one of the great, poorly explored spiritual resources of Australia. In the huge spaces of the Outback, ordinary souls expand into splendid and often innocent grotesquerie which the cramping of urban surroundings might transmute into ugly, even dangerous forms. And it may be, in the end, that humour is the touchstone for the viability of any import here. I have thought at times that our patron should be St Philip Neri, for Australia really seems to be where God puts a sardonyx to the lips of Western man and teaches him to laugh wisely.

The Rallies

If the sort of vernacular Shinto I have been describing is partly a matter of looking afresh at old importations, as well as finding a sense of shared identification in phenomena we haven't always noticed or valued, most of the other rituals of heightened meaning I want to talk about in this segment are more recent imports. We didn't invent them, and our having them, as it were, second-hand weakens and exacerbates them at once, and may help to give them the sour, angry stridency some of them exhibit at times. They're things we joke about less, and a good deal of group or class identification lies behind whether we get a laugh or not.

There is an interesting, often noted but poorly explained significance in the fact that, while both have earlier antecedents, the two most notable mass ritual forms of recent times arose, or in the one case rearose, in the early sixties, spreading worldwide from a number of centres with extreme rapidity and practically in tandem; I refer of course to the pop or rock concert and the political rally or demonstration. It is also interesting that, with the coming of economic recession in the Western world, the latter form has once again declined and become fairly fitful, while the former continues unabated. Both command an intensity of involvement that is much stronger, or at least closer to the surface and more vehement, than almost any churchgoing. A fair few people who attend such manifestations also go to church, both here and, perhaps more commonly, in some other countries. Their demeanour in the two cases, however, tends to be quite different, because different ends are being served. And of course a good many who go to the modern mass rituals wouldn't be seen dead in a church. There is an evangelical analogue of such mass events in the revival meeting, a reality in some overseas countries, notably the United States, but never really acclimatised here. And there are equally clear analogues in the regimented yet fervent rallies of Hitler's Germany and other modern dictatorships.

If wildly different overt content, ranging from heavily amplified love songs to exhortations to crush Malaysia or slaughter the Jews, can elicit strikingly similar behaviour in crowds that listen and scream their approval, it is clearly not very useful to evaluate and argue about the messages that are being presented. Rallies, mass concerts and demonstrations have had a variety of effects running right across the moral spectrum from genocide to the preservation of irreplaceable buildings and helping to end the war in Vietnam. Their effects therefore aren't the essential point of the transaction either, though they may most certainly be evaluated by the rest of us, and credited where beneficial and resisted where evil. Such evaluation can never be done from within, however. At least not by participants.

The essential elements in what we may call the liturgy of a rally are probably three in number, the *enemy*, the *secret* and the *sharing group*. The enemy is necessary to give participants the delicious sense of being a beleaguered but heroic band; if he did not exist, he would have to be invented. With rock fans, an older person not absolutely in the groove soon realises that he is not going to be allowed to understand and sympathise, and probably won't get any marks for trying, since the point of the thing is partly its psychodrama of rebellion against an outmoded and unjustly dominant adult world. The secret is the exciting new perspective on things which exalts the recipient and makes him or her significant, while still perhaps safely anonymous, and exalts at least the fantasies of the lowly by substituting for their lonely imaginings something far more vivid and imminent, something which they can take with them out into the dull world of bewilderment and dreary work, or dreary unemployment; when it begins to fade, the glorious picture can always be renewed at the next rally — or replaced by another one. Most important of all, though, is probably the sense of belonging to a group, to a "generation", to the Circle, the Chosen Company, the In Crowd, the supportive nexus empowered to judge, to demand compliance and to punish by exclusion. This is very close to the thing which can make soldiers fight on with magnificent courage when their cause is hopelessly lost and all belief in it has left them; loss of belief long before the end is sometimes the dark secret of victorious armies, too.

The dynamics of the group-mind are fraught with all sorts of strange paradoxes, one of which is a profound distortion of the sense of size: a mass movement which has captured a whole nation and converted a majority of its citizens to its world-view may still behave like an embattled band, while a handful of activists with no significant following may believe that they are the determining force in a nation's life and the wave of the future. In the atmosphere of a rally, almost any group of participants will see itself in both of these perspectives at the same time. The group and the mass rally are of course not quite the same thing — except that they are, so convergent are their attitudes and behaviour. We may say that the large rally is the core group writ large and diffuse, while the dedicated core group is the large rally distilled. Within the catchment of the large rally, there will usually be several smaller core groups who enjoy the special exaltation of being Inner, and it is very often these rather than the mass membership who will actually enact the works which the broader rally calls for, and perform, or make, the necessary sacrifices. Not all of those who roared Sieg Heil actually operated the gas chambers. I have heard activists in some of the dedicated core groups of the women's movement say that, to be one of their number rather than merely a supporter, it is indispensable to have had an abortion. To be fair, I have also heard members of the movement say that, while women lack self-determination in most areas of life, they will tend to have abortions to prove their power over at least this one central area, as

Some Religious Stuff I Know About Australia

well as to revenge themselves on a confining mystique.

One advantage which the rally and its core-group analogues have over Christian observances is that they deliver the goods, in a very immediate way. They produce the spiritual and emotional effects which people seek from them, in much the same way that technology delivers the devices and supplies we want from it. If, as some commentators have held, technology is magic which works, the rally and similar practices are magical and effectual in the same way. Occult practices, whose vogue has paralleled that of the rally very precisely, can be seen as retarded forms of engineering. The difficulty with all these things is, they only deliver what we think we want. The Spirit gives us what we need, and doesn't necessarily heed our petitions. God may not even rescue us from cruel death when we implore Him to. Being God, He can see both sides of death, as we cannot. This is hard to bear — but the alternative is to seek your spiritual supplies from sources which provide, in the end, only what cannot satisfy you, since what humans imagine to be their salvation can't logically be anything greater than the human measure. "This world of appearances," writes the Australian poet Robert Gray, "is the Diamond." True, perhaps — as a poet myself, I certainly think it is true — but it is not the Light. There is impressive power in what we can imagine, but no transcendence. There is great depth, sometimes, in our perception — but, again, no transcendence. Political commitment, art, drugs and the like may be effective for quasi-religious (actually magical) purposes such as establishing an identity for oneself, or acquiring protective prestige, and some of them may even mimic transcendence, but it is not the true otherness to which we are, as it were, keyed in the depths of our being. Without that transcendence which is the only coin the soul recognises, you are left restless and unfulfilled, though clinging perhaps so fervently to the substitute you have found that, in order to crush down your unadmitted disappointment, you may be capable of any enormity that serves to exalt the supplier of your substitute and bind you to him. Pooling your strength with that of all those who depend on the same supplier, you may even change the world — but it remains the world. All you have done is to rearrange the pattern of joy and pain, bewilderment, disappointment and dominances. The hunger of the soul remains, even if we feed it on our very heart and mind and on the lives of millions of the innocent. The first of these is the essence of ideology, the second is its ultimate tendency.

Jesus Christ came out of a milieu similar to our own, in that it contained millenarian hopes and a tradition of political-eschatological rallies aimed at throwing off an oppressive foreign-dominated establishment. Superficially, some of the events of His ministry on earth look like rallies, and it is likely that many of those who flocked to Him intended them to be. He differed from modern demagogues, however, in not giving the people what they thought they wanted, even in an impressively "improved" version. Not being the creature of His audience, as every demagogue finally is, He gave them difficult truths, valid for all time and all peoples, when all they wanted was a hero-king who would drive out the Romans, restore the local glories of their small nation — and maybe give them a taste of the joys of empire in their turn. If He had yielded to that demand, He could have been a success in the world's terms, and eventually just another name in the history books. Instead, we all know what happened; David Campbell has a poem in which Christ is crucified because of His failure to be the creature of the crowds: "We played you music and you would not dance." It is a strange, urgent, but queerly equivocal poem, oddly unlike most of David's work, but these days I find myself asking in the case of most poets: Show me his or her Strange poem, the one (or maybe more than one) that is unlike the rest. That's likely to be the genuinely contemplative one as distinct from the competent or professional ones, and so may be the one in which the Spirit peeped forth.

In comparison with the core groups and cells of modern movements, there is no doubt that Christian churches, in the West particularly, often fail to provide that sense of warm mutual support and reinforcement they must once have provided. And there is often a canting, constrained quality about these things when we do provide them, what the Canadian novelist Robertson Davies calls the "unreal, stricken quality of religion". In an age when self-consciousness often sees itself in terms of its problems, we can seem all too ready to leave a lot to the individual dealings of the soul with God. The care of church members for one another, like the priesthood of all Christian believers, tends to be almost entirely delegated away — or, if it isn't, the sort of caring control and surveillance a community provides is often resented. Why did a person come to the city, if not to escape from that cloying hometown stuff and find some excitement in independence?

Elias Canetti remarks, in his book *Crowds and Power*, on the very great distrust of the Catholic Church for crowd phenomena, and its concern to slow such phenomena down into a measured, uneruptive ritual; he calls us a "slow crowd". This is an interesting view, and true as far as it goes. Unlike groups for which excitement and ecstasy are the point, the purpose of Catholic ceremonial is slowly and solemnly to construct a bridge between the ordinary and the spiritual realms, so that life and strength may flow from God to us. It is also meant to bridge over our inner divisions, so that health and power may flow across these too. Unlike art, this ceremonial does not rely on freshness or novelty to attain its effect; the familiar itself becomes the ever-new as we enter more deeply into it. The efficacy of the whole process depends not at all on the passionate noise of our desires and yearnings, but on the receptive quality of our stillness. It has emotional results, and emotive meaning, but at heart it is not a matter of emotion, which would be just another source of "noise" blanking out receptivity. In the Free Church service of my childhood, with its emphasis on the sermon, there wasn't enough receptive silence; there was no sense of ceremony deepened to the point where human activity briefly fell away and God was present. Not the God we theorise and chatter about, but God, the incommensurable, the Strange, speaking health to our soul in rapt silence, as we take Communion with Him.

The Supermarket and the Common Dish

With the decline of the normative position of Christianity in the West, we now live in a sort of spiritual supermarket, full of competing systems and brand names. This is partly the result of higher education, of course, and the technology of the paperback book, but that is not to sneer at it: it is also a visible manifestation of need, and quest, and even of pilgrimage. Christianity in the West may, by now, be almost the religion to which people characteristically *return*, after trying many other options. And we should never forget that the paperback pilgrim, like the follower of the rallies, is very often a person of large spiritual gifts which are in desperate need of expression. The supermarket situation is also in part a result of the twentieth century's anthropological revolution; the cultures of mankind are now on display to the literate and TV-watching Westerner as they never were in any previous age. The rhetoric of decolonisation in the Third World has flowed back to us and quite properly shaken our old superiorities. As the traditional societies enter upon their Industrial Revolutions, the cities and universities of the West are becoming a kind of cultural museum in which the loved monuments of everyone's tribal or agrarian past are stored, handled and misunderstood. It is natural that people bored with their own traditions, or angry with them, should draw upon this museum and take up alien systems which can never threaten them, because they can never really enter them. I have known several Australian and British and American "Buddhists" whose real motivation for being so was patently a fear of commitment, of being hurt again by family or other attachments. It was a way of sanctifying indifference and solipsism, of being religious without belief — and sometimes of being aggressive without being frank about it. We have seen a lot of that sort of thing in Christianity, too, in competitive holiness and pious bullying, so it's not hard to recognise a variant form. But that form issues in numbness and loss of the ability to love. It is a lumpen aristocracy, one which reduces everything to a single snobbish level of indulged illusion. How sad: the peasants believe, in their unenlightenment, that they are hungry.

So far as I can judge, from a lot of experience in the milieu, there's nothing very distinctive about supermarket spirituality in Australia, apart perhaps from a natural interest in Aboriginal tradition and the greater difficulty of fitting cyclic pagan systems to a place where the seasons are both back to front and subtle, and where nature often forgets to be effectively cyclic for years at a time. This is very bad news for the more innocent dabblers in witchcraft, who claim to be interested in reviving an allegedly universal primordial religion of the Stone Age (for which there is no good anthropological or archaeological evidence; ancient religions, so far as we know much about most of them, seem always to have been very varied and by no means always tuned to the cycles of nature). It will probably confine them to the towns and piped water. The main danger they're in is that of being drawn into the flesh markets of that high-society Satanism which seems to pop up in our country from time to time, and which may well be related to the excruciations of a tiny old-money caste driven to Gnosticism and worse by the shameless success here of the Lower Orders. The loathing of "ordinary" Australians and all their works evinced by some of our privileged folk is very striking, and an important theme in our literature. It may, sadly, be a permanent corollary of egalitarian aspirations.

We have said that Australia is perhaps the proletarian evolution. This is more a matter of manners and style than one of politics, and political parties which try to reflect or exploit it often end up baffled. This is the thing which tends to make privilege, "high" culture and some of the groups we have been discussing defensive, self-conscious and, at times, strident. It helps to accentuate in them that modern tendency to constant prickliness and social anger which, perhaps paradoxically, they now share with self-conscious defenders of "traditional" values. Since the early sixties and the rise of the universities, we have seen a process not so much of heavy Americanisation (the Californication of Australia, as someone has called it) in our country as of the ultimate democratisation of formerly aristocratic attitudes. If the people who tend to sympathise with the rallies and the spiritual supermarket, but who also value education and social concern, can be termed an emergent class in our society, different from but ultimately convergent with

Some Religious Stuff I Know About Australia

older colonial privileged groups, it is possible to see the religious preferences of that class as humanist, with some embroidery of occult or Oriental borrowings and a tendency to be anti-Christian. Over against this new class, the religious tendency of what may be called majority Australia may best be described as Residual Christian, with side servings of such themes as stoicism, luck, heroism in the strict sense of survival through the memory of one's supreme achievements in approved fields, plus pieties of various kinds, for example towards the extended family, among country people especially, or towards dead comrades, among ex-servicemen. In majority Australia, chivalry, in the sense not of equivocal gestures towards women, but in the more central sense of the thousand-year effort to Christianise and civilise raw pride and Lawrentian swagger, still carries force. So, lamentably, does a measure of racism, and the sad shamanism of alcohol, as beautifully and sympathetically described in David Ireland's novel *The Glass Canoe*. On the other hand, majority Australia has produced, along with most other things we think of as distinctively Australian, the two human figures which we tend to recognise as peculiarly our own, the Battler, who may be man or woman, and the Larrikin, who has tended to be male. Because of denominational strife in the past, there are sanctions in majority Australia against too-visible display of religious differences. Piety is very often suspected of hypocrisy, and it is usually bad form to "talk religion", unless one is a cleric and doing so, as it were, professionally. But if Australians are reluctant to talk religion, they are often eager to talk spirituality for hours on end, so long as sect is kept out of it and no attempts at recruiting are made. Some folk in remoter parts of the continent rarely talk about anything but spiritual concerns, in cloudy, sometimes confused, sometimes penetrating terms of their own.

Many people in majority Australia are of course practising Christians, but even among these, perhaps as a result of the centuries of Puritanism, there is a tendency to confuse morality with standards of behaviour, and to run a shame culture rather than a moral one. The downgrading of guilt and the coercive use of shame, of course, are also features of the new class; there is some intersection between the two groups here. If both classes are capable, at times, of a peculiarly cold-eyed, contemptuous authoritarianism, it is perhaps instructive to remember that the first white Australians weren't all convicts; some were warders and guards, and quite a few played both roles at different times. Common to both classes, too, is a great deal of Cargo Cult acquisitiveness and something of a consumer attitude to life and values, though the objects sought are different and class-determined. The important new class newspaper the *National Times* is practically a consumer guide, to approved attitudes, books, wines, indignations, causes and even eccentricities, and the earlier *Nation Review* performed the same service in its time, though arguably with more tolerance of variety, and perhaps more innocence, being less tightly market-researched.

Although we may regret — and I suggest that Christians should logically also oppose — the divisiveness of class, it is futile to pretend it isn't there. Just compare the attention and respect given to people in, say, a public hospital when they speak Broad, without educated vocabulary to alleviate the impression, and that which they obtain by speaking Flash convincingly. The much-decried apathy of Australians is often a misnomer for sensible imperturbability. If we were to seek a common denominator for majority Australia, it would not lie so much, I think, in her widespread and almost instinctive rejection of the rallies (I well remember the man who described Woodstock to me as "the Nuremberg of Peace and Love"), nor in its disdain for spiritual chatter, pretensions to being free from guilt and evil by one's own mere say-so and the like (the brutal term used here is *bullshit*), so much as in her harsh rejection of those somehow privileged to escape the common lot. This is a very negative way of putting what is a deeply proletarian feature, one encountered in the older societies as well but perhaps more powerful and noticeable here. Seeing it in a more positive light, I would be inclined to use a term I invented in a verse novel I wrote a few years back, and call it the ritual of the Common Dish, that vessel of common human sufferings, joys, disappointments, tragedies and bare sufficiencies from which most people have to eat in this world, and from which some choose to eat in order to keep faith with them. This dish is the opposite of the medieval Grail, which was a vessel attained only by a spiritual elite. To refuse the common ration, or to fail at least to recognise and respect it, earns one the contempt and rejection of battlers and all who live under the laws of necessity. It is a harsher vessel than the Christian chalice, and not identical with it, except perhaps for the saints, but I believe it lies close to the heart of Australian consciousness, and can never be safely ignored. It is the fountainhead of much of the conformity so often deplored in our society, and much of the art of living in Australia consists in judging, continually and if possible gracefully, just what distance we may wander from the common table and how often to come back.

A Note to Coreligionists

For many historical and other reasons, some of them Australian and our own fault, Christianity is no longer On Top in Australia, though the great majority of Australians continue to believe in God. Others writing in this book (*The Shape of Belief*) will have gone into the modalities of this more effectively than I could do. All I have to add are some personal impressions. The first of these is that the experience is probably a salutary one for us. The time for ecclesiolatry, the worship of the visible church instead of God, is past. We're no longer free to indulge our bad habits of boring people, bullying them and backing up respectability; we're no longer in a position to call on the law to do for us what we should be doing by inspiration and example; we're no longer in a position to push second-rate thinking and an outworn picture of the cosmos, where God is Up, we are in the middle and Hell is Down; we're no longer free to indulge the internecine warfare of denominations that has so harmed God's cause on earth for the past four centuries; finally, we're not going to be universally accepted as a spiritual elite, so we'd better get on with being what our Founder told us to be, which is the salt of the earth, the baking soda in the loaf of mankind. Salt and baking soda aren't privileged substances, but they're pretty essential ones.

The second of my impressions is that, while our vision is no longer the dominant one, and may never have been, neither is any other at the moment. There is as yet no other vision abroad in our society which commands the same authority as ours does, the same sense of being the bottom line, the great reserve to be called on in times of real need. Many of the themes of the rallies are necessary problem-solving and little more, and much in the spiritual supermarket is fair-weather stuff, adjuncts to a prosperity which may now be vanishing. Unbelief, once a daring and rather aristocratic gesture, must by now have exhausted most of its glamour; it is certainly no longer exclusive, or particularly rebellious. Much the same could be said of sexual indulgence, pornography and the like. Having by now surely lost most of its flavour of forbidden fruit, sexual licence has to justify itself in terms of whatever real satisfaction it can give; its utility as a bait to draw people out of traditional ways and beliefs, and if possible into new allegiances, must by now also be wearing thin. The reaction against Victorian values has now lasted longer than Queen Victoria's reign. And it will be difficult, at the very least, for the cult of unremitting youthfulness and physical beauty to survive in the era of ageing populations which it has helped to produce. By now, liberal humanism is as badly fragmented by dissension as our witness ever was, and its fiercest adherents are often covertly uneasy at its lack of gentleness, its readiness to force the facts and its desolate this-worldliness. What misery, to be forced to be Interesting all the time or face cold relegation. What horror, to know one will be obsolete and Irrelevant sooner or later, before the arrival of unending death. The style of unrelenting adulthood forces people on to the thorns of tragic complexity, to face the strange intractability of the world, the mobile but irremovable Shadow on all things, and often when people who subscribe to it relax for a moment, their eyes are seen to contain an almost desperate appeal: please prove us wrong, make us believe there is more to it than this, show us your God and that Grace you talk about. We are more widely judged on our own best terms than we think, and more insistently expected to be the keepers of the dimension of depth than we find comfortable. We will be punished if we do try to live up to what we profess, but we will be punished much worse if we don't, because so many of our enemies are relying on us. If we say God and Christ and stand by what we've said, we don't stand alone, but we do have to expect some splinters in our shoulders. We should not, I suggest, be tempted to see ourselves as a team that has to win for God; He is not helpless — and anyway His idea of a win is the Cross, which may be the place where the truly irresoluble contradictions, by which our life in this world is torn but also perhaps powered, meet and get the only resolution they *can* obtain, that is, a living continuous one, which we've agreed to take part in after all.

It is possible, if we must think in terms of doing rather than being, of *actio* rather than the equally potent *passio*, the Passion of the heart of our tradition, that the most urgent tasks facing our faith at this juncture have not got to do so much with the reconversion of the disaffected (Christ said that He came to minister to the sick, not the healthy, and most of the disaffected would probably consider themselves healthy), as with the reconciliation of Black and White Australia and improving the contents of the Common Dish from which Third World people, including our own few such, have to eat. That, and some positive fostering of the contemplative life in a country which has not widely valued it hitherto, except in the figure of the bush hermit, who has tended not to be a specifically Christian type here. We need to strengthen our intellectual presence in this society, while always remembering that a modicum of true vision, or a truly holy life, is more to the point and more effectual as witness than any amount of combative argument. It might not be amiss to point out though, that a good deal of talk about religious decline is in fact incantatory, an interested prophecy constantly reiterated by those who *want* religion to decline. Disentangling the facts from the ill-will is an unstated purpose of this essay. Sentencing by assumption is a familiar tactic of some secularist groups. There are other practical tasks, of course, which concern some of us, if not all. If, for

Some Religious Stuff I Know About Australia

example, we are concerned about abortion, as some of us are, perhaps it is time not merely to combat it, but to offer, without being at all superior about it, to take the threatened babies into our own families and care for them for as long as their parents don't want them or can't look after them. For this and a hundred other purposes, it is most important for us simply to *be* here, to serve and receive the desperate if they come to us, and pray for them whether they come or not. Or simply to be here keeping faith, which is given to us to keep.

Movements which Christ initiated are still dominant forces in the life of the world. To cite just one instance, I think that the Kingdom of God, which is not solely of this world, *is* slowly coming closer to being more clearly figured in this world, in part through the steady push towards human equality in many countries, and I say that in the teeth of all the great crimes which have been committed in the name of that evolution. God works through His enemies as well as His friends — because in the security of His Godhead he possesses the unutterable nobility of full freedom and can choose not to have any enemies. He offers to share that freedom with us, since without Him we could neither attain it nor dream it. Those who can handle something like that degree of freedom we sometimes call saints, when we recognise them in our midst, but God doesn't intend that they should remain forever alone in their sainthood; they are meant to be models and forerunners for us all. And it is probable that there are a great many whom only He knows to be saints, hiding their status from most eyes, including perhaps especially their own. We who are not saints are caught up, not by God but by the logic of our choosing to delay sainthood, in a combat we keep thinking is new (or even Modern) because of the novel shapes and pressures it keeps presenting, a physiognomic struggle between those who somehow accept grace and those who bear the distorting strain of trying to block it off, to act without it or against it. This, I think, rather than the usual superficial divisions between Right and Left, Black and White, religious and irreligious etc., is where the real lines are drawn. By that very grace, though, no one is irremovably fixed in his position. And we should remember that it is often hard to know which side of the line we, let alone others, are standing on at a given moment. Religious practice does, or should, develop the ability in us to discern our own position, at the same time as it makes us wary of judging the positions of others. But when I come to meditate on topics such as grace, I don't finally trust myself to talk about them in prose. For the important stuff, I need the help of my own medium of poetry, which can say more things. Here is how I talked

about grace in a poem called *Equanimity*, which opens in the world
of Sydney suburbia and goes on:

Fire-prone place-names apart
there is only love; there are no Arcadias.
Whatever its variants of meat-cuisine, worship, divorce,
human order has at heart
an equanimity. Quite different from inertia, it's a place
where the churchman's not defensive, the indignant aren't on the
                                                         qui vive,
the loser has lost interest, the accountant is truant to remorse,
where the farmer has done enough struggling-to-survive
for one day, and the artist rests from theory —
where all are, in short, off the high comparative horse
of their identity.
Almost beneath notice, as attainable as gravity, it is
a continuous recovering moment. Pity the high madness
that misses it continually, ranging without rest between
assertion and unconsciousness,
the sort that makes hell seem a height of evolution.
Through the peace beneath effort
(even within effort: quiet air between the bars of our attention)
comes unpurchased lifelong plenishment;
Christ spoke to people most often on this level
especially when they chattered about kingship and the Romans;
all holiness speaks from it.

From the otherworld of action and media, this
interleaved continuing plane is hard to focus:
we are looking into the light —
it makes some smile, some grimace.
More natural to look at the birds about the street, their life
that is greedy, pinched, courageous and prudential
as any on these bricked tree-mingled miles of settlement,
to watch the unceasing on-off
grace that attends their nearly every movement,
the crimson parrot has it, alighting, tips, and recovers it,
the same grace moveless in the shapes of trees
and complex in our selves and fellow walkers; we see it's
                                                         indivisible
and scarcely willed. That it lights us from the incommensurable
we sometimes glimpse, from being trapped in the point
(bird minds and ours are so pointedly visual):
a field all foreground, and equally all background,
like a painting of equality. Of infinite detailed extent

Some Religious Stuff I Know About Australia

like God's attention. Where nothing is diminished by perspective.

Written as a chapter for *The Shape of Belief*,
edited by Dorothy Harris, Doug Hynd and
David Millikan (Lancer Books, 1982). First
published by permission in *The Review*,
Melbourne, 1982

Locum at Lyons Road — My Years at Poetry Australia

The antecedents of *Poetry Australia* magazine stretch back through the years of its forerunner *Poetry* magazine to the Barjai group in Brisbane in the forties. The young Grace Perry was conscious of that development, and it was in those days, around 1944, that she first thought of a literary magazine that would concentrate on poetry and have the dual aim of encouraging beginners to develop their gifts and publishing the best work available from Australia and abroad. The conception was international from the start, and opposed to the ghetto tradition of Australian writing still understandably prevalent at that time. No such magazine had ever existed in Australia, and there was no way a young medical student could fund one on her own, so the future Dr Perry joined the Poetry Society in Sydney and shaped their magazine towards her vision. A woman of immense energy and cheerfully overwhelming presence, she worked unremittingly to build up the magazine's subscription list and secure the best writers for its pages, and her decisive editorial judgment may have been as threatening to the genteel weekend versifiers and romantic solipsists of the Poetry Society as her thrustful enthusiasm. In the end, the editorship of *Poetry* magazine was wrested from her in one of the palace coups to which such societies are prone. Furious at this, she instantly set up her own magazine in the image and format of the one she had been developing, and prudently forestalled any future usurpations by putting the new journal, called *Poetry Australia*, under the imprint of her own specially created South Head Press. *Poetry Australia* would generate a circle of its own, and indeed already had one before the rupture, but never again would its editor be at the fickle mercy of a literary society. It is interesting to relate that those who took over *Poetry* magazine were quite soon thrust aside in their turn, and the magazine was reborn as *New Poetry*. And with that, I suppose, the respective rallying banners of the famous Seventies Battle of the Books were raised.

From the first, the newly hived-off journal had the format and style it still bears today. The ultimate model was *Poetry Chicago*, but the eschewing of editorial statements or biographical notes, the

Locum at Lyons Road — My Years at *Poetry Australia*

insistence on using the best printers and the best paper available and securing the best possible standards of production and binding, even details such as running the names of contributors in "coat-hangers" above their work, these things were all carefully designed by Dr Perry and have worn well through twenty years. In a period in which most major literary magazines have been the property of universities and open to grey wads of publish-or-perish academic prose and its verse equivalents, *Poetry Australia* has resisted, even in dire moments of poverty, the siren offers of universities to acquire it and give it a subsidised home. Many university scholars have been its friends, but none has been allowed to become its keeper. In its independence, it has preserved a definite if hard-to-define personality of its own, marked by an openness and a hospitality to poetic variety greater than any other Australian magazine can boast and a refusal to be totally solemn. It has been something of a redoubt for poetry as a profession rather than an adjunct of academic study. By refusing ever to state any editorial principles beyond the original dual aim I mentioned above, it has never found itself in the position of having to repudiate, or live down, any fixed poetic theory. Nor has it ever bothered to refute any who accused it of having a covert "line" or being in the grip of any particular literary cabal. Instead, it has often published its accusers, if their work was good enough, and some of them even got their start in its pages. Australian poets, and many from elsewhere in the English-speaking world, owe *Poetry Australia* and its founder a tremendous debt, one which to this day is not always repaid with the generosity it merits.

I had known Dr Perry and her magazine almost from the time of the great hiving off, and indeed the rumble of that event had caused the odd pane to quiver even in my remote quarters. I'm pretty sure I first met Dr Perry in the course of some readings given by Geoffrey Lehmann, Keith Smith (now of *Earth Garden* magazine) and myself at the Ensemble Theatre in North Sydney in 1963. I occasionally published poems in the magazine in the years which followed, and regarded it as a good venue for the long poem especially. *Poetry Australia* had always been hospitable to the long poem or sequence, and many notable Australian biggies have first seen the light of publication there. Vincent Buckley's "Golden Builders" sequence shared an issue with my "Walking to the Cattle Place", and other first airings would include Mark O'Connor's "I-land", Hal Colebatch's "Crowhurst" and "Coastal Knot" sequences, Chris Wallace-Crabbe's "Shapes of Gallipoli", Geoff Page's sequence "Buried and Unburied Voices", my own "Buladelah-Taree Holiday Song Cycle", Alan Gould's "Songs of Ymir" and "Marine Photographs", and a fuller version of Allen

Persistence in Folly

Afterman's searing "Truganini and the Old Lady of Cracow" than he later chose to print in his Angus & Robertson collection *Purple Adam*. The list is not exhaustive and apologies are proffered etc. The above list doesn't even include sequences published, as it were, serially in the journal, such as Bruce Beaver's "Odes" or Geoffrey Lehmann's "Ross' Poems" and "Nero" poems, nor have I mentioned sequences from overseas such as one of Pound's late Cantos.

I had occasional contact with the *Poetry Australia* circle, and was sometimes amused by its medical atmosphere. There was an important outpatients side to South Head Press, and several crumbling storm-racked heads were valued and cared for by its founder. This is a side of the enterprise which need not be dwelt on, and indeed to dwell on it would violate some privacies, but it can be said that a good deal of help and rehabilitation came of it for a number of poets. If Grace Perry was one of Australia's great innovative editors, she was also a born physician generous with help for anybody around the literary world who needed it.

In mid-1973, Grace Perry asked me to become, in effect, acting editor of *Poetry Australia*. A number of things lay behind this request. Continuing ill health had reduced Dr Perry's once boundless energy, and she had begun living more and more in semi-retirement in Berrima, conserving her strength and concentration for her own writing. Berrima, of course, is two hours' drive from the house in Lyons Road, Five Dock, which had long been the journal's headquarters. The same address contained Dr Perry's medical practice, in which she had installed a locum, and secretarial work for both the practice and the journal was done by the cheerfully indefatigable Mrs Carmel McEnally, *Poetry Australia's* only paid helper. Mrs Mac has never previously been given any public tribute for her unending labour on the magazine's behalf, and since I loaded a lot of that labour on to her over the years, I think she deserves a place in literary history, and I am happy to give her one herewith. In an administrative sense, and as the person who fielded innumerable phone calls and visits to the Five Dock office, she was the real linchpin of the whole South Head enterprise for many years.

A good deal of voluntary labour on the part of members of the *Poetry Australia* circle had always been a vital part of the enterprise too, and much of this had been forthcoming during the difficult time when Grace Perry's energies began to flag. But volunteer work ultimately has its price, and among the unspoken parts of my agreement with Dr Perry when I became acting editor was an understanding that volunteer work by some people shouldn't continue to be the cause of any fuzzing of editorial standards, or

Locum at Lyons Road — My Years at *Poetry Australia*

any indulgences for deserving friends. This did not need to be spelt out, nor did valuable goodwill need to be lost by spelling it out. The moment had also arrived for the magazine to regain the goodwill of various poets alienated from it in the great hiving off, and they could more easily be reached by someone from outside the *Poetry Australia* circle who had not had any part in the historic Poetry Society split. I use the word "historic" quite advisedly here, as much subsequent divisiveness in Australian poetry really dates from that quarrel. Politics only came into it later on, commonly as a stalking horse or the camouflage of ambition. At the beginning of my term as acting editor, as at the end of it, Grace Perry obviously felt that the magazine needed to widen its reach and draw contributions from as broad a pool of Australian and overseas poets as possible; the common perception of a tight *Poetry Australia* circle was restricting this necessary expansion.

Hearsay tells me that when I joined *Poetry Australia* there was some resentment on the part of the old circle, but that is only hearsay and deserves no great credit. I did attempt, not always successfully, to cut back on very indulgent reviews of the Old Guard's books, but I probably compromised that by one or two indulgences of my own. Commissioned material, such as reviews, is always more difficult for an editor to reject or modify than unsolicited contributions are. Dr Perry knew of my slight experience as an editor a good few years before, when Geoff Lehmann and I jointly edited the Sydney University magazines *Hermes* and *Arna*; she may even have known about my apprenticeship on the right end of the blue pencil at *Honi Soit* in the very early sixties, when the university was highly literary and didn't yet call it politics. In the mid-sixties, she had got me to collect and edit a special Canberra-Capital Territory issue of *Poetry Australia*, one of the special regional issues which the journal published at that time and which, as an idea, it has now revived: late in 1982 I guest-edited a combined ACT and West Australian issue, the linkage between them being that both are regions remote from the main metropolitan redoubts of cultural power.

My early ACT issue came much too soon to catch the quite remarkable efflorescence of poetry in the national capital which happened in the mid-seventies, and indeed I had to scratch to fill even the slim format *Poetry Australia* had in those days; I padded the thing out with a portentous introduction and a couple of long poems of my own — I was eligible to include these because I lived in Canberra at that time. We only moved out in 1971, just before the efflorescence, and the great good fellowship among Canberra's poets which marked it, had become visible. My ACT issue, though, must have suggested to Dr Perry that I had something of an editorial "eye", a thing she herself was extremely well qualified to judge.

An eye for poetic quality, even nascent quality in beginners' contributions, is the one absolutely essential requirement in an editor, and belongs to the craft side of our profession, the side which is hardest to defend to prosaic and analytic minds. Especially hostile ones. It stands to quantifiable criteria and operations as, say, decency stands to abstract justice, less easy to characterise because more complex, more subtle and for these reasons ultimately a higher value. Because the editorial eye, through practice, usually does its work with what a lay observer might consider appalling swiftness, some have been tempted to see it as mere personal taste or prejudice. This mistake is perhaps more common among the rejected, but it can be an honest view. It ignores, though, the way in which all editors find themselves accepting material whose sentiments they may loathe, simply because they know the material is good as art. Because they are scanning for just one very specific essence, namely, the poetic experience; if there is no trace of that still, breath-altering resonance in the text, that's the end of it. If there is, consideration then begins. Is there *enough* of that essence present, could it be brought out more clearly by paring away surplus wordage, modifying the presentation etc? And the sour view of editing ignores the real joy which lies in discovering good work, especially by new names, and the participatory delight of helping authors polish their work to its best potential. Also, all poetry editors, I'm sure, would testify to the difficulty of finding *enough* material to fill their pages without betrayal of a certain standard. Restrictive prejudice would make this task all the harder, if not impossible. It is no easy matter, even with the whole English-speaking world to draw from, to amass sixty or seventy pages' worth of useable verse every three months. Not against the competition of dozens of journals at home and abroad, and particularly the hard competition of high-paying prestige journals in London, New York and such places. All of which, if no one has guessed, was one reason for *Poetry Australia's* doing the odd special issue, just to let stocks of contributions build up for a bit longer.

The arrangement was that, as acting editor — or poetry locum, as I called it — I would take responsibility for editing, design and production, while Grace Perry would retain overall direction of the journal and deal with its financial and administrative side. I would, by choice, keep out of the book publishing area of South Head Press, and I was never particularly effective in the continuing work of getting subscriptions. Indeed, I never took more than a cursory

Locum at Lyons Road — My Years at *Poetry Australia*

look into the packed file drawers of the mailing list, the one which agents of a rival magazine once tried to burgle, and I confess I often failed to be around to put the two thousand copies of our peak circulation into their preaddressed envelopes for posting. I did desultorily visit bookshops with requests that they stock the journal, but other members of the old *Poetry Australia* circle were more efficient than I was at this, until their enthusiasm waned. Beyond judging the last Farmers Poetry Prize in 1975, I took only a limited part in the biennial *Poetry Australia* Write-Ins at Macquarie University.

Professor Ron Dunlop traditionally did the painstaking work of preparing the magazine's annual index, and his willingness never waned. Nor did that of Dr Perry's lawyer John Millett, the Managing Editor of the magazine. His freely given help was sometimes crucial, notably in the complex negotiations which made the special Francis Webb memorial issue possible — the talks on that went on for many months, between Webb's sisters who had inherited his literary remains but lacked experience of the publishing world, their advisors and various publishing interests having claims on Webb's work. The difficulty of the negotiations can be glimpsed behind the very carefully drafted statement we printed on the inside cover of *Poetry Australia* (number 56, 1975). A magazine needs a good lawyer, and *Poetry Australia* was fortunate in having John Millett. If I seem to be paying tributes right and left to people whose work on and around the magazine made my job easier, I can only say that I was grateful to them, and hope that deserving figures not mentioned here will accept that I have singled out only those whose work I actually saw being done.

It was my main and continuous task, especially after the first few issues of my acting editorship, to go over to Five Dock every few weeks and "read the drawer". This meant sifting through the one or two deep filing cabinet drawers which filled up with contributions seemingly within hours. Business letters were sorted out by Mrs Mac and sent to Dr Perry if she was in Berrima, or dealt with by her if she was staying at Five Dock. Within a few hours, I would reduce a pile of work eighteen inches or two feet thick to a loosely stacked half-inch or so of work good enough to publish unaltered, plus perhaps a like amount of work showing enough gleams of quality to warrant my scribbling editorial suggestions all over the manuscripts and entering into negotiations with the authors. And then there would be all the verse submitted by people wanting evaluations, advice and the like. This was a firm part of the magazine's effort, and all seekers of evaluation and advice got it, often at length. A very few resented the hard things I sometimes

Persistence in Folly

had to tell them, and even without that the strain of bringing the bad news to people about the worth of their cherished effusions never grew less.

It was particularly hard to tell doting mothers that their children's treasured poems were of no real worth beyond the family circle, or to inform lonely souls that the sub-Tennysonian keepsake verses they had been writing in their exercise book for decades contained no freshness or promise. It wasn't easy to reply to prisoners and their wives with the sad truth about semiliterate versifying done in gaol, or to write sympathetically to the obviously insane about their Mauds and Aeneids of confusion and inner violence. It wasn't even an unmixed delight to write time and again to determined contributors whom one longed to publish if only they would consent to grow and develop. One persistent contributor frustrated me endlessly by refusing to slow down her writing rate and work over just a few of her poems till they reached the necessary standard, a standard she kept falling below only by a small margin. She was quite capable of falling below it twenty or thirty times a month. I think I grieved for every single case of just too little talent, every case where the number of silk hairs on the sow's ear just could not be made to increase despite all rubbing with editorial unction.

If I had ever doubted the truth of *Time* magazine's old crack about more people writing poetry than reading it, I would have lost it in those sessions of reading the Drawer. Over and over I had to write the same messages: cultivate concision, try to be more vivid, learn about imagery, remember poetry is an art not a confessional, cultivate precision, avoid waffle, don't rely on vague generalisations, let us see and feel with you, avoid ancient poeticisms, and, most commonly of all, please *read* some poetry and try to get an idea what it actually is. Read good poets, read some modern poetry, read the following authors whom you can easily find in your local library or bookshop, read literary journals, even ours. Research your market, as an elementary step (I rarely put it quite that bluntly), but first find yourself some published models to guide your beginnings and give you some standards to aim at. In private conversation, editors of all sorts of stated aesthetic and political loyalties agree that these are the things you have to tell contributors endlessly. And it's fresh news to every one. They seem never to respond to published statements outlining these things: each one seems to need telling personally, and editors quickly realise that they cannot assume that contributors have ever read any examples of the art they're trying to practise, let alone anything about it.

Locum at Lyons Road — My Years at *Poetry Australia*

I was always more prissily reluctant than Dr Perry to push *Poetry Australia* at contributors, especially hopeless ones, as their model and guide, and was initially even uncomfortable about the subscription form which went out as part of our standard rejection slip. I now realise I was being overscrupulous, and that this was perfectly justifiable and realistic. Only a very privileged level of subsidy would support such a pretentiously high-minded refusal to take anything from people who had shown their interest by contributing to the journal. Magazine subscriptions, in the field of poetry anyway, are surely built to a large degree on the rejected who hope not to stay rejected.

As my years as locum editor went on, the Drawer never grew less copious, but the amount of material coming directly to my home address steadily increased, till towards the end I was receiving and sending out dozens of letters a week on my own account. A few times, in an effort to keep up the turnover of the tiny bush post office in my home district and so forestall its closure, I posted a month or so of such correspondence from there. Rationalisation, so called, still managed to have its determined way with Bunyah Post Office. In line with the nursery function of the magazine, I often published work which really had only a fingernail over the rim of acceptability, in order to encourage authors and help them to grow. And sometimes the method worked and they did grow. In many other cases, inevitably, they didn't, and eventually had to be turned away, a sad process requiring much tact.

What I used to dread were importunate phone calls and dreadful uninvited visits. One man whose best work I liked and whom I published extensively over the years used to turn up on his large motorbike with a bulk supply of beer which he would then mournfully share with me for hours while negotiating the acceptance of more poems. If you think that sort of pressure works on poetry editors foolish enough to let out their private address, you are right. If ever I get a chance, and the necessary backing, I dream of running a journal of imperiously high standard — I even know the name of it: *The Cream* — with no nursery function at all, or anyway only a very high-level one. For that, I will need a silent phone, a secret address and not only the hide but also the nose of a rhinoceros, which is both sensitive and fearsomely armed.

Although I was surprised and delighted by the very real editorial independence which Dr Perry gave me in the running of her magazine, I did not institute any very important changes of policy or design. I did abolish the old practice of paying a slightly higher fee for a poet's first appearance in print, as being hard to administer and fairly irrelevant, and I did manage after a long time to get our fee raised from eight to ten dollars per page of verse. I shifted our jacket designs decisively away from the vague coloured squiggles and Rorschach blots of the past. During my time, we had some very handsome covers, the Dürer *Concatenation* on number 50, for example, or the Vesalius anatomical drawing, illustrative of the then state of our finances, on the combined issue number 60–61. Another one I was proud of was the photograph of Grinling Gibbons' *Lace Cravat* which appeared, as a wordless exhortation to craftsmanship, on the cover of number 64. Towards the end of my acting editorship, I was beginning to use graphics by Australian artists prepared to give us the use of their work for the twenty dollars a time we could afford to pay. Number 67 carried a monotype by Peter Laverty, and number 70 an engraving by Salvatore Zofrea. I did not move to institute the biographical notes on contributors which most magazines carry, since I thought that the policy of omitting these and leaving readers to face the poems without external pressure of any sort was a good one.

What I have called our nursery function had to be done invisibly and confidentially, and I agreed with the notion that it might be good for beginners and unknowns to see their work alongside that of the most accomplished, free for once of the profession's obsessive pecking order. Quite often I found that the poem or poems in a particular issue which pleased me most and stayed in my memory were by people with no particular fame, some of whom published in the journal only once or twice and then vanished from my ken. Number 67 (1977), for instance, contained perhaps the best poem written by the late Jennifer Rankin, who died tragically young; this is "The Sea and Other Stories", the fruit, in part, of her apprenticeship to Ted Hughes; it also contained Geoff Page's "Buried and Unburied Voices" and Mark O'Connor's brilliantly successful experimental sequence "I-land"; it contained Alan Gould's powerful "Sea Eagles — North West Island", and good things by Gwen Harwood, Andrew Taylor and Martin Johnston. And I am still haunted by the ending of Hal Colebatch's "One Tourist's Cologne": "Our van can barely crawl through/the quaint medieval streets, where every house is new." Altogether a good issue, including the prose at the end. Yet without prejudice to those the poem which I still remember and treasure from number 67 is Joan Aronsten's "Ad Infinitum":

> A trickle of sand on the grave's edge
> moves with limitless momentum.
> The mass follows and hurries downhill into the pit
> as time, with its last thrust
> has rushed through the body

ravaging all but the spirit.

• • •

The flowers lie in hopeful profusion
but there is no end to the sand
that is moving towards them.
Already it is creeping towards the shadows
of those who turn away.
They turn to tread the impetus
that moves about their feet.

We never heard from Joan Aronsten again, though I certainly asked for more of her work, and I have not seen her name in other magazines.

Lately there has been something of a campaign by a few critics who claim that I created a cabal in the magazine (something they would understand from their own practice) and that certain poets are "acolytes" of mine. This is quite false and would not be worth combating were it not for the insult it offers to a number of good younger poets and the way the story has apparently resulted in their being denied critical notice and even funding. Those who deal in "generations" and other quasi-journalistic groupings of poets have tended to see me as the creator of a "generation" over against their own, a younger generation subsequent to their own which threatened to relegate them to obsolescence. It is a tormented if dramatic way of looking at the phenomena, and my own view is merely that I had the good luck to discover a number of younger poets well worth publishing and encouraging. Perhaps I didn't so much create a generation as discern one — but really the whole concept is too coarse to describe literary realities accurately. Any journal which has been going for some years tends to gather a pool (I don't like the term "stable") of regular contributors, and it was my task and intent at *Poetry Australia* constantly to widen that pool by attracting and encouraging new poets. Among those now vilified, in fact, are some poets I inherited on joining the magazine, as well as some who began to publish there during my time as acting editor. Poets already contributing when I joined include Geoff Page, Laurence Spingarn, Bruce Beaver, Peter Kocan, Craig Powell, Hal Colebatch, Tom Shapcott, Norman Talbot, Mark O'Connor, Chris Wallace-Crabbe, Roger McDonald, Allen Afterman, Judith Rodriguez, Eric Beach, Rhyll McMaster, David Campbell, Bill Beard, Jennifer Maiden, David Malouf — the list is by no means exhaustive — and among those who began publishing in the journal during my tenure were Robert Gray, who made his debut with us in number 50 (1974) (I remember my chagrin at misspelling his surname in the issue!), Peter Goldsworthy, Andrew Lansdown, Jennifer Rankin, Geoff Lehmann, Peter Porter, Kevin Hart, Peter Redgrove, Alan Gould, Gary Frances, Jennifer Compton, Gary Catalano, Philip Mead, Andrew Sant, Susan Hampton, William Burns, Paul Lake, Herbert Kuhner, John Foulcher, Jamie Grant and Dennis O'Driscoll.

Some not named in these lists whom I also encouraged failed to develop, some peaked and faded away, some who had started out with us moved to other magazines and regarded it as a matter of allegiance, in the manner of that time. Some of those who set great store by allegiances elsewhere would make occasional guest appearances in our pages, sometimes after writing me tentatively snotty letters asking "whether they would be considered" etc. I was amused at the self-protective tactics of this, and always wrote back telling them not to be mad, that they'd be welcome to submit their material, but making no false promises as to its acceptance. Usually it was perfectly acceptable, but no one ever had automatic entree to our pages, a thing which even a few very dignified senior poets had to learn the hard way. Not all rejectees, however, allowed their rancour to persist and become enmity. Only a few did that, just as only a very few resented the impartiality of my black Pentel suggestions scribbled down the margins of their manuscripts or conveyed in the postcards which became my preferred form of letter-writing when the press of correspondence grew too hectic for formal letters.

Perhaps the people who accuse me of having acolytes, though, have merely picked the wrong names. I do have some, or so I am told by friends who have read the verse and even the prose of all sorts of unexpected people closely, but I find that touching rather than offensive. Just so long as the adage about hating the one you feel you've wronged or robbed doesn't earn me more dislike. I would rather be a peacemaker than carry one on my hip, and some of the names I was happiest about attracting to *Poetry Australia* belonged to people anciently on the other side in the Poetry Society split. Just before leaving the magazine, I was particularly rejoiced to receive some poems from Roland Robinson, the first editor of *Poetry* magazine after *Poetry Australia* hived off from it. That seemed a breach well worth healing. The return of Bruce Dawe to our pages after a coolness not caused by the great rift was also deeply pleasing.

Concerning the much-touted internecine battles of Australian poetry in the seventies, perhaps it is enough to quote a poem by the Hungarian poet Endre Ady, as translated by Paul Desney and published in my first issue, number 49 (1973):

HERCULES OF NECESSITY

How I would like to peter out, a coward —
Tom Thumbs are watching for my fall —
But Hercules I must remain after all.

How soft-headed the dwarfs are;
If they would but leave me alone,
By Christ, I might break down on my own.

But they wag their tongues, swarm about,
Harass me and, to their loss, drive me on
To always new beliefs, fires and song.

• • •

Poor Hercules of necessity. I stand by,
Winning every struggle with my sad rage,
While my dream and my death are delayed.

Nobodies, gnomes, all wretched shams around me,
A little respect and quiet is long due;
I'll never die if this should continue.

Some may be tempted to take that poem autobiographically, but I think it is better applied to the battle itself. Let it have its full radiance, though.

My acting editorship lasted from late 1973 to late 1979, comprising issues 49 to 72, though there were four issues during this time which I did not edit. These were number 52 (1974), the Dutch-Flemish issue, number 56 (1975), the Francis Webb commemorative, number 59 (1976), the American Bicentennial issue compiled and edited by Noel Stock, and the Scottish and Irish Gaelic issue, number 63 (1977), which I initiated but which was edited at my request by the Scots Gaelic poet and scholar Derick Thomson (Ruaraidh MacThómais). I did the ordinary production work on all of these issues, with Dr Perry or alone, and in the case of the Dutch issue I corrected and improved the Dutch editor's halting English translations. Proofreading the special issues was always hard work, but at least the stanza left off the end of one Dutch poet's poem was omitted in the English facing-page translation as well. The stanza was dropped in the manuscript delivered to us, as I had later to explain to the victim when we met at Poetry International in Rotterdam. The Dutch and Webb issues were special projects of Dr Perry's own, the American one was an initiative of Noel Stock, and the Gaelic issue was my idea. Sales of all four special issues were good. The Dutch Government took 7500 copies and the Belgian Government 500 copies of that issue, and our print run on it was ten thousand, large for a specialist literary magazine anywhere.

With the Gaelic issue, the Irish Government took six hundred copies and paid promptly, while Professor Thomson took five hundred on behalf of the Scottish Gaelic magazine *Gairm* and never paid us for them. I have always been mystified by this, and do not ascribe it to dishonesty; some firm justification for it existed in the Professor's mind. When I wrote asking about payment, he told me that we hadn't paid his contributors, so in the end we asked him to pay them out of the money due to us and send us the residue, as we had been waiting for his payment in order to pay them! I never heard another word from him, and when I was in Scotland in 1981 as part of the Scottish-Australian Writers Exchange scheme, he refused to attend a party held to welcome me officially to Scotland. The Gaelic issue which he did for us was splendid, however, and attracted much favourable comment abroad, becoming, as the Webb did, something of a textbook in various places.

Poetry Australia had always had, as part of its international aspiration, a strong interest in translation, and I continued and developed this. It is interesting to recall that the great Poetry Society split was brought about by Grace Perry's intention of doing a special issue devoted to a foreign literature in translation, something which terrified parochial spirits at the time in Australia. Each of my issues contained a proportion of translated material, and I commissioned a number of reviews of books of verse in translation, notably Kevin Hart's important review of the large Corvina anthology of modern Hungarian verse and Alan Gould's equally stringent and perceptive treatment of a Macedonian anthology.

Through a visit I made to the Struga Poetry Evenings festival in Yugoslavia, a good deal of material from various Balkan lands came our way, along with Austrian poetry; much of this came to us in versions made by Herbert Kuhner in Vienna, who became a firm friend of the magazine. One at least of the poets we published more than once in translation was the noted Slovenian author Edvard Kocbek, whose work is proscribed in his own country. We carried translations of Voznesensky, Yevtushenko and Peter Vegin by Igor Mezhakoff-Koriakin and others, and David Campbell's and Rosemary Dobson's versions of earlier Russian poets. We published many of Laurence Spingarn's lively translations from the Portuguese, and a great many of Mark Scrivener's superb versions of German poems from the classic canon. Many of these were old friends of mine, too, and it was a particular pleasure for me to enter into editorial collaboration with Mark on them; in my last issue, number 72, he amazed me by making a sprightly English rendering of a poem I had thought quite untranslatable, Morgenstern's *"Der Werwolf"*. It would be tedious if I recorded here all of the translations we published; it is probably fair to say that, among the world's literary magazines, we were one of those most concerned with this particular form of retrieval. Once only did I publish a translation of my own, done by the familiar method of collaboration with an expert in the original language; this was my rendition of Fazil Hüsnü Daglarca's "The Evening of the Amnesty", (number 64, 1977), done with the help of Talat Halman, the Professor of Turkish at Princeton. Looking back, I wish I had done more translating for the magazine, but the happy pressures of editing and of my own writing always got in the way.

As several magazine editors have found, it is not easy to run an international journal in Australia if you are in any way dependent on government subsidy, as practically all literary magazines in this country are. The Literature Board sees it as its function to subsidise Australian literature, not that of other countries, and gets nervous about any high proportion of foreign material in a magazine. We partly got around this by never, or only once (number 68, 1978), identifying the countries of residence or origin of our contributors. This was, of course, another reason for our eschewal of biographical notes, and is the philosophical basis of my including a number of overseas names in my lists of regular contributors above. Damn national boundaries: the nationality of our contributors was *Poetry Australia*, divided into two provinces called Airmail and Surface Rate. Over the years the magazine published great numbers of American, New Zealand and Canadian poets, large numbers of British and Irish ones, lesser numbers from Africa, Asia and the Pacific Islands, though quite a few Papua New Guineans appeared in its pages. It may even have been of importance in the literary history of several countries in which it was not domiciled. Nigel Krauth, in his anthology *New Guinea in Australian Literature* (UQP, 1982) says that the indigenous literature of Papua New Guinea really began with the publication of Kumalau Tawali's "The Bush Kanaka Speaks" in *Poetry Australia* in 1969. The only important English-speaking area I don't remember receiving contributions from was the Caribbean.

Although the record of the magazine over its whole history would show a very respectable roll call of the sort of local and overseas Great Names which magazines tend to chase in order to gain prestige, I was perhaps a little too diffident and lacking in hierarchical awe to go headhunting in this way with full conviction. We did secure contributions during my acting editorship from such overseas notables as Ted Hughes, Seamus Heaney, Richard

Murphy, Czeslaw Milosz and the Canadians Margaret Atwood, Earle Birney, Dennis Lee and several more, but I was also inclined to send up the whole business of Names at times, by including the names of poets translated in our pages in the Contents. That way, we gained the lustre of contributions from people like Michaelangelo, Du Bellay, Goethe, Heine, Leopardi, Montale and many more. For swank and my own entertainment, I also ran Margaret Diesendorf's excellent German translations of Grace Perry, and a fine Latin poem with accompanying English rendering sent us by William Fleming (number 69, 1979):

THE POLITICIAN'S PROGRESS
Rufus, cura penes quem est civicorum,
cum non servierit loco suo ipso,
tum urbi, tum patriae, hemisphaerae tum,
nunc se recipit ad versum Catulli,
"ad claras Asiae volemus urbes."
Quo spectat? Studet orbi non servire.

OTHERWISE:

Having failed to serve successively his constituency,
His State, his country, his hemisphere,
Rufus the politician now adopts the verse of Catullus,
"Let's fly to the famous Asian burghs."
What *is* his aim?
He seeks, ultimately, to fail to serve the globe.

Although a fair number of excellent articles and many good reviews appeared in *Poetry Australia*, during my tenure as acting editor, I was never as happy about the prose component as I was about the verse. I did manage to reduce the proportion of highly indulgent reviews of mediocre work, but I was never able to eliminate that common fault of Australian magazines. And somehow I never, or rarely ever, managed to obtain as many first-rate general essays and articles as I might have wished. Only Noel Stock provided a reliable supply of those, and it would have been good if we could have varied his well-considered opinions with others equally well presented but from different points of view. Most general discussion of poetry in the magazine was presented in the course of review articles. In a way, I suppose, this reflected my own editorial practice, which was always more akin to case law than Roman-style prescription and statute. All the same, it would have been worthwhile to have some of that "talk about standards" adumbrated by Jamie Grant in one of his reviews.

When I speak of general articles on poetry and related matters, of course, I do not mean the sort of gaseous and politically motivated rhodomontade common at the time; that would have been easy to obtain, in bulk. During my six and a half years, I tried out a good many prose contributors by way of commissioned reviews and projects for essays, and generally found that poets made the best reviewers. For one thing, they were less likely than academics to mistake promise or empty excitement for real achievement, or to fudge the question of quality in favour of often-illusory innovation. They were less in thrall to theory and ideology, and less prone to write up far-fetched "qualities" in poets' work in order to display their own discernment. One academic critic who never disappointed me with special pleading or lack of good sense was Pam Law, of Sydney University, and I was always happy to get the lucid, well-considered prose of the Dublin poet and critic Dennis O'Driscoll. The justified acerbities of Jamie Grant made him, and me, a host of enemies, but his clear-eyed appraisals of two or three fairly major reputations still stand as models of a level of reviewing we have needed and feared during the period of Australian poetry's rise to shaky maturity over the last three decades or so.

Although I was active in reviewing during my days at the magazine, I always refrained from publishing my prose there, in line with the tradition against editorial statements. *Poetry Australia* never went in for the syrup and treachery of interviews, but it might have been good if we had more of the sort of personal statements and observations on art represented by the piece by Czeslaw Milosz in my last issue. If I had stayed on, I might have looked for more such pieces to enrich our prose section, though I might then have had to endure more dithyrambic exaltations of the sort provided us (in number 68, 1978) by the senior French-Canadian poet Rina Lasnier.

I remain grateful to many people for the good days I had at *Poetry Australia*, to Dr Perry for lending me her cherished journal and not imposing any close supervision of my running of it, to the poets and prose writers who supported it, to Dick Edwards and Rod Shaw for their geniality and the miracles they accomplished in translating my optimistic paste-ups into practical pagination — "Yes, it's a deep page, Grace, but Edwards and Shaw are clever men; they'll make it fit!" I am also grateful to Dr Perry for her tolerance of my indifference to the magazine's frequent financial straits, and for our merry cutting-and-pasting sessions at Berrima, Five Dock or Bilgola Beach. I am only sorry she failed to tell me plainly, in 1980, that she now wished to have her magazine back in her own hands. Many parts of our agreement had always been unspoken, and in the end that one was too, and I was left more or less to deduce that my term had ended. I was briefly sore about that, and the confusion it caused, especially among writers who found their work suddenly rejected after I'd accepted it. That cost me a deal of face, but I've since grown it back, and hold no grudges. Since my time, the magazine has moved to Berrima and, after a few hitches and a fairly disastrous temporary change of printers, has returned to Edwards and Shaw and to fair health. It has done a very good commemorative issue on David Campbell, and appears set to survive for years to come, despite the stringencies of recession. It has been called the most open and the most genuinely pluralist of our literary magazines, and that, precisely, was the ideal I tried to serve when I was running it. The desperation of some people to pin a "line" on it has never really succeeded, though it may in the end have been an underground factor in Dr Perry's decision to replace me.

About my last issue, I remember, there was a buzz of comment that I was turning *Poetry Australia* into a Christian magazine. Shock! Horror! To hell with pieties about censorship when dread Christianity threatens to trench upon the received literary sensibility. Behold, the non-god of secular humanism is a jealous absence. I suppose the panic was caused jointly by Kevin Hart's poems and Milosz's article in that issue, and it does worry me to think that neither might have been allowed space in any other Australian literary-intellectual journal, except *Quadrant*. I hope *Poetry Australia* will always remain so open. It sometimes seems to me that Australian intellectual and artistic magazines are much farther down the road to quasi-totalitarian consensus than those in other English-speaking nations. I wasn't really trying to turn *Poetry Australia* into a quality Christian journal, but it is possible that we need one.

During the present stringencies, and for another reason I will name in a moment, it is probably especially important that at least a few independent literary journals survive. By independent, I mean journals open and responsive to the profession and to the general reader, rather than in thrall to universities and splinter groups within them. Curiously, the proliferation of university-based journals seems to be continuing despite the recession. Scrutiny of the motives of sponsors should not stop when sponsorship comes from government or from public institutions. Historically, literary modernism and university English departments rose to prominence together, and it is at least arguable that the willingness of some English departments to found or bail out small magazines evinces a wish to prolong this symbiosis. Experimental modernism is a sort of half-wild cow from which daring critical reputations can be milked, particularly in provinces where better critical standards do not prevail. And it can all be done on the cheap, because to be reliably desperate, the cow needs to be kept hungry.

There is a perhaps crucial weakness in small-press low circulation literary magazines of the sort we have known since the dawn of modernism, and that is the way they perpetuate a ghetto atmosphere in which writers are led to expect token payments for their work and a perpetually marginal status. The Literature Board and the various writers' unions in this country, like their counterparts overseas, exempt the small magazines from paying full Society of Authors or Journalists' Association rates for their material; necessarily so, if such magazines are to exist at all. The independent ones, that is. Oddly, though, universities also take advantage of these exemptions to pay token (perhaps we should say "gentleman amateur") fees to writers who contribute to their pages, though in the matter of salaries they pay their academic staffs fully and, from the point of view even of writers enjoying intermittent Literature Board support, lavishly. It is an exaggertion, perhaps, but not wholly unfair, to see universities as the last of the great feudal patrons. Much aristrocratic scorn is heaped by small-press advocates on vulgar commercial magazines, of which we have had precious few of quality in this country till recently — at least since the very different era of the old *Bulletin* and the *Lone Hand* — and it is true that the small presses do afford opportunities for tyro writers to get published and refine their skills, as well as for uncommercial literary experiment, cyclic though that often is in its breakthroughs.

We are all grateful for the seedbed the small magazines offer our talents early on, but it can often happen that a writer will grow beyond the seedbed. He or she may then wish to reach a wider public, and be treated in a more professional way. The recourse for Australians in the past, at this stage, has been to seek publication overseas. For prestige and perhaps a greater tolerance of diverse viewpoints, it will probably be necessary to go on doing so for quite a while yet; economics and distance, as well as metropolitan assumptions in the older English-speaking world, militate against the creation here of magazines truly influential in a world sense, though I am still not convinced they are impossible, given an unlikely coincidence of large-scale investment and editorial excellence.

On the home market, though, we are beginning to see the arrival of a wide-circulation quality press, with the advent of the *Age Monthly Review* and the return of the *Bulletin* to literary publishing. A valuable precursor of both was the old *Nation Review*, which also paid proper award rates, and the short-lived attempt to revive it as *The Review*. Most recently, I gather the West

Australian magazine *Artlook*, which began a few years ago as a news-sheet about the arts, has joined the ranks of journals paying close to ASA rates for poetry and short fiction. As more such publications emerge, able because of their major backing to overcome the postage and transport costs which tend to cripple the small magazines in this country, and able to pay the rates which might make freelancing possible in this country even for poets, the traditional literary magazines may be driven into a gradually narrowing remnant space in which they cater ever more obviously to beginners, hobbyists, propagandists for unpopular extremist causes and writers not talented enough to break out of their obsolescent ambit. If this happens, and of course it is happening now, the traditional "little" magazines will tend to become puddles of ugly rancour available to eager stirrers. What we may call the mediocrity threshold in the small magazines will become more obvious; it is already their unhappy secret, and I will not be thanked for mentioning it. It is possible that, in the future, no journal of whatever size will be able simultaneously to fulfil the dual aims Dr Perry set out with. In the end, I suppose, the history of *Poetry Australia* has consisted, in part, of a continuing if inconstant battle, concealed by the editors even from themselves because it was partly within us, against the mediocrity threshold. At its best, though, the journal has managed to rise above sounding like a mere literary magazine; I usually find those a misery to read.

Quadrant, April 1983

Eric Rolls and the Golden Disobedience

Among a host of lesser and sometimes quite justifiable omissions from the recent *Oxford History of Australian Literature*, the really surprising one was the fourth wheel of our literary wagon, non-fiction prose. In its place there was a very exhaustive bibliography queerly out of whack with the rest of the book, with long entries listing the works of writers barely mentioned in the text and often no entries at all for writers treated at length. My view of the importance of non-fiction prose is echoed, ironically, in the apology for its absence given by the editor, Professor Leonie Kramer, in a prefatory note to the *Oxford History*: "Our most difficult decision was to omit a section on non-fictional prose. Documentary writing, memoirs, essays, diaries, letters and general prose have a special importance in Australian literary history, because of their quality and their influence upon other literary forms. But in the space available we could not have included this material without serious distortion." Perhaps the space available should have been expanded or transcended, or the distribution of elements within it rearranged. I gather that in a future edition, possibly even the second one, the omission will be put right. Space could be made by cutting the bibliography back to its General component, and perhaps publishing a revised bibliography-by-authors as a supplement. I suggest this partly because I do think bibliographies important, and partly because I don't like to see anyone's hard work go for nothing.

Non-fiction prose, though, is pretty clearly a vital part of our whole tradition, and is now perhaps the sector of Australian literature where specifically Australian themes, tones, concerns and even identity are most freely allowed to persist. There, we are even permitted to learn about the past and have continuity with it, without charges of "bush epic" and "costume drama". We are permitted to recall and draw on non-fashionable vernaculars, and to examine things for their interest rather than their relevance. In matters of style and tone, there is less pressure to appear always in cord jeans and Adidas shoes, and less pressure towards what I call display prose, the sort which calls attention to itself constantly and with more or less subtlety, wearing its maguey-fibre shirt with a knowing flair. In the absence of such constraint, non-fiction prose may occasionally develop modes and strategies of its own, drawing on native elements and, I believe, creating possibilities for fiction, poetry, the drama and even film. A book which does this, I think, is Eric Rolls' regional-ecological history *A Million Wild Acres*, and I would like to look at its manner, over and above its matter, though the two are finally impossible to separate. It seems to me at once to represent and to extend a tenuously surviving native tradition, and to do things which could be extremely fruitful for fiction writers, poets and others to examine. In its manner as much as in its matter, though the effect is more spectacular there, it is a deeply disobedient book.

Because most scientific and scholarly writing in Australia has tended to be technical and constrained by professional disciplines, with no points given within those for literary excellence, non-fiction writing in this country favours Australiana and matters of Australian rather than universal significance. When we think of Australian non-fiction classics, these are mostly books about our country and its people; Dakin and Banfield and Mary Gilmore are names which come to mind, as do Geoffrey Blainey and Manning Clark, Bill Gammage and C. E. W. Bean, Gavin Souter and Germaine Greer (the last-named partly escapes the Australiana net, though her *The Female Eunuch* does stand as a distinguished cousin to a host of routine excoriations of Australian life and culture, the various Godzones and Australian Stupors). Other names which would have to be added to the list would be Francis Ratcliffe and Rachel Henning, T. G. H. Strehlow and the Berndts, Robin Boyd and Hal Porter — the list keeps lengthening in the mind, approaching Legion and dizzying us with its dance towards and away from and across the borders of classification. A lot of our poetry, for instance, has a strong element of non-fiction about it, and much of the tone of prose works that grapple with the realities of a new, strange continent. In the fields of polemic especially, but also elsewhere, we may begin to wonder just where the borders of fiction, poetry and non-fiction lie. That, of course, is a whole field of study in itself, and its results may tend to undermine our categories altogether. For my purposes here, it merely demonstrates the risky artificiality, the unreality even, of leaving non-fiction writing out of consideration. How can you write at length about Hal Porter's novels and merely glance at his autobiographical writings, without distorting your whole account of the man's achievement? How can you look only at Mary Gilmore's poetry, and short-change her greatest achievement in the *Old Days Old Ways* books?

Eric Rolls and the Golden Disobedience

While not failing to credit Professor Kramer's reasons for leaving non-fiction out, there are emphases in the *Oxford History* which militate against its giving a full account of a literary field strong, as we have said, on Australiana and matters of national concern. The *Oxford History*, following Patrick White's strictures against "dun-coloured" journalistic fiction of the sort once prevalent here — authors such as Katharine Susannah Prichard, Kylie Tennant, Frank Hardy, the Palmers and others have a pretty thin time in Dr Adrian Mitchell's long essay on Australian fiction — is ruled by European-style criteria of High Art rather than any wish to register all local outcroppings of literary significance, though it puzzlingly fails to compare approved Australian works with their overseas coevals, and so operates in something of a vacuum as regards its own criteria. The *Oxford History* is concerned to oppose a test of high literary quality, not as promised but as actually achieved, to any and all prescriptive or extra-literary programmes. And I think this is perfectly proper. I have often inveighed against the corruption of our poetry anthologies, all of which select their contents on grounds which include many considerations other than poetic excellence. The *Oxford History*, though, is particularly opposed to the legend of the nineties and to prescriptive views of Australian literature and culture derived from that legend, and here we may be justified in suspecting the presence of the demon Politics. It would of course be contrary to all decent pluralism to object to a High Tory history of Australian literature — and I don't think the *Oxford History* is such, at least not in its Poetry and Drama sections — but it is also fair to say that our whole culture owes an immense debt to the older left traditions. I freely acknowledge my own debt. Without such books as Russel Ward's *Australian Legend*, or Manifold's *Who Wrote the Ballads*, I would not be the writer I am. Without major default, no single ideology "owns" any important subject matter.

Non-fiction prose pretty obviously has as great a potential for moulding and changing opinion as any other branch of literature, and nowadays when the other branches do effect changes in our sensibility or world view it is with the strong help of non-fiction writing. How much of the revolutionary effect of modernism in, say, poetry arose from the texts themselves, and how much from the commentaries and the early proselytising critics, men such as I. A. Richards and F. R. Leavis? To cite a case in which non-fiction prose had far-reaching efforts in Australia, C. E. W. Bean's decision to write the history of the First AIF from the standpoint of the ordinary soldier arguably set our whole basic attitude to Australia's part in that war and those to follow, and largely determined the form our commemorations would take in the long run, in spite of official overlays of Empire sentiment. Where other countries' traditions in military history had always stressed the generals and leaders, ours would be unique in its emphasis on the citizen soldier, or the citizen-as-soldier, and would even do less than justice to our one really great commander, Sir John Monash, a general of international significance. It would be interesting to trace which of the great themes and images of our imaginative literature, the Explorer, the Voyager, the Inner Emptiness, the Alienness of the Bush and so on, arose from non-fiction sources and which were created by poets and novelists. I do not know the answer in any particular case; I suspect that the alleged alienness of the bush had mainly poetic origins powerfully reinforced by D. H. Lawrence on his visit in the twenties. But even with this one I suspect there would have been antecedent reportage by diarists and writers of descriptive prose in colonial times. The same may even be true of Mateship, which we think of as a great "folk" discovery of the short-story writers and poets of the eighties and nineties of last century.

If non-fiction writing is powerful in establishing views which gradually become accepted reality, it is arguably even more powerful than imaginative literature in overturning such orthodoxies. Imaginative literature is unique in its power to give to materials that vivid life which we may call poetry; it has no unique power to make discoveries, though it probably makes some, and certainly deepens and consolidates many. When it goes against an accepted view, however, it lacks the sober documentary force to sway tough-minded and "realistic" spirits, or deeply committed ones. It may delight them and weaken them, but it will not usually convince them on its own. And yet it is possibly poetry which does in the end convince and convert, conferring reality on successive constructs — but that is as likely to be the "poetry" of a remembered distillation of non-fiction prose as the actual poetry of verse or imaginative prose. I think poetry is the principle which controls reality, and I doubt there is any more final truth, but when I say that I use the term poetry in its widest sense. We are ruled, and sometimes martyred, by successive large loose "poems" which become the governing paradigms of our world.

It is a commonplace, of course, that poetry can even drive out personal experience. I grew up near and often in the great forests of the New South Wales lower north coast; our house was less than two miles from the edge of the Myall State Forest, and four more large State forests lay within the ambit of my childhood; my father had been a bullock driver and timbergetter in those forests before he married and started dairyfarming — and yet even I was almost seduced by the myth of the alien bush, as I began learning to write poetry. A received sensibility almost had me subscribing to its agenda, in spite of my awareness that the bush wasn't alien to me at all, but a deeply loved vastness containing danger and heavy work, but also possessing a blessedly interminable quality which was and is almost my mind's model of contemplation. It was years, though, before I had a character in a verse novel discover that "the bush is sensible; it'll kill you, but it's — decent".

The part of the bush I grew up in is first mentioned in Eric Rolls' book on page 70, as he describes the surveys carried out by Henry Dangar to find suitable country for the newly formed Australian Agricultural Company:

The one area left that seemed likely to contain the company's grant lay between Port Stephens and the Manning River. In February 1826 Henry Dangar made a thorough reconnaissance. And he found good land. There is beautiful cattle country around Stroud, Dungog, Gloucester and Taree. Further east, though it was obviously not the rich farm land that Dangar would choose for himself, there was fair open grass land. It was not the wooded tangle of today.

The poor grassland country down around the Myall Lakes, now all under eucalypts and red-barked angophoras and great tracts of paperbark forest standing in rushy grass on white clay soils (where the AMP Society has not bulldozed the bush to put in superphosphate pasture for its cattle), was deemed suitable for fine-wool sheep, and the world of the local Aborigines was destroyed to accommodate them. Within a few years, footrot and the soils' deficiencies in copper and cobalt, defects unknown to nineteenth-century science, had wiped the sheep out. And with the Aborigines no longer there to burn the country over continuously, the lonely Myall Lakes scrublands we know today, with their tremendous wealth of wildflowers, began to cover the grassland over. Back in the hills I come from, north-west of there, the rainforest which had always withstood the Aborigines' fires in moist gullies began to expand as the settlers and cedargetters usurped the black people, then retreated again before the white man's axes and crosscut saws. The scattered clumps of sclerophyll forest, never large or dense in Aboriginal times, began to surge outward, spreading down off the ridges to cover the valley flats which had carried only a few trees to the hectare in pre-European days. When my father was a young man, he and his brothers could ride everywhere in "the State", as they called the vast forest reserve near their home, seeking the giant timber trees that stood among the younger spindlier growth. As my father told me recently, "You hardly had to make roads for the bullocks then. You could see through the bush for hundreds of yards." Now, you could barely get a horse through most parts of the Myall State Forest, among the vines and wattle thickets and dense stands of young trees which flourish there after eighty or ninety years of mill logging and sleeper cutting. And if modern use by trucks and tractors has not kept them open, it is a job even to find the bullock roads of forty years ago. Fifty years ago, my father and his brothers happened on a promising quartz reef in a clear gully, and the assays were promising. I remember seeing the shaft when I was a child, but when Dad and I went to find it again a few years ago, we couldn't even identify the right gully, among the masses of lopped heads of trees and surging second growth. The bush out there would be far too thick to go possuming in now, as Dad and his brothers and cousins used to do on moonlit nights. Their great-grandfathers had learned from the Aborigines how to "moon" possums, perhaps even while they were still working for the Australian Agricultural Company at Stroud.

It is Eric Rolls' controversial and perhaps revolutionary contention that the forests of Australia as we know them are no more than a hundred to a hundred and thirty years old. Apart from the tracts and patches of rainforest that follow the eastern face of the Dividing Range from far north Queensland down almost to Victoria, and a few large pockets of sclerophyll forest mainly in areas of high rainfall, he contends that Australia bore the appearance in pre-European times of a vast parkland kept open and well grassed by constant burning off. It was a *paysage humanisé* and *moralisé* which the Aborigines had maintained for untold centuries; the wilderness we now value and try to protect came with us, the invaders. It came in our heads, and it gradually rose out of the ground to meet us. As Rolls writes (page 400):

> Those who value our forests and wish to preserve them declare, as in this extract from *Save Colong Bulletin*, November 1976, "More than half the forest in eastern Australia — the dry sclerophyll and savannah woodland — has disappeared since European settlement." Hugh Tyndale-Biscoe of the Society for Social Responsibility in Science (ACT) irresponsibly exclaimed in *The Sydney Morning Herald* of 18 September 1978 "there is no equivalent in Britain to our great primeval forests." Over and over one finds similar statements in modern writings. What forests? How many trees make a forest?
>
> "Everywhere we have an open woodland," wrote Charles Darwin on his 1836 visit. "Nowhere are there any dense forests like those of North America," explained *Chambers Information for the People* in an article on "Emigration to Australia" written in 1841. Such statements are made over and over in early writings. De Beuzeville was aware of them. He reasserted them in his *Australian Trees for Australian Planting*. "Even along the ... gullies and the contiguous streams," he quoted, "the country resembled the 'woodlier parts of a deerpark in England.'" In the seventy-two forests declared in New South Wales in 1879 the tree count of those assessed varied

from two and a half mature trees to the hectare inland to eighty on the tablelands and coast. The Forestry Commission in experimental plots in the Yerrinan section of the Pilliga forest found that sixty-year-old White Cypress Pines thinned in 1940 to two hundred to the hectare produced the best timber over the next thirty years, but, if thinned to six hundred to the hectare, they produced the most timber. Nowhere, in a search lasting months, did I find reference to former stands of timber as thick as those modern thinned stands.

The author goes on to describe, in the same passage, the few stands of relatively heavy timber which existed at the time of settlement, places such as the future Nundle Forest Reserve first sighted by Oxley, where a density of a hundred and fifty mature stringybarks per hectare as assessed in 1879 was enough to form a canopy and permit the growth of large tree ferns which do not grow in direct sunlight, and the mountain ash gullies of Victoria. He also refers to the large jarrah and karri forests of south-western Western Australia, though he doesn't add to his case by mentioning the frequent references to expansion of those forests since settlement. On visits to Western Australia, I have read many accounts of those forests which state, how truly I don't know, that places where giant trees now grow in profusion were wheatlands a century ago. After pointing out that the great eucalyptus growth on the Dividing Range and on every little hill in central western New South Wales, the Bimble Box swaths in the west of that State, the long forests of river red gum on the western drainage and the coolabah forests found on plains subject to flooding are all post-settlement growths, he candidly details the destruction of much of our rainforests and the idiotic overexploitation of *Toona australis*, the red cedar which, apart from Tasmania's Huon pine, is Australia's only truly long-lived tree, living for upwards of two thousand years but tragically hard to regenerate artificially. Even the cedar grew only sparsely in its brushes; good stands averaged one great tree to the hectare. Modern timbergetters have learned the hard way to be secretive about the odd red cedar they know of in the forests, often passing the location of such trees on to their children as a sort of inheritance, or at least waiting many years before felling the big solitary treasure trove they have been saving up. When such a log comes in to a city mill, it is an event; I remember the arrival of a red cedar log at the Asquith mill in Sydney a few years ago, a middle-sized stick taken from private land on the northern rivers which earned its owner eleven hundred dollars after cartage. A decent-sized red cedar log nowadays can easily fetch five or six thousand dollars at auction. In case conservationists may worry that he is undermining their cause, Rolls goes on to point out that while there are now more trees in Australia than at settlement, just as there are more

Persistence in Folly

kangaroos, this does not make proper care of our forests less important. "Our forests are vulnerable," he writes. "Their concentration puts both plants and animals at risk. They are the packed containers of so much that has gone from the rest of the country." And he describes the shortcomings of many of our forestry authorities, with their ignorance of soils and their persistent temptations to monoculture. One man up our way hated the sterile plantations of slash pine (*Pinus elliottii*) north of Tea Gardens so much that he waited over twenty years, then, in a searing drought-stricken summer, put a match to them and wiped out half the stand in a fire which must have been an orgy of expensively fragrant destruction. Rolls describes right and wrong ways to conduct the woodchip industry, which he regards as sound and necessary, and deplores the sneaky, servile way in which several State governments have sold off forest resources in secret deals.

Except for the rainforest Aborigines of north Queensland, I have never heard of any groups of Aboriginal people who habitually lived in thick forest, nor have I ever read any legends which had a good word to say for it. In my home region, people who spoke the various dialects of Kattangal used to enter the thick brushes along the Manning River each year to bring down flying foxes for food, but stories from the region tell of cannibal spirits (*doolgarl*) which inhabited the riverine forest, so we may imagine the hunters did not hang about in there when they had got their quota. There are legends, not mentioned by Rolls, which describe the permanent destruction of forests by fire — the Rubuntja fire-ancestor legend from Central Australia is an example — and stories of the gradual widening of the sky as ancient forests disappeared; these may go back thousands of years and describe a process which began as Australia became drier. Forest does not provide good hunting ground for nomads equipped with long spears and throwing weapons. Spears would catch and break in thick bush, and boomerangs would be lost in it. Similarly, animals would have too much cover, and get out of sight too quickly when startled. Fire, we know, was regularly used by Aborigines to flush out and drive game, and the green feed which came up quickly after burning attracted grazing animals. Rolls is not alone in citing numerous early European references to Aboriginal fires seen burning in places from Tasmania to Cape York; in his *Triumph of the Nomads*, Geoffrey Blainey devotes a whole chapter, titled "Australia, a Burning Continent", to the fire-husbandry practised by the first Australians. We are becoming familiar with this concept now, and coming to appreciate the unique adaptation to fire of dominant floral and faunal communities in this country. Most people, for instance, must by now have heard of the leaf-regenerating epicormic buds in eucalypts, and be aware of the many plants whose seeds only open when a fire cracks their hard coverings. And country people know the way birds will gather as soon as smoke begins to rise from a paddock, butcherbirds, kestrels, satin birds and kookaburras appearing as if from nowhere and dodging through the smoke to catch grasshoppers, lizards and other small animals driven from cover by the flames. It would be fascinating to know how far back they learned to do this, and know the answer to the various chicken-and-egg questions which the unique fire ecology of Australia poses for evolutionary theory.

Rolls' general theory of the Australian forests is anchored in the particular story of one forest, the Pilliga (from Kamilaroi *peelaka*, a spearhead), which lies beyond the Dividing Range in New South Wales and extends from Narrabri in the north to Coonabarabran in the south. Its eastern extremity is close to the village of Baan Baa and in the west it peters out around the small town of Baradine. It is characterised by a mixture of eucalypts, acacias and callitris trees, usually known by the collective name cypress pine, and is enormously rich in birds, animals and flowering plants. Rolls writes (page 1):

When John Oxley saw it in 1818 there was little forest there as the word is used now. The meaning of forest has grown with the forests. "Brush" he called it in small areas, "a very thick brush of cypress trees and small shrubs." "Scrub" he called the stunted growth on the dry ridges, "mere scrub". Most of it, about 800,000 hectares, was a "forest" of huge ironbarks and big white-barked cypress pines, three or four of them only to the hectare.

We would not now call it forest. "But it is open grassland" we would say in bewilderment. "One would scarcely have to clear it to cultivate it." ... What Oxley saw he did not like. "Forbidding ... miserable ..." he said, "a sandy desert ..." Oxley was using the term "desert" in the sense of deserted, not dry. It was a decidedly wet desert in August 1818.

Slowly, with a leisurely accretion of detail from sources that range from printed books to previously unread family diaries and Lands Department archives, Rolls tells the story of how European animals, plants and humans spread northwards on each side of the Dividing Range and took over this belt of sandy country. It is not purely human history, but ecological history he gives us, showing how the real explorers were as likely to be escaped cattle and introduced grasses as men. By the time the hard men of the infant colony and their convict slaves arrived to take up new country, cattle had usually preceded them and begun compacting the ancient spongy soils with their hoofs, driving out the native ground-plants with the chemical and light-occluding properties of their huge droppings. He is unsparing of the rapacious human landtakers, but

Persistence in Folly

will not take the easy course of repudiating them. As he writes (pages 11-12):

The tormented community generated its own men. Some hard gobbets indeed were thrown up. Those attracted later as settlers were the same type — capable, adventurous, and extraordinarily adaptable, difficult, crude, vigorous, dishonest, selfish, violent. They differed only in the extent to which each of these qualities was developed. Some were more violent than others, some less adaptable. They developed Australia.

If these men had remained in Britain they would have had no influence on their times. Society would have restrained them. In Australia they moved outside the law. It is no use wishing they were different. To do so is to dispense with our culture. No other men could have done what they did. Australia might have been abandoned as a British settlement.

If it had been abandoned, of course, the bush cattle and introduced plants and Mr Brumby's horses would still have gone on spreading. And since in a world rapidly heading towards being crowded, no large area of even marginally exploitable land could expect to go on supporting only a beautifully adapted small population of hunter-gatherers, some other nation or nations would have invaded Australia and brought destruction to the world of the Aborigines. Rolls does not theorise or agonise about the morality of the invasion, but he also does not seek to evade its ruthless violence. We are given a sense of that curious meshing of warfare and accommodation which commonly comes about on frontiers:

From the beginning of settlement there was an astonishingly close relationship with the Aborigines. It was rare for a white man to be killed by unknowns. When a shepherd in a lonely hut was speared, if he saw the man who threw it, he knew him by a name. And, when stockmen rode out to shoot Aborigines in retaliation, they counted the dead by name. But the names they called them were cursory and degrading: Bobby, Saturday, Sunday, King Billy. Most Europeans could not be bothered learning to pronounce Aboriginal words and in choosing names for Aboriginal acquaintances they took less trouble than teamsters in naming their work bullocks.

There are black people still alive in northern Australia who bear such names. From time to time, casual killings and small massacres turned to pitched battle. On Boorambil station in 1827 or 1828 — we may call it a station, though the term didn't originate till 1836 — a large force of Kamilaroi tribesmen attacked white stockmen sheltering in a well-built hut with rifle slots in the walls. It is possible that the Kamilaroi had issued a formal challenge to meet and fight on a stipulated day, but the handful of white men did not come out and line up to meet their challengers in the honourable traditional way. When spears and boomerangs thrown against the walls in derision did not bring them out, the black soldiers stormed the hut and tried to unroof it. They kept attacking for hours, and perhaps as many as two hundred were shot, most of the young men of the tribe. This battle is known from two slightly differing accounts, one handwritten by William Gardner, one in a book published by the bushranger Martin Cash.

The story of the Pilliga forest is one of advance, disappointment and retreat by pastoralists and then by small farmers. It is possible that we have never had so penetrating a study of the realities of settlement before; certainly I do not know of one which interrelates the human and non-human dimensions so intimately. Also, and it is a country man's point, Rolls realises that more of Australia's history took place outside the law than within it, and more attempt was made to hide than to record it. He has a knack, born of sympathy and human knowledge, for detecting the outlines of concealed knavery even a century old. History is not just the propaganda of dominant groups, but also the public record of approved classes of human beings, and there is a way in which country people in Australia are apt to miss out on their due by being neither acceptably Upper nor recognisably proletarian, and their wary reticences compound this still further. Given rapid changes of ownership of runs, by chicanery, bad luck, disease, opportunism or poor judgment of country, and changes in government policy such as John Robertson's Selection Acts of the 1860s, few were able to amass large stable fortunes. Dynasty and great wealth are features of many parts of the New World of European settlement, but are far less important in Australia, and the difference sets us off from many apparently comparable societies. The ecological result in the Pilliga was that neglected runs and failed selections went under surging masses of gum and cypress pine seedlings by the 1870s. Cypress pines came up ten thousand to the hectare, and soon there was no room for grass to grow. Foxes and competition for grass destroyed the rat-kangaroos which had previously kept the seedlings nibbled down, and the disappearance of the Aborigines meant that burning off was no longer regular and cyclic. Happening occasionally, sometimes as a result of lightning strike or accident, fires had the opposite of their historic effect: they now induced the appearance of millions of seedlings. The blue-green *peelaka* spearheads of cypress pine trees filled up the country. Rabbits, arriving soon after the first great spurts of growth, tended to keep the forest in check to some extent, until myxomatosis in the fifties of this century wiped the rabbits out, and bush fires in the same decade were followed by soaking rains. After the fifties, the Forestry Department, which had assumed that milling in the Pilliga would eventually cut the timber out, began to think in terms of sustained yield from the region. And unless the periodic threat of a new international airport in the Pilliga "scrub" becomes a reality — let us hope Rolls' book makes that less likely — the area may at last have reached some sort of natural balance of human and non-human life. Not that such balances last forever.

Reading and re-reading *A Million Wild Acres* with all the delight of one who knows he has at last got hold of a book that is in no way alien to him (I begin to understand the sheer relief of a black Australian who has at last obtained a book written by one of his own people and not by whites) I was struck by the almost pointillist way in which he writes history. The book has historical sequence, and is arranged in chapters, but its logic is really accretive, made up of strings of vivid, minute fact which often curl around in intricate knottings of digression. Patches of timeless life are shot through with patches of sequential narrative, and vice versa. In the chapter on bird life in the Pilliga, we suddenly get a thread of human history and a fascinating needle of speculation. After telling us about the feeding habits of many of the birds in the forest, and their reliance on pollen and nectar from flowers, he writes (pages 390–1):

This extensive pollen feeding helps to explain the pollination of Australian plants. Anyone, scientist or layman, asked today "What is the principal pollinator of native flowers?" would answer "The honey bee". The honey bee was brought out with as much care as the first rabbits — Gregory Blaxland's hive travelled in his cabin — and spread with settlement. In many districts it has been principal pollinator for no more than a hundred years. One wonders whether more efficient pollination allowed the heavy growth of modern forests. Could the honeyeaters and lorikeets or the little (native) *Trigona* bees have coped with thousands of hectares of massed flowers or millions of extra solitary bees found enough holes or dug enough burrows to store their individual honey pots?

Historical sequence in the book shifts constantly from the drily economic to the personal, and report is charged with reminiscence. For instance, on pages 181–2 we read:

Thomas G. G. Dangar married Catherine MacKenzie, daughter of the man who grew wheat so early at Wangen. He built a good home on Bullerawa. No one in the north built mansions costing a hundred thousand pounds sterling like Thomas Chirnside or Sir William Clarke and several others in the Western District of Victoria. But whereas homes on most northern runs were valued at about two hundred pounds, the home on Bullerawa was valued at two thousand.

By the river he built huts to house twenty-five exconvict workmen who had grown too old to work. He supplied a cook who called them to meals by ringing a big brass bell. Thomas Dangar later donated the old bell to the Pilliga school.

Eric Rolls and the Golden Disobedience

W. C. Cormie, the son of David Cormie who was manager for Thomas Dangar, used to watch the old men bathing naked in the Namoi when he was a child. The cat o' nine tails had so scarred their backs they seemed to be covered in scales not skin.

The events described belong to the seventies of last century, and on the same page we revisit the sprouting acacia and cypress pine seedlings now beginning to take advantage of the depletion of cattle numbers by drought, and also of runholders' attempts to destroy spear grass and wire grass by burning. In that decade, stock routes are invented and gazetted, and sawmilling begins in the Pilliga for the first time, at Narrabri on its northern fringe. As elsewhere in the book, everything is in motion yet held in a sort of dynamic tableau, measuring some thousands of square miles by about 160 years. In contradistinction to most European art since the Middle Ages, there is little sense of foreground and background, that perspective of heroic agents acting out their drama before a series of sketched-in theatre flats, the Renaissance schema by which the aristocratic principle was able to triumph over an older Christian "field" (the sense of Everyman, or Piers Plowman's Field Full of Folk) in which prominence was reserved for supernatural figures. In Rolls' presentation, things human and non-human are all happening interrelatedly, and the humans barely stand out. Through a fusion of vernacular elements with fine-grained natural observation, and a constant movement of back-reference, he breaks through sequential time not to timelessness but to a sort of enlarged spiritual present in which no life is suppressed. We feel that the myriad activity of the book's "field" does not cease when we move our gaze through it and over it. Of all art, it reminds me distantly of Pollock; perhaps "Blue Poles", which I take to be as much as anything a painting of equality, was an appropriate purchase for an Australian Government to make. It also reminds me of just a few Australian works, Boyd's Breughelesque paintings such as *The Mining Town*, with their myriad active figures mostly held below the high horizon line, or Geoffrey Lehmann's vernacular-meditative *Ross's Poems*. It is perhaps a nascent New World form of vision, struggling to emerge from under successive impositions of neo-aristocratic style derived from abroad. When I look at a piece of art which mimes community or commonality in something like this way, it gives me an obscure sense of homecoming I rarely get from, say, the theatre, with its dominant and subordinate characters, its conflict and its merely human interactions. This may admittedly be a preference drawn from poetry, in which the rocks, the trees and the animals are as important as the human figures and all things can be taken as referring to the human anyway without stressing the point.

In the laconic, discursive and yet economical pace of its narration, and in its dry tone, Rolls' *Million Wild Acres* reminds me at times of the Sagas, particularly I suppose the Icelandic *Landnamabók* or Book of Settlements. And yet there are differences. Rolls' book presents a complex system greater than any of the agents in it, but does not call it fate, or indeed refer it to any metaphysic. It has a much larger quotient of meditation than a saga story, but it is usually a meditation based on elegaic and unobtrusively intense scrutiny of detail, as in the beautiful brief accounts of older country lore, of bells and bullockies' commands and the way to oil seasoned pine planks. And, as the sagas only occasionally do, he treats his human and non-human agents pretty much on a par. This par we may call ecological consciousness, and see it as a new form of a very ancient sense of the interrelatedness of all things. A way of expressing this which we find in surviving fables and fairytales is to make the animals and even the trees talk. Rolls' animal figures do not talk, and so don't offend modern rationalist expectations, but he shows us their lives in vignettes which capture their unidealised behaviour, sometimes in situations we have imposed on them. An irritated sow in a sty bites off the penis of an importunate boar, a homosexual steer provides relief for young rig bulls. Any kind of aristocratic sensibility is liable to scorn such things as mere peasant anecdote, fearful perhaps of being itself caught in a web of laconic storytelling which might deflate prominent or highly polished humans and reduce them to a memorable feature here, a perhaps devastating recollection there. The Reverend Samuel Marsden, for example, merits less sympathy than that possibly happy steer, and gets no more space. Rolls merely writes of Marsden hauling a miller before him one Sunday morning and fining him because his mill was desecrating the Sabbath. Marsden's own mill turned throughout the hearing. Or there is the picture of "sedate, scientific and religious" Lieutenant Dawes, of the Royal Marines, tramping through the hills in the year after settlement with his bags for collecting soil samples and his habit of quizzing the Aborigines about Noah and the Flood. The Aborigines had certainly heard of a flood, and Dawes was delighted. Anecdote, which is of course not exclusively a bush or a peasant thing, has some threatening relativities about it, and can be merciless in an equable way which gives power to the powerless. It is a music of equality.

The anecdote of course, based as it is on interest and selection of detail, may carry tyrannical potentials of its own. A lot depends on the breadth of the group it appeals to, and the complicity it seeks. We need to ask whether, in a given case, anecdotes and details are

Eric Rolls and the Golden Disobedience

being selected in order to impose a world view or reflect one. Are we looking at the familiar journalistic trick of selecting details and presenting them blandly in order to shift our perceptions towards a view which the writer is covertly pushing — always telling stories that make religion seem foolish, for example — or are we looking at an attempt to mime the balanced complexity of reality according to something like a common view held by a broad range of society? Of course one may do a lot to change a common view by adopting a common tone: that is a familiar post-nineties strategy in Australia. I think Australian readers have already come to see Rolls' book as genuinely representing a broad rather than a sectional sensibility, however, and existing on a plane we instantly recognise as common Australian property rather than the atmosphere of an elite. I have heard conservationists growl at Rolls, and call him "that old fraud", but I can't see how he damages their cause; he may, indeed, have burnt off a derivative form of ecological consciousness and let one more truly adapted to Australia spring up. He gives an originally imported notion the "sound" of common acceptance, partly by freeing it from overtones of a mandarin desire to reform and civilise us. And so there is no strain of intimidation in our assent to his book.

The ruling literary culture of our time exhorts us to many disobediences. Very many of these are fraudulent or by now worn out, but there is a disobedience I value and call the golden one — and that is disobedience of the dominant literary sensibility itself. It is often wise, in the New World, to write literature as it were against the grain of Literature, because then you avoid the resistance which literary claims very often provoke, perhaps at a deep level, in the minds of readers whom Literature as usually understood in late-colonial societies often seems to threaten with relegation if they resist its assumptions. We have grown used in recent years to highly mannered forms of prose fiction, many of them derived in this country from Patrick White's method of dabbling small exacerbated qualifications of extreme sensitivity over narrative and character alike in ways which constantly threaten to snub us if we do not render abashed assent. Few writers, perhaps, have followed White's other trick of inverting ordinary snobbery and transposing it into mystical election, but a myriad other transformations and inversions of snobbery are around, to the point where the marks and shibboleths of enlightenment and competitive modernity have become a study as intricate as the quarterings of European heraldry encountered by Voltaire's Candide. Canny writers such as Frank Moorhouse, of course, can get away with holocausts of damaging exposure of fashionable circles by remembering always to have their narrators do approved things and seem to reflect the reigning sensibility. But even playing tricks on a divisive and alienating mandarin tradition is not the same as discovering new styles and departures in art, and perhaps freeing it to reflect more of reality than a received sensibility allows. In its steady "middle" voice, Rolls' narrative seems to be attempting nothing less than a complete account of its large subject. The whole truth, with no let-outs of polemic or withheld sympathy or portentousness or even of the chic brilliances which often disguise hollowness of vision. In its very different tone, and in a context of half-personal documentary rather than fiction, Rolls' enterprise may be seen as Proustian. But only tangentially, because in achieving his effect of completeness Rolls has done something which the aristocratic literary traditions of Europe make hard even to conceive: he has penetrated to the condition of the best "primitive" art. In painting, the term *primitive* refers to art executed by people without formal training; in literature, where it is much rarer as a genuine and productive thing, we may take it as meaning unaware of the received sensibility. This is quite different from Latin American "Magic" Realism, currently rather fashionable in Australia and elsewhere, which is a sophisticated appropriation of some primitive techniques. The hollowness of Magic Realism lies in the way it affects to love the People, but really considers their life too boring on its own, and so heightens it with implausible surreal incident and fantasy. In six and a half years as acting editor of a poetry magazine, I only twice encountered work of quality produced by genuine primitive poets; these were Carmen Blomfield, of Armidale, whose strange, utterly individual and yet deeply communal poem "Lament for Kangaroo Flat" I published in *Poetry Australia*, and Allan Jurd, of Lismore, whose poems had a tumbling fecundity of observation and an oddness of imaginative angle which cannot be faked. Rolls' own early "Sheaf Tosser" poems had a comparable "primitive" quality which impressed many good judges who could see beyond the roughnesses and repetitions. It now seems that this essence in his early poems has stayed alive in Rolls and kept him from conformities, so that he might consummate it three decades later in a prose masterpiece.

Claims have been made that Rolls' *Million Wild Acres* will be seen as one of the great books about Australia, rivalling *Voss, Such is Life* or *Capricornia* as the "ultimate statement about national experience". The book has a larger scope, perhaps, than any of those, but I am unsure of the precise meaning of that term "ultimate statement". Rolls' history probably contains as much poetry, in the wide sense, as any of them, without their dimensions of fiction, and none of its poetry consists in "purple" writing. Interestingly, two of the three books named draw upon vernacular elements of our culture, and use yarning as an element of their construction. *Such is Life* at once creates and celebrates a new "Australian" sensibility based on conscious exaggeration of the actualities of the itinerant workers' yarn; while pretending to be a structured novel it is actually a meandering picaresque entertainment that flows rather like the Murray River, with infinite bends and lagoons of minor incident and newly sprouted forests of comic meditation. In this latter regard, *Capricornia* is fairly similar, with emblematic characters who undergo much disaster but little development.

Rolls' book is more classically "laconic" in its tone than either novel, and proves just how long a laconic performance can go on without tiring the reader or ceasing to be laconic. The only part of the book which did drag a little for me was in the early chapters minutely detailing the spread of settlement north and west from Port Jackson. Those were the chapters which, dealing with times beyond living memory, were most affected by documentary history, and closest to merely sequential narrative. Later in the book, human characters could emerge in a way which owes little either to literary fiction or to historical writing. Figures of timbergetters and rabbiters, Forestry officials and farmers are then simply named, with perhaps a word or two of designation when we first meet them, and are thereafter apt to re-emerge in an apparently casual way when needed to tell a story or anchor a statement of fact. They appear with the sudden naturalness of old friends mentioned in a fireside yarn, and reveal themselves while contributing to the flavour of the narration. Writing about the great bushfire of 1951, for example, Rolls allows a number of figures to play their small parts and vanish again (page 305):

Initially some of the firefighters were not worth feeding. With so little equipment they saw no point in risking their lives for a bit of scrub. They played cards and let it burn. A young sleeper cutter, not mentally normal, could not resist lighting a few extra fires. Others risked their lives trying to cut breaks with the little graders. Noel Worland worked the first sixty-three hours without sleep. Ned Edwards spent thirteen days and nights at the fire, his brother, Roy, eighteen.

Arthur Ruttley was sent up to take charge. He organised big bulldozers from coastal forests, five new graders from Sydney, water tankers from the RAAF. He flew in a plane load of forestry students to get experience. He recruited local volunteers and enough cooks to feed several hundred men. He kept everybody working. They put the fire out in three weeks.

Noel Worland watched the forest for further outbreaks from a De Soutter aeroplane flown by Dick Burt of Baradine. The high wings were made of plywood and they drummed as the plane came in to land. The noise got louder and louder till at touchdown it seemed the plane must disintegrate. Dick Burt's cattle dog rode with Noel on the back seat and licked his face while he was spotting. Each time he pushed it away it growled venomously.

Every individual figure in that passage, except the unfortunate sleeper cutter who is perhaps still alive and anyway better unnamed, has the dignity of his name; there is no recourse to the lazy (or superior) passive voice: bulldozers *were organised*, five graders *were got* from Sydney etc., and no reliance on periphrases such as "one man spent thirteen days and nights at the fire". The difference, though apparently small, is the difference between democracy and aristocracy, or between community and elite culture. Naming implies respect. And by naming a great many of his human figures. Rolls almost paradoxically gives them as great an individuality as the birds, flowers, creeks and cattle breeds of his narrative. Not all European-style writing about milieux which combine nature and the human dimension bothers to do as much.

It is possible that the sobriety of Rolls' book and a few like it reflect more exactly than any past fiction the temper of vernacular Australia. Attempts to work from the vernacular tradition in creating imaginative fiction have tended to result in a laboured flatness, as in much of Prichard, arty falsity and inflation, as in Patrick White's *Tree of Man*, in arch rumbustiousness and grotesquerie, as in David Foster's *Moonlight* and a hundred lesser novels, or honourable eccentricity, as in Furphy and Herbert. Only one recent novel based on vernacular life which has made me prick up my ears in the way I always hope will happen is David Ireland's *Glass Canoe*, which does contain suggestive shapes and captures of rhythm. Rolls' "field" method of telling history and depicting a milieu all at once may suggest new possibilities, however, to writers of fiction. It is even possible that the novel, as a form we have adopted from elsewhere, may not be the best or only form which extended prose fiction here requires. Its heavy emphasis on the human, on character and the development of character, may tend to lead us into repeated misrepresentation of our world. Man and his classes and disputes may not be *important* enough, here, to sustain such a form. So many of our novels are portentous in their essence, piling up sensibility and brilliance on themes which cannot quite bear them, trying to exclude space in order to attain intensity. And the novel's inbuilt bias towards the individual may be fatally at odds with the communal basis of much of our life, though truly developed individuals are, I think, rare in our fiction; disguised humours and types, the Intellectual, the Bushman, the Liberated Woman, so often take their place and fatally short-change real individuality. This parallels (feeds, feeds off) a deadly habit of self-stylising we may always have gone in for, in preference to

Eric Rolls and the Golden Disobedience

developing full selfhood. Again, there is something anti-ecological about the novel: in its assigning all of agency to humans, it may be seen as a product of the overhumanised landscapes of the old world. Rolls himself repudiates the distinction between fiction and non-fiction, holding that it rests upon a confusion of the concepts of *imagination* and *fantasy*, or as the eighteenth century termed them, fancy and wit. Real things are *imagined*, in live writing, that is, they are deeply understood and made into images that touch the mind, whether the context is historical or projected.

It is good to have Rolls' great book in a time when so much of our literature seems in the first generation of widespread tertiary education to have become urgently mandarin, obsessed with the markers of consumer Style. It is hard to make unwelcome caveats when a culture long taught to despise itself achieves a tentative self-confidence and goes all out to capture the talismans of "high" culture, in this case Style and highly visible Sophistication. Style here, though, has tended to stylise its subjects, and sophistication of the sorts we have been exhorted to admire tends to issue in gestures of conformity with currently received literary values, over against the life very many of our people lead. We may construct beguiling networks of artistry, but in the back of many Australian minds there is often a suppressed dismay even in the midst of admiration, a feeling that some more essential network is being short-changed, dismissed unjustly, not got right. Our fiction is long on exhortation, on revision, on a habitual social scorn we have been three-quarters persuaded to endorse, but somehow it so often estranges us from something in us which goes on wanting to be represented, to be spoken in its true words. And so, almost behind the back of our learned proprieties, we welcome time and again books of non-fiction, books which articulate even some part of our deep experience as a people, and speak to us in a level, balanced, undecorated voice we "hear" as our own. To cut through alienation by simply ignoring the received sensibilities which produce it is a form of what I call the Golden Disobedience, and that disobedience seems at the moment to be available to non-fiction writers in greater measure than to other writers of literary texts. Poets may come next as writers to whom the Golden Disobedience is available. Novelists and playwrights, with honourable exceptions, seem to come a poor third. Rolls sidesteps all the received literary manners, and tells "people's" history in a way which belongs to them rather than to most these days who would speak of The People. And in doing so he creates a great work of art in which a central native tradition is renewed, altered and immeasurably deepened.

Quadrant, December 1982

On Being Subject Matter

If I sometimes boast that I was Subject Matter at my university before I graduated, that is partly a rueful admission of the inordinate time I took in graduating. I entered Sydney University in 1957, stayed there, educating myself and avoiding employment, until the early sixties, and then came back in 1969 to complete the two courses I had left hanging when I ceased going to lectures in 1960. I never got a mark above bare Pass, and my degree of Bachelor of Arts was probably the least distinguished the university ever conferred. I do think, though, that in my case the degree should be called Bachelor of Arts Studies; I am demonstrably married to my art, and it is only towards academic studies that I behave like a bachelor. I have understandably never put the letters BA after my name but I might be tempted to append my true distinction, the degree of Subject Matter. Les A. Murray Sub.Mat. It is a degree at once distinguished and democratic. In anthropology, sociology, medicine and many other fields, every single human being holds it.

Of course, I would only have been Subject Matter in a very minor way before 1969. It should be remembered that regular courses in Australian literature, especially undergraduate courses, are an innovation. When I drifted out of university in 1962, they were available only, I gather, at the Universities of Toulouse and Leningrad. In Australia, Brian Elliott had pioneered Australian courses at Adelaide and plans were well advanced for a Chair of Australian Literature at Sydney. There may have been other developments in a similar direction elsewhere of which I am not aware. I do know that, in the university as in high school, my generation was never exposed to Australian authors. We had, unknowingly, said goodbye to those in primary school when we finished Dorothea Mackellar's *My Country* and went beyond the excellent, varied old New South Wales *Schools Magazine*.

Poetry, though Scots Australians of my grandfather's generation venerated a limited range of it, was for us a remote and unreal form of writing which referred to the seasons and flora and class-ecology of an archipelago off the north-west coast of Europe, and seemed to deal in sentiments mostly quite unacceptable to boys of the future Third AIF. At least, it seemed sissy on the surface and that was enough for us; we could not be coaxed or driven to look deeper, and most teachers then had too little conviction about — or even understanding of — poetry to force it on us.

It was an option they nearly always allowed us to evade, often not even trying to teach it: "You won't do the poetry question, so I won't waste my time taking you through it." I almost managed to get right through high school without any serious engagement with poetry. I had read *The Rime of the Ancient Mariner* with some fascination in fourth year; also I had read *Paradise Lost* — indeed, all of Milton — in a single long weekend sometime in my teens, but that was for the science-fiction. I remember being irritated by the wordy, cumbrous manner of the story's telling; the poetry stuff seemed to make it stiff and preachy. In the end, I enjoyed *Samson Agonistes* more. That was a yarn I had enjoyed in the Bible, about a God-favoured Big Bloke who tore the gates off towns and slew enemies wholesale, and ended up as one prepared to pull the factory down rather than work. But I am getting ahead of my story.

I can scarcely have been Subject Matter earlier than the year 1966 because it was only in 1965 that Geoff Lehmann and I published a joint first book, called *The Ilex Tree*, thus giving readers some sort of very early conspectus of our work. We would both thereafter have been mentioned in odd lectures — indeed, we were told this was happening — and part of the impetus for this may have come from a favourable, possibly overgenerous, review of the book by Kenneth Slessor in the *Daily Telegraph*. That, and perhaps the kind review we were given by Roy Fuller in the *London Magazine*. We deserved some such rewards, perhaps: ANU Press, emphasising its great magnanimity and daring in taking on a pair of young unknowns, had offered us a contract under which we received no royalties. And we were green enough to agree to it.

My work was in its infancy in *The Ilex Tree*, of course, and it is probably surprising that the first Honours thesis on it was written only five years later, by Dianne Ailwood in 1970. This was published in *Southerly* (3/1971). There have been a fair few since, some submitted to universities cosmically remote from my native Bunyah. It gave me special pleasure to hear the brilliant young Teresa Altamore, of Sans Souci and Calabria, formally defend her thesis on Aboriginal art and my debt to it in Ca' Foscari, the University of Venice's palazzo on the Grand Canal, one morning in 1979; it was an excellent piece of work and deservedly got her a *Magna Cum Laude*.

Without any flippancy, I am grateful to all of those who have chosen to study my work. Partly because of their numbers, I imagine, the Tasmanian education authorities began setting it for study in schools in 1978 and those in my home State followed suit in 1979. This showed considerable magnanimity since I had never been a fashionable writer and had been known to say hard things in print about educators.

Many of the hard things I wrote about educators arose from a campaign to upgrade Federal Government patronage of the arts which began in 1969 with a policy paper I wrote for the Labor Party. In this paper and in an expanded article published in the *Australian Quarterly* in 1972, I pointed out the extreme discrepancy between the wages and conditions of educators and the often-desperate, hand-to-mouth existence of the living authors and artists they taught about. My case for expanded patronage was based on the injustice of treating middlemen handsomely while leaving the primary producers to suffer in irrelevant outside jobs or actual penury. This may have been the last major contribution of genuine old-style Country Party thinking to Australian public life. Many educators were slow to recognise the obligation they incurred by commenting on living authors' texts, and few admit it with any candour even now.

In 1971, desperate for a job of any sort (though also heartsick at the prospect of having one and so losing most of my real working time), I approached Professor Leonie Kramer, of Sydney, and asked her to use her influence to get me some sort of employment around my old university. Not an exalted academic post, of course: research assistant, translator, even trolley-pusher in Fisher Library would do. She refused to help me and I wrote her an intemperate letter demanding that she remove all of my work from the university's Australian literature courses.

Professor Kramer's reaction was to call in the university's lawyers to determine whether I had the right to bar my work from study in this way and, when they concluded that I didn't, she issued a memo to her department ordering that study of it should continue. About fifteen months later, the new Literature Board came into existence, and has since been able to alleviate the lot of many more writers than the old Commonwealth Literary Fund was able to — though the central problem is still far from being solved.

By no means all of my dealings with universities have been unhappy. In late years, I have been Writer-in-Residence at the Universities of New England, Stirling, Newcastle and New South Wales for a term each, and have spent the odd week at a few other tertiary institutions in much the same capacity.

Writerships in Residence are a rather mixed blessing for writers and probably a rather uncomfortable graft within the academic

On Being Subject Matter

body corporate. They have — or are hoped to have — some public relations value for the institution (Behold, we are patrons of the arts!) and possibly also represent a channel through which unadmitted conscience money can flow, but they draw upon English departments the envy of other scholars competing for scarce funds — "Here we are, desperate for a new gas chromatograph, and you waste university money on some hairy scribbler who's not even an academic."

Students' reactions to the writer on campus vary quite unpredictably, but there is always an initial period in which you see very little of them. Those who come along for a talk, at least at first, are usually mature age students or people with only a peripheral connection with the place; young students suss you out for a while before they put in a tentative appearance. And when they do come, the men especially are apt to be highly tentative and defensive until you gain their trust. And that goes double for members of university writers' clubs. At Stirling, I spent two months in seclusion from all but the friendly staff — then, in my final month, a caucus decision seemed to have been taken in my favour, and I found myself yarning with dozens of Scots and English students in the department and the university watering holes alike.

I usually learn a lot from my conversations when I'm at a university; I've always liked learning things by word of mouth. People in English departments like to fill gaps in my literary education — "Thank you for showing me this Ben Jonson chap: boy, he can write!" — and I gain wondrous knowledge and often wondrous vocabulary from professionals in other fields, though some scientists aren't entirely happy to see the sacred terms of their specialty used like recycled Roman tombstones in the construction of baroque works of art.

There are odd points of discomfort in some residencies. It can be slightly sticky to meet an academic critic who has been busily extracting prose meanings from one's verse in order to refute them and prove that one is a snake-oil doctor, but hypocrite affability will usually defuse that situation. A much worse pitfall, though, and one which the writer may not see at all until he or she has tumbled into it, is caused by the sad envy of those academics who are failed writers and know it. One may earn their savage public wrath merely by existing and writing well — and one may suspect nothing until the lightning crackles out of a clear sky into a critical journal. There is a tiny minority in English departments (writers often exaggerate its size) who will never feel truly compensated by their regular wage and lush conditions.

Writers who become Subject Matter differ widely in their response to the fact, especially in the degree to which they are prepared to assist students. Some, understandably valuing an often hard-won privacy, decline to make any statements at all about their work; some will give interviews and the odd public address but will avoid the distractions of anything like stumping the country and visiting schools and universities. Judith Wright has increasingly eschewed personal statements, and Patrick White has never made public comments about his writing. And this is perfectly proper. Such people allow their work to speak for itself. Students of geography don't expect a mountain to come into their classroom and explain itself. It simply exists and lets its investigators make their observations and hypotheses, which in turn are replaced by different observations and different hypotheses. Other writers, perhaps more foolishly obliging, perhaps less confident, make themselves more available to those who would or must study them.

I don't accuse Tom Keneally of foolishness or lack of confidence, but I know that one year he hired Sydney Town Hall and addressed a vast concourse of school students who were studying a novel of his. Others — and perhaps Tom, too — have talked to students on radio or television, as I have done, and taken opportunities to present themselves and their work in university and college seminars. Given the ambiguous modern entanglement of literature with education, these are forms of publication, and the presence of the author in the flesh can give a fillip of reality to literary studies without which those may never come alive for some students. Particularly for the conscript sort. And there is also, for some of us, the subversive hope of using the institutional set-up to reach and fire potential readers, as it were, over the system's head or behind its back.

The dangers of ego-tripping are of course patent, but there is arguably some value, for other writers as well as oneself, in bearing live witness to the reality and the craft of writing. Without this, many students may go on believing, perhaps only unconsciously, that the whole business of creating literature is somehow remote and a matter of no more than dry intellectual calculation. Or they may be seduced by stereotypes, by some image of trendily disreputable ravers or elegantly asthenic figures with long hair and Parisian berets. And who has ever seen a real poet who looked like that?

My friend Wayne Hooper, who is in adult education, once told me the most educative thing I ever did was to enter a classroom. Stereotypes crumbled to dust at my diffident Clydesdale approach. If only the students knew it, the outward cheerfulness of that approach masked an inner quaking familiar to all fat people with memories of the sort of treatment they endured as fat adolescents in schoolyards long ago. For early training in sensitivity and a balanced view of the nobility of humankind there's nothing like it, but merely crossing a schoolyard, even today, can fill me with muscle-tightening horror. Perhaps an element in my readiness to address school students was a delight in repeatedly facing down a personal demon.

One doesn't, I think, make up one's mind all at once about what one's attitude to making public appearances is going to be. To a considerable extent, one can drift into it. Friends who are teachers invite their friend the writer along to talk to their students. Institutions offer a trip and, usually, a fee — though this isn't an invariable rule: my old school didn't. They also provide a crowd whom they may see as students but whom the writer sees as an audience. Balancing the reading with the teaching, the show business with the education, is one of the strains but also one of the arts of this new field of performance.

The writer must learn the techniques of satisfying both educators and students without currying favour with either. Seeking to play upon tensions he may imagine to be present between teachers and taught is shoddy and self-defeating, and I was never tempted to try it. The tension is not always there and, even when it is, teachers and taught are involved with each other, while the visiting writer is at best a guest, at worst a transient freak show, but always an outsider in the situation. He must never be defensive, but he should not appear unduly assertive, either, and eccentricity only invites the reactions which have kept artists on the margins of life ever since the renegade Plato put us there. I have always found a sort of egalitarian honesty the best approach, partly because I don't have to fake it.

Without sacrificing or glossing over the fact that you are only interested in art of the highest standard — for theories which hold that all people are artists, all attempts at art are valid and of equal dignity, etc., are fraudulent, desolating nonsense and most people of all ages know it — show yourself prepared to talk to young people and their teachers as intelligent people worthy to be told the fascinating ins and outs of a great and ancient profession to which you are wholly committed. And you will usually gain their trust.

Being friendly without unction and genuine without any little lies hidden about you will get you a hearing and often beneficially change students' perceptions of art itself. This simple recipe may not, of course, be enough when facing doctrinaire groups, but those are not usually encountered in schools or in adult education. They are by no means the rule even in universities, though there the danger of tripping over passionately held theories and shibboleths is notoriously greater. And it is of little use going near venues where the audience has gathered partly to see controversy and fireworks among the artists, rather than art. Unless they have changed a great deal since I gave up attending them, major arts festivals in this country are pretty nearly impossible. Would David Oistrakh take his violin to parliament? And expect ears coarsened by dissension, rhetoric and the noise of competing egos to hear his more delicate nuances? He might beguile them momentarily but at the risk of damaging his instrument and his touch and possibly suffering gross insult to boot.

One further rule I always observe, with groups of all ages, is to prepare nothing in advance. If you are really master of your material — and certainly you should be if the subject is yourself and your own work — you can afford to speak impromptu. That way, you have room to interest and surprise yourself and make discoveries even about things you have discussed dozens of times before. If I developed a spiel, I would disgust and bore myself even possibly before I bored the audience. I am grateful to many students for discoveries they have made or helped me to make about my poems. Any performer — and that is what probably a majority of poets have to be today, at least part-time — is nervous about scenes where the audience is allowed to talk back, but that is the nature of the new education-based variants of the public reading and I have gained benefit from the fact.

As with any performance, there is always at least some "edge" in facing a class. You quickly learn to size up the potentials. In a school, if all the boys are down the back and all the girls in the front seats you know you are going to have to work hard, because the boys will be inclined to resist you. If there are several teachers in the room and they're all sitting up at the front — or even merely sitting together — all will probably be well. The prospects are grim if they are standing, and particularly grim if they are disposed strategically around the walls like warders with invisible truncheons in their hands. Standing teachers are an ominous sign. Even more so if the male ones (it's usually the male ones) wear expressions which suggest that they'd really rather be in the pub, or that they didn't know what to do with their lives but there was this teachers' college scholarship offering.

The size of a class is surprisingly unimportant, though intimacy and real exchanges are naturally more likely if it is small. I have had successful sessions, though, with groups of four or five hundred, good rapport while I was speaking and during question-and-answer sessions. You need to be able to see the whole group without constantly turning your head. Curved seating or any sort of wrap-around arrangement plays hell with essential eye contact and other physical cues. Standing to face a class is all right, I suppose, but I usually find it more relaxing, more informal and less suggestive of

On Being Subject Matter

domination, if I can sit — preferably on a desk or table, so as to gain a little height from which to project my voice.

When you go to a school to address students you enter the classroom as a privileged visitor, often as a welcome diversion from the normal grind, and you are the beneficiary of class control and good behaviour established for you by teachers. None of this will make your visit a success if you bore or disappoint the students, but you do owe the teachers the loyalty of not undermining them with what you tell their students. Teachers bear the long burden of repeating things until they are understood and assimilated, and the misery of never getting through to some at least of their pupils. They can be forgiven if their day-in-day-out performances lack the pizzazz of your single hour or so; they lack the authority you have as the Horse's Mouth. Teachers sometimes have a bumper sticker on their cars which goes: "If you can read this, thank a teacher." In my case, I learned to read at home when I was four and didn't enter a school or meet a teacher till I was nine. But it was a teacher who opened my eyes to poetry just before I left school, to such effect that I was set on the course of life I would follow. In class, students will often seek opinions and interpretations from the distinguished visitor which will contradict what their teachers have told them. Often you will not know exactly when this is going on but it pays to be cautious about it. I do warn students against common errors in dealing with poetry — against the still-widespread habit of looking for symbolism in everything, for example. As Freud said, a cigar is sometimes just a cigar. And the subject of a poem or of an image in a poem is frequently more important as itself than as a pointer to something else.

Poetry makes things real, restoring their life and our perception of it, and the ways in which things in a poem refer to the wider world aren't usually as simple as the ordinary school notion of symbolism would suggest: the knack of reading on several levels at once isn't hard to suggest, though, and is usually picked up readily by senior students. I also warn them, as good teachers do, that there is no one Great Golden Interpretation that will get them through their exams. If they want something of that sort, as many sadly do, I give them several. As they warm to me, they will often give me theirs — which I often can exhort them to trust ... "Yes, the poem will bear that reading. What is in the poem supports it. It's good. Now, I've sometimes thought this, too ..." When that starts to happen, what may have seemed an onerous and artificial exercise begins to be fun as students catch on and begin to trust their own perceptions.

Shockingly to some, I even admit that I don't really mind analysis of my poems. A good poem, I tell them, should be indestructible and should recover its mystery and resonance as soon as analysis stops. It should be alive and inexhaustible, able to wait when you tire of it and come up fresh and vibrant when you return to it, even years later.

I ask students who don't like school not to take their revenge on poetry just because they first met it in school. I regret that poetry has to be any part of the grading and relegating mechanism which our education so pervasively is, but I tell kids that poetry has to be part of education because it is the very point of education, as exam-passing is not. There was a point in my own schooldays before which I had not "got" poetry, and before that illumination it was impossible to convey anything to me about it, beyond the most basic rote material and surface fact. After I had twigged, however, everything about the subject would henceforth follow, and I needed no more guidance from teachers. The next help I would need would come from colleagues. I think this moment of illumination is a key thing, perhaps in any field of study, and I always hope to be the one who can somehow cause it to happen or start happening in the students I speak to. In nearly any class, of course, there will be some to whom it has happened already, and those students are easy to spot.

I am not a teacher, and my time with any class is necessarily very brief and concentrated. Giving as little heed as practicable to age or grade or presumptions about my hearers' intelligence, I pay kids and adults alike the compliment of telling them the best I know in one large heap they can sort out for themselves when I am gone. They rarely seem to mind my being very demanding on their powers of assimilation. I tell them how I wrote particular poems, those on their course if their courses are structured around the study of set poems, and surprise some by revealing how imperfectly I usually understand a poem when I first write it; all I have to know is that it is "right", that it is achieved and has its own life. I might never have thought deeply and, as it were, interpretatively about particular poems if I had not been asked to talk about them to classes of students. Students usually find it illuminating to be told the nodal points, the initial images, thoughts, etc., from which particular poems grow.

I usually tell them a bit about the literary life, about publication, magazines, the book trade and such like and frequently underline the distinction between vocation and employment with the hope that the two will not have to be distinct in their own lives. In all of my talks, I stress the idea of literature as a profession rather than as a mere adjunct to education. I often gently correct prevailing critical misconceptions, such as the belief that Murray hates the city and loves only the bush, and tell them about the relatively few core concerns any writer has — the topics to which he or she will perennially return, as it were, on a spiral of development; moving away from them for a while and then coming back to them with a fresh insight at a later and maybe higher stage of evolving wisdom. Whenever things flag, I read another poem or two — always including some not on their course.

In trying, as it were in one hit, to counter the widespread neglect and disdain of poetry students encounter outside the educational national park in which it shelters and is vivisected these days, I suppose I try at once to normalise it and show how special it is. To do this, I have somehow to separate in the minds of my listeners the ideas of excellence on the one hand and snobbish superiority on the other. Our education does, for complex historical reasons, tend to fuse those ideas together, and the worst obstacle I continually encounter is the dispirited self-relegation of students and teachers alike in all but the poshest places. This curse is marginally more prevalent, I find, in the country than in the city — though poorer urban areas are as rife with it as any bush town. If there is one quasi-political (but really spiritual) line that I try to push it is opposition to mandarinism and all other forms of consumer hierarchy, opposition to the notion that anything good can be somehow "too good" for some people or "over the heads" of a majority.

As I have said, the interaction I have with classes of all ages is usually good. Disruptive behaviour and attempts to stir the distinguished guest are rare. Out of probably hundreds of schools I have visited, I only remember one in which a class rejected me, telling me quite frankly that they hated poetry and would never read it again as soon as they escaped from school. I still smart from that defeat, even though the class was only a dozen pupils strong. I simply failed to click with them, and can't help thinking it must have been my fault. More or less subtle attempts at disconcerting or exploiting the speaker occur very occasionally, as once in a girls' school outside Sydney, where one member of the class tried, in the midst of a discussion of vernacular culture and the like, to get me to comment about the parliamentarian Ian Sinclair, then under investigation for possible misconduct. Of course I sidestepped the trap, since I knew nothing of Mr Sinclair and since the case was both sub judice and quite irrelevant to what we'd been discussing. It turned out, of course, that Mr Sinclair's daughter was a member of the same class. The teacher told me this afterwards, and I'm afraid I described the other girl as a little bitch. Really gormless questions from students are quite rare, and when they come I do my level best to rescue the questioner from embarrassment, by desperately finding some deep point of interest in his query or by almost any other means to hand. I have been a lifelong asker of stupid questions myself, and anyway can't bear to see people laughed at. The only such questioner I remember being unable to rescue from ridicule was the poor boy in one class who asked, about my poem "The Widower in the Country", "Was his wife dead?" I simply could not, off the cuff, do better than reply sadly, "That's how you get to be a widower." Adult classes, of course, contain people with more experience and more ability to talk about it, and sessions with those often become thoroughly enjoyable conversations. Talking about my poem "The Burning Truck", in which boys who have been hanging around the streets discontentedly go running after the apparently miraculous vehicle that burns but is not consumed and won't stop, a lady who had been through the Blitz in England snorted decisively in one of my classes "Hmpf! Creatures like that creep into their holes like rats at the first sign of an air raid; you'd never get them back into the streets to follow a burning truck or anything else!" I protested mildly that such things could happen in fiction, surely, and that there were many literal and less literal Burning Trucks people commonly chased after in our time if they were bored with ordinary life, but she was unconvinced. The word "canaille" burned too hotly in her mind.

I did have a consultative say, over duck casserole in a French restaurant, in the choice of my poems to be set for the New South Wales Higher School Certificate in 1979–80, but I neither had nor wanted any part in marking exams on them. Indeed, I have only ever seen three or four of what must have been thousands of school essays on my work; one, by a boy at Pennant Hills High School in Sydney who had previously preferred the bush ballads to any modern verse, struck me as truly excellent. He said things about my poem "An Absolutely Ordinary Rainbow" which seemed accurate and which interested me from an artistic point of view. And that is what an artist wants from critics, even more than praise. Approval without real understanding can be a desolating experience. I have had a very good run from the critics, by and large, and have no scores to settle, but the reviews and essays I value and remember are those in which the quality of response answered in some way to the labour, the illumination and the delight which went into writing the poem or poems under discussion. I remember, for example, the illumination that came to me from an essay in which Harry Heseltine pointed out that "An Absolutely Ordinary Rainbow" was written from the point of view of the crowd rather than the weeping man who stands at its centre, and that perhaps to side, as it were, with the crowd rather than the central figure might be an Australian characteristic. That helped me with my thinking on many Australian things afterwards. Some less helpful forms of criticism are at least amusing. There is that magnanimity, for example, which allows you a triumph but fills the chariot with slaves who whisper dire things in your ear: *You are the last of your line. You will run out of themes. All glory is fleeting.* Or the mild Tiptoe method, for minds eaten out by brilliance and the hard labour of spending the seventies finding some saving virtue in rubbish; such minds have usually lost all recollection of simplicity, and cannot bear to see the obvious. I remember one senior academic who successively asked David Malouf and me what we thought James Dickey had meant by a reference to cattle "feeding together in the night of the hammer". When we both told him, quite independently, that it primarily referred to the way cattle are sold by the knock of an auctioneer's hammer and taken to be slaughtered with a hammer-blow to the head at the abattoir, he was amazed. Surely some deeper interpretation was called for. Coarser forms include Fishnet (or Dragnet) criticism, which sees all things in terms of schools, and the Secular Rosary style, which is obsessed with decades.

The least helpful sort of criticism is the kind I call Inquisitorial, which presumes to investigate one's work in terms of an ideology or programme alien to it. Even where this isn't a cloak for ordinary rivalry and jealous ambition, it can tempt people to falsify the work in order to attack it. Tactics used include what I call the Targeting method of criticism, in which epithets are suggested or actually applied to a writer — *conservative, Establishment, reactionary, decadent, Jewish-cosmopolitan* etc.: the inventories of totalitarianism are long and the items remarkably interchangeable — in order to get him or her despised and harassed by activists and fellow travellers who need not look at the evidence for themselves, and may indeed not dare to. A variant tactic is to drop the target author in the path of an oncoming fashion or Cause. A related technique is the Chain of Presumption, which pretends that the writer's whole range of opinions can be deduced from a specimen position he is seen to hold, or perhaps merely to express: if he believes A, or F, he must also believe B, C, D, E and G. To dislike nudity on the beach is to support racial oppression in South Africa. Application of these methods can already, in Australia, get writers barred from particular magazines, can cause favourable reviews and indeed all reviews of their work to be suppressed, can cost them school and university settings and government funding, can get them defamed and insulted in public, and can provoke professional sanctions against other writers who speak well of them in print. All of these things have happened here. As with so much of criticism, the story which is told is less interesting than the one which might be. The main merit of all such criticism lies in displaying to the public the real implications of the ideologies espoused, and what life would be like for artists and people generally if they came to power. Such criticism is the case law, epitomised in advance, of prospective police systems. More subtly deadening, though, are the effects of the received literary sensibility, that pool of assumptions and habits of feelings of the literary-intellectual caste out of which all the ideologies ultimately flow. It is my old enemy, the RLS. It hates my religion, it disdains and patronises my people, it yearns after aristocracy, it marinades its every word in contempt. If it could, it would make all art its prisoner. I tend to judge the worth of writers and critics alike by the distance they maintain between themselves and the RLS. At the same time, I know that the entrance to literature for most people leads through that sensibility. As we begin learning to write, we assimilate it like tribespeople learning a culture-language, one in which the warmest, most native and homely things cannot be expressed. We have to wrestle with it if we wish to tell any but its prescribed versions of the truth, and it pulls at us like a strange gravitational force, trying to think for us, to snub us out of our most distinctive insights, to proscribe unapproved subject matter, to control and harness unpredictable delight. However extolled, no work written in conformity with the RLS can be better than second rate, and if you are interested in attempting to write supremely well you have to essay a freedom beyond its reach. The joyful surprise there is that such freedom can restore you to the community of a broad readership.

The great secret weapon against the RLS, against Literature with a capital L, is that impenetrable mystery the reading public. Because the RLS cannot fathom or reliably conquer that, it affects to disdain it, and even ascribes class characteristics to it intended to evoke disdain. The dreaded Bourgeois, the unspeakable Mid-Victorian, the despised Housewife. I suspect, though, that the reading public is very much terra incognita, poorly explored and inadequately mapped by anyone. I find it continually surprising. It may in the end be purely a matter of individuals, of myriad singularity, for which all descriptions involving collectivity are inappropriate. The most surprising people, if we give any credence at all to stereotypes, turn out to be readers of literary books — and sometimes of the *Women's Weekly, Bugs Bunny* and the *Proceedings of the Australian Institute of Engineers* too, all in the one day. I have had letters from readers of poetry as diverse as station cooks, surgeons and banana growers. An old lady on a train, one of the "Geriatric" caste so despised by today's Lawrentians, may be seen deeply immersed in T. S. Eliot. A floorwalker from David Jones, his carnation of office still in his buttonhole, may be seen deep in Dostoevsky in his luncheon break. I have seen these phenomena, and had letters from their like. No one even knows what causes people to buy books. We can investigate *who* buys books, but on the matter of which books or why we can only speculate. The Literature Board early in its life, around 1973 or '74, conducted a large study on the matter and arrived at no firm conclusions. Even the effect of reviews remained unknown. Reviewing and advertising must have some effect, we think, and yet we don't know for certain. Scores of books of verse published in the seventies and extravagantly praised by friendly critics ended up on the remainder tables, having sold twenty to fifty copies in eight or ten years. On the other hand, Kevin Hart's collection *Lines of the Hand*, which was practically sent to Coventry by reviewers, has sold extremely well. Readers seem somehow to have sniffed out its quality in the few bookshops which carried it.

Many publishers, including my own, rely on reviews as free advertising, and yet there seems to be some evidence that advertising as such is more effective. Roger McDonald's excellent *1915* really had quite a lacklustre time with the reviewers when it came out; few praised it unequivocally. On the other hand, it had energetic backing from its publishers, the University of Queensland Press, with large ads for months on end in all the leading publications. It became the book of the moment. People were made conscious of it, to the point where they would look for it, pick it up, dip in — and I have a suspicion, which I can't prove, that the crucial things happen at that point of dipping in. All I can really describe is an almost simultaneous complex of things which happen when I pick up a book in a bookshop. My eye runs over the print, sampling it here and there, inviting it to continue and focus the impulse which made me pick it up, looking for whatever may connect with my interest or surprise me by extending its range; I even seem to feel my nostrils constrict as I search for the book's tone, its flavour, its likely relations with reality (by which I don't mean just the everyday kind), as well as the quality of its argument, which doesn't have to be high, the quality of its humanity and its quotient of literary devices. All sorts of subliminal, half-physical things are probably also happening, more or less as they happen when we encounter a new person and discover what our attitude to him is. This process of sussing out a book happens in a quick lucid blur, rapidly forgotten if the book fails to grab me, and is really, beyond all reviews or puffery, the chance the book gets. I am probably a quite impure sample, though; after all, I am in the business of writing and publishing books. All the same, I don't think my practices have altered very much since long before I became a writer as well as a reader. The main evolution that has brought in its train is a growing ability to see through Literature to — literature. And to that much-scorned quality of *enjoyment* which may be what other, non-writing readers even more ruthlessly seek from books.

If the Unknown Reader is our best defence against the RLS, it is pleasing to know that in this country, for reasons we can only speculate about, poetry enjoys a much larger readership in proportion to population than in most Western countries. The normal print run of a new book of verse, a slim volume in trade parlance, is the same here as in West Germany, a country with four times our population. When I told people in the United Kingdom about the sales figures our best-known poets attain, figures which I know for most of them from trade sources, they were incredulous. No poet in Britain, not even the most celebrated, could match them. "So what's the strength," asked my clansman Glen Murray, editor of the Scots Nationalist magazine *Cencrastus*, "of this legend about Australia as an uncultured land of illiterate philistines?" "It is bullshit," I replied, answering his smile with one of my own. In this late-colonial country, so patronised and excoriated by its ruling literary sensibility, we not only have a better poetry book market than most other Western nations, but our poets often sell better than all but a very few of our novelists. Having said these things, though, and having praised the Unknown Reader as one of the safeguards of my artistic freedom, I have to pay tribute for my sales also to people driven to read me by the fierce giant Curriculum. As Subject Matter, I have to realise that some of my readership at least is conscripted. I apologise to all conscripts, and fervently hope they find my work such that I can be forgiven. Teachers tell me that they like teaching my work because students seem to enjoy it. I can't imagine they all enjoy it; I have too much faith in human differences to believe that. So long as those who dislike it dislike it on its merits, rather than for any thought-police reasons, I'm pretty well satisfied.

As well as the financial benefits which start to accrue visibly, if not copiously, when one passes from the degree of Subject Matter to that of Set Author, there is this final satisfaction which one has almost from the beginning, even before one is properly accredited as an Occasional Topic. With one's first reviews, there is the thought that, while society may treat writers and other artists as bachelors' children in the matter of worldly rewards, our profession must have some high importance, since it is subject to public scrutiny of a sort granted to no other. It is hard to imagine regular published reviews of barristers, for example, or cardiac surgeons. Think of it: "With his move to the cardiac field, Mr Brodribb-Cleaver appears to have left behind the timid bourgeois formalism of his earlier appendicectomies and acquired an almost daredevil attack in his incisions. His suturing is as sensitive and finely considered as ever, but his bypass work shows a new insolence, and he has brought a neo-*tachiste* profundity to our perception of the mitral valve. With the appearance of this superb stylist, Australian heart surgery has come of age."

Bulletin Literary Supplement, Easter 1983